I0653345

SECRETS: BOOK 1

THE SAULIE BIRD
(Circles of Safety)

Eliza Quancy

⌊C

Lame Crow Press

First published in 2020 by Lame Crow Press.

Book design by Paul Way-Rider based on a photo by Kumar Harsh at unsplash.com

ISBN (paperback) 978-1-913669-08-9
ISBN (ebook) 978-1-913669-09-6

For Jill Tennison

'I have seen the bird of paradise and I shall never be the same again...'

from *The Politics of Experience and The Bird of Paradise* by R.D.Laing

1

Saul and Layla are not my mama and papa. I've asked. They don't know where my birth-mother is or my father. Don't know who they are. Saul says he found me in a hibiscus bush when I was a baby and brought me home. Sounds unlikely but that's what he says and Layla tells the same story. Why haven't they got any children I ask, and they tell me that Layla can't have babies so that's why they got me. They had baby things all ready when I arrived. It's a confusing story.

One day when I am fifteen, I decide to run away down the mountain. I've got to find my birth-mother and father. I've just got to. Saul and Layla are the best, but still, I've got to find my own people. They won't tell me anything and Saul will never take me with him when he goes down to the city to sell the wooden things. Layla and I never go. We stay here in Keroko. Our little place is called Keroko and it's all by itself in the mountains in Central Province. Our house is the only one here and Saul didn't build it. It was here when they came. It's on stilts (fat wooden poles) so it's safe from animals and we can sit under the house in the shade. It's made of local wood and bamboo and the generator was already here when Saul and Layla came. Who made it I ask, but they don't know. Or won't say. One or the other.

I am ready to go. I have thought about this for a long, long time but I was scared. I am still scared. Partly I'm afraid of going down the mountain by myself because I shall be in the bush alone at the night times. And partly I'm afraid of what I might discover when I get down there. But mostly I'm afraid of Saul because I know that he will be angry with me for going and Layla will think he is right.

It will be easy to find the way down because there is only one track. I wait until Saul has gone on his journey to the city and then one day more. Then I wait until Layla is in the garden. She works in the garden every morning now that I'm older while I do the school exercises by myself. We go through them together in the afternoons. Today, I pack my bilum so that the bag stretches with all the things I need to take. Layla made this bilum. In fact, she often makes bilums and Saul sells them along with the wooden animals. It's red and green with diamond patterns. I've tried, too, but I'm no good at making string bags. More patience, I'm told. I need to be patient. Saul says that Layla is not strict enough with me, but she takes no notice.

I try hanging the bilum on my shoulder but it's heavy and cuts in, so I carry it around my head like Layla taught me with the bag hanging down my back. I'm taking my laptop and my phone, an exercise book, pens and some clothes. I've stolen some money from Layla's purse and I'm sorry about that but I know that I'll need it. And now I'm off.

I nearly run to begin with but remember that I shouldn't. It's a long way down and soon I'm walking steadily. I've been taught that it's dangerous to run when you're going downhill (and impossible to run when you're going up). So no running. Down and round and round and down, the track winds steadily down the mountainside. It's quite overgrown and sometimes not easy to see. Nobody passes me. Not a surprise. Nobody lives near us. Nobody comes to our place. Ever. I'm nervous and I keep on listening. Think I can hear a cassowary crashing through the bush, but it's not close. They can rip you open with just one kick. The birdsong echoes in the air and bounces through the trees. Clear, separate, chirping sounds. Sweet and loud.

My phone rings. It's Layla.

'Where are you?' she asks.

'I'm sorry, Layla,' I say. 'I'm going down the mountain,' I hesitate. 'I'm going to find my birth mother,' I pause, 'and maybe my father.'

'It's dangerous,' she says. 'Come back, baby. Come home.'

'I'm not a baby,' I tell her although I know she doesn't mean it like that. 'I've got to go.' There's a long pause. She's upset and I'm sorry.

'And where will you look?' she asks.

'I don't know,' I tell her. 'Don't know yet. But I'll think of something.'

I do have an idea but I don't want to say. I know which road it is where Saul found me because he told me about it. I know the name of the road but I don't know which building it was. I'll have to look for a hibiscus bush in front of a building and start from there. Or maybe the bushes will have changed. Not much to go on but that is all I know. I've come prepared. Got two cooked kaukau and a bottle of water. I laugh about that. The kaukau won't last long, but I'll manage somehow. After I've found my birth mother and father - or at least my mother - I'm going to come back. Don't want to speak to her, just want to have a look and I told this to Layla on the phone.

All she said was, 'Oh, Aulani. Oh, my dear. Oh, Aulani.'

Mostly, she calls me Auli. My name sounds the same as 'Owly' and I like that. I would like to be a wise bird but no, they tell me, that's not what I am. My name means 'traveller'. Just 'traveller'.

It is a long way down the mountain and when the night comes, I am still not down. I go into the trees and gather firewood so I can light a fire. I've remembered to bring some matches from the shed where Saul keeps them. I light a fire and sit beside it. I am tired but can't sleep. I am frightened. I have never been on the mountain alone at night but it will be worth it. They won't tell me about my parents and I have to find out. Perhaps they don't know.

For hours, I listen to the night animals making noises in the bush. Night-time isn't as quiet as you'd think. There's a silence and then something yelps or howls. Or swishes. That's worse because I don't like snakes. After a long time, I sleep but wake up as soon as it's light. I feel hungry and thirsty and dirty and stiff. I find a place with water trickling over the rocks and I wash and drink and fill my bottle.

Layla and Saul keep phoning to see if I'm all right, but I'm worried that my battery will run out so I don't answer. I text them saying not to worry and that soon I'll be back. Layla says that Saul is coming to look for me so I text again to say that I am already in the city. He won't find me. I'll be home soon.

It's not true. It is evening before I finally reach the road at the end of the track. This is where the city starts. I am thirsty and very dirty. Two days now and I've eaten both of the kaukau and drunk all the water. I keep looking for a stream to fill the water bottle but there is nothing like that

in the city. Of course, there isn't. I know all about cities because I watch tv and I've looked on google, but still, it
comes as a shock. It is dirty and smelly and full of cars and
trucks and people. Hundreds of people. All going somewhere. Like ants but not marching together. Can't believe
it. Thought it would be nicer.

2

Nobody notices my dirty state. They all walk by. Don't speak. Keep on walking past. More and more of them. All busy busy. I look on google maps but it's draining the battery so I do it as little as possible and set off to find the road Saul told me about. It doesn't take long to find it. Name is Three Mile Road. I know it doesn't mean three miles of road because I've looked it up. I guess that it means three miles from somewhere. I've had a look at it on Streetview, so it is just as I expected. A lot of low plasterboard houses all single-storey some bigger than others, a couple of stores and then some larger buildings. And all the houses seem to have bushes in front of them. Our house is smaller but more beautiful. Our house is made of cedar wood with bamboo patterns woven into the walls.

Was I born in one of these white plasterboard buildings, a store perhaps or a big house? Probably not a store. I giggle and my heart calms down a bit. It's all just as it is on tv. I'll have to walk up and down the road and have a closer look. There must be a clue somewhere. I'm tired and Saul keeps ringing but I'm not answering. I set off down the road and haven't walked very far when I see a sign 'Three Mile Hospital'. Wow. That must be it. That was quick. This must be the place. I must have been born in a hospital and there won't be another one. I stand and stare at the outside. Lots of bushes, mostly bougainvillaea, but that means nothing. It's a hospital so bingo, I must be there already. I walk in.

'Can I help you?' asks a small, round woman wearing a blue uniform. She is sitting at the Enquiries desk. I tell her that I'm looking for my mother. I was born here fifteen years ago and found in a bush outside. She laughs, but not unkindly, and asks me to explain. I tell her again. Saul said I must have been thrown out of the window. Impossible, she tells me, the windows here have louvres. No space for a baby to get through.

'Have the windows been changed?' I ask. 'It was a long time ago.'

''No,' she says. 'The windows are the original ones. The place was built in 2001. When were you born?'

'2000,' I tell her, 'I was born in the year 2000.' So we both know that it's not possible that I was born in this place. In any case, she says, we would have noticed if a baby had gone missing.

To be honest, I have thought about this myself and wondered why nobody had noticed there was a baby missing. She must think I'm mad, but she smiles at me and wishes me well. Doesn't seem surprised. Are there people turning up here all the time looking for their birth mothers? Asking if they were thrown through a window? Before I leave, I look for the washroom (I've seen washrooms on tv) and I find it. It's impressive. I count five toilets and go into one behind a door. It's got a little bolt so I decide to lock it. There's a lever to flush it afterwards. In the big room there are five washbasins and everywhere is clean. I have a wash and tidy up. There's no-one here. Fill my water bottle. Feel much better now I'm clean again but there's nothing I can do about my clothes.

Above one of the washbasins, there is a mirror. I've never seen myself in a mirror so I go to have a look. My

hair is frizzy like Layla's hair and it's about the same colour. Light brown from the sun but darker at the roots. Not
as big as Layla's but still it's all right. I like our hair more
than Saul's. His hair is black and short with small tight
curls - almost like no hair or a sheep's hair - and he keeps
it like that. Always very short. And he's black. Looks nice,
but I like being brown like Layla. I think I look like her
even though she's not my mother.

My blue meri blouse looks dirty and I wonder about
changing. I've got another blouse in my bag but I don't
know how long this searching is going to take so I think I'd
better save it. That's all I can see. Just my face and part of
my blouse. The mirror is not very big and it's quite high up
on the wall. I smile at myself and wonder why we haven't
got a mirror at home. Actually, I've asked about a mirror
but Saul said we won't have one. It encourages vanity.

Back outside, I feel tired and disappointed. Sit down for
a bit at the side of the road but I don't think people do that
here. Everybody I see is walking. Nobody is sitting down
and two people give me a funny look so I get up again and
start walking myself. Up the road right to the end where
the houses stop and then back again. There are buildings
only on one side so that makes it easier. Apart from the
hospital, the two stores and the houses, there is a small hotel. Nothing else. I've found nothing. I'm hungry and tired
and will need to sleep somewhere. I'm just thinking that
Saul could tell me where the place was, if only he would,
when my phone pings.

'Try the hotel, Aulani.'

'Thank you, Saul,' I reply and wonder if he's a mind-
reader but then I think that he doesn't have to be because

I told them why I was coming and I've told Layla that I am already in the city. She will have told him.

He would never tell me which building it was. Only the name of the road. That's all he would say. I walk back towards the hotel feeling tired but at least my hands and face are clean. I find the place and look at the bushes. Hibiscus. My heart beats faster, but I look at the windows and my heart sinks. Louvres again with flywire on the outside. Impossible to throw anything through those.

I walk in and see a desk with no-one there. A bell says 'ring for attention' so I do. Someone comes but it's an Aussie woman with jet black bouffant hair and a huge chunky necklace. I've never seen anyone with hair like that not even on tv and wonder how she's got it to stay in that shape. It looks stiff and hard. A very strange *waitpela meri*.

'What can I do for you?' she asks.

'I'm looking for my birth mother.' I start to speak and see her eyes flicker for just a second before her face sets back into its smile. Face is stiff the same as her hair.

'And how can I help you with that?' she asks.

'When I was born, I was thrown out of a window and I landed in a bush. That's where I was found. This is the place.' I watch her face as I say this but her smile doesn't shift.

'Not here,' she says and looks me over. I see her looking at my dirty laplap and meri blouse. Looks at my feet. No shoes. I see in her eyes what she thinks of me. 'Haven't you seen the windows?' she says. 'It's not possible to throw anything out of our windows and certainly not a baby.' She tries a little laugh, forcing herself to be polite.

'Then they must have been changed,' I say. 'This is the place where I was born.'

'This is a hotel,' she says, beginning to sound irritated. 'It's always been a hotel.'

'It's the right place,' I tell her. 'I know it is.'

'Sorry,' she says as she steps out from behind the desk and walks away down the corridor, leaving me standing there. She doesn't sound very sorry but there's nothing I can do. I'll have to leave and there's nowhere else to try. This is where Saul told me to look and I don't think he would lie to me. My phone rings again.

'I'm outside waiting for you.' It's Saul and I don't know if I'm relieved or cross but mainly I'm scared because he will be angry. He's there outside the hotel. I can see him standing by the gate.

'Was this the place?' I ask, wanting to know before the anger streams out of him.

He nods. 'What did you find out?'

'Nothing,' I say and feel myself begin to tremble, but Saul says nothing and sets off up the road. I follow. He's going too fast. He is angry. I'll get it later, but first, he takes me to a small house full of people and I'm given a mat in a room with a lot of other girls. I'm not used to sharing, but I go to sleep as soon as I lie down. I'm exhausted.

The next day we leave at dawn and start the climb back up the mountain. It will take three days to get back to Keroko. I think it's strange that we live there all by ourselves. Just the three of us. I've kept asking about it. Why is there no village? No people at all? But neither Saul nor Layla will give me an answer. I'm sure there must be a reason. It's hard work climbing up. Going down was easier and much quicker. We walk in silence and I follow behind.

When we sleep, Saul lights a fire and gives me a mat but we don't talk. Maybe just a word. He is angry and I am miserable. He will beat me when we get home and we both know it.

3

When we reach our house at last, Layla is gone. We look for her everywhere but she is gone and her clothes are gone. We phone her over and over, but there is no reply. Saul's black face gets darker. Like thunder. He was born in the North Solomons. Buka. They are all black there Layla told me. Not the light brown colour of her people. And what about my people I wonder, where is my village and what do my people look like? I think sometimes that I come from the same place as Layla because mostly, I look like her.

'Give me your phone,' he says.

I hand it over.

'Go to your room and wait.'

I go there.

I am hungry and thirsty and I want my phone. Want to ring Layla. Where is she? Layla is my mama, my proper mama, the one who loves me. Where has she gone? I lie down. I'm weary but too scared to sleep. Frightened of Saul. He'll come in sooner or later. My body is stiff and tense. Heart pounding. I hear him clicking his phone and hear him leave a message but I can't hear what he says. Must be to Layla. Where is she? Oh Layla, where are you? I need you. It gets dark but I don't sleep. We use kerosene lamps to save the generator fuel but Saul doesn't bring one for me. Then I hear his footsteps. He is bringing a lamp. I can see the light and the shadows swinging on the wall.

There is no door to my room. Only one door in our house and that's on the toilet where the shower is. Saul stands in the doorway and puts the lamp down. It's almost dark but in his hands, I can see something glinting. Like metal. He walks towards me.

'Lie down,' he says.

I lie down on my mat. I was sitting with my back to the wall when he came in.

'Put your feet together.'

I do as he says and watch while he fastens each ankle into a metal holder. There is a little click as each one snaps into place so that my legs are chained together. He tests each one to check that it's locked and then pulls the chain to check that it won't come loose. And that it's not too long.

'Now you know what shackles are. Get up,'

I struggle to get up. Half fall down. Try again and sink back on to the mat. Saul watches.

'Get up,' he commands. 'Stand up, Aulani and walk towards me.' He moves away and stands in the doorway. What has he done? Is it a joke? He'll take them off again, won't he? I fall back on the mat but he tells me again to walk towards him.

'I can't,' I say. 'I can't walk in these.'

He walks towards me and asks for my hands.

'Hold them out.'

Slowly, I stretch out my hands. He pulls out his knife and cuts the palm of my right hand.

'Now the other one.;

'No, Saul. No.'

'Hold out the other one.'

There is no choice. He cuts the palm of my left hand and blood drips from me.

'Now get up or I'll lock your hands as well.'

Somehow I get up and shuffle towards him.

'Closer,' he says. 'Closer,' then, 'turn around.'

I get there. I turn around and he ties a scarf over my eyes.

'Now go and lie down,' he says and leaves the room.

I reach up to untie the scarf he's fastened around my head but the wounds in my hands open up and the blood pours faster as I pull at the knot. Can't get it off and I look for the mat in the dark. Don't find it. Lie down on the floor. I shake. Don't cry. Can't believe this has happened. Saul doesn't behave like this. He is strict but fair. Beats me sometimes but not often. I can't believe that I am lying with my feet chained together and oh, the pain in my hands. Oh, Layla, where are you? It's because of Layla. Suddenly I think I know. She's gone and he blames me.

The next day he puts antiseptic on my hands and binds them up. The scarf is gone.

'You've got to work,' he says. 'You need your hands.'

'I can't work,' I whisper. 'I can't walk.'

'Yes, you can,' he says. 'But you can't run away.' He pauses. 'Like you did last time.' He pauses again and looks at me so that I am forced to drop my eyes in respect. 'You've destroyed our family,' he says. 'Now you will work and you will serve me. I will make you clean again.'

What does that mean I wonder? Make me clean again? I think he's gone mad but don't dare to argue with him.

Saul goes out and leaves me alone to sweep the house. While I'm sweeping, my phone rings. It must be Layla. I look around for the phone and then I see it. My phone is on Saul's shelf, the one above Layla's but I can't reach it. Can't climb on anything with the shackles. I can see her name on the display. Layla, it says. Her name lit up. Green on black. Layla. It rings and rings and then stops as I sink to the floor and sob. Oh Layla, where are you?

The days go by and I manage better with the shackles. Getting down the steps out of the house is difficult. I fell the first time and slid all the way down but I've learned how to do it without falling. My hands heal and I garden, clean and cook. No studying. That's all finished. No phone. No laptop. No books. But no beatings. Saul leaves me alone. He gives me clean clothes but no panties. He cut off my panties so I could wash and shower but after that, didn't give them back. They won't go on over the shackles and he won't take the shackles off, but he leaves me alone. No more shuffling towards him. No more cutting. No beating. Just shackled, that's all.

Night after night, I cry myself to sleep but I find that crying doesn't help. After some time, my tears stop and my heart hardens. I learn to hate and go about each day with the hate growing bigger, turning my heart to stone and spreading into my whole body. Into my soul. I'm turning completely into stone, rock hard. I hate Saul but I can't run away. Or shuffle away. I wouldn't survive because I couldn't get far. I can't reach anyone. Can't reach Layla. She's gone and there is no-one else.

I try to talk to him.

'Where is Layla?' I ask.

'I don't know,' he replies.

'Why did she go?'

He looks at me and says nothing. His silence means that she went because of me. Saul idolises Layla. She was his whole world and now she is gone. His anger gets cold and hard not hot like it was to begin with.

One day he comes to me in the garden and orders me into the house. I shuffle towards the steps that lead to the veranda. It's the only way into the house and every day it is hard.

'Faster,' he orders and I try, hating him with every step. 'Go to your room and lie down. You need a rest.' He laughs. Saul never laughs. He hasn't smiled or laughed since Layla went. His laughter is more frightening than his anger. I go and lie down but he doesn't come. The time passes and afternoon comes. It must be time to cook. My hands are dirty from the garden and I need the lavatory. Slowly I get up and shuffle towards the shower room. There is no sound from where he is. I go in and use the toilet, wash my hands. Go back to my room and lie down again. Still no sound. I watch a gecko run around the walls and make its knocking noise. Tap tap tap. The light changes and the crickets start to chirrup. Louder and louder. It's evening. The dark is coming. There is no light from the living room. He hasn't lit the lamp. I am afraid so I don't sleep. I can feel my heart beating. I can hear it in my ear.

Then he comes.

'Turn over.'

I do.

And then he rips me apart and when he leaves I'm bleeding. Broken and bleeding.

4

My phone doesn't ring anymore and neither does Saul's. In the mornings, the birds sing and in the evenings, the crickets chirrup. After that, the night brings noises. I think there's a carpet snake in the roof but it won't hurt. I hear it sliding about. There are no spiders or ants because I clean and clean. The ants are hard to keep out. Every day they are back but the house is spotless despite my shackles because if Saul sees a dirty mark or spilt food, he beats me.

More important even than the cleaning is the circle. Every day, I have to check the circle and brush it round. Like Layla, Saul won't tell me why I have to do it. It seems like a waste of time, but I can see that he thinks that the circle is more important than anything. And Saul no longer helps with it like he used to do. It's only me. I shuffle round and round and I'm careful. He doesn't speak to me and I remain silent. When I'm in the garden and he's not in sight, I try talking. Just softly to see if my voice still works. It sounds croaky.

Every day, he's vicious. Rips me apart and whispers that he's driving them out, driving them out, driving them out. Often more than once, and my hatred grows. He says he's making me clean and driving them out. Driving what out? I can't keep living like this, but I do. I learn to cope. When Saul comes into my room, my spirit slips away and stands by the window. Watches this large, heavy man ripping my body, but I'm not inside it. Day after day, I leave my body behind. I've learned to do this and it helps. Sometimes I go further than the window and almost forget to come back, but always I do come. Something makes me remember and brings me back. If I can't protect my body, I shall die and I don't want to die. Most of the time, I don't want to die.

I plant pumpkin seeds and watch them grow. I used to love eating pumpkin and Layla made the best pumpkin pie. I don't like any food now. I eat to survive. I garden to survive. I clean to survive. There is no way to escape. There is no way to escape. The thoughts repeat. But maybe, maybe there is just one way to escape, just one way to do it. One way out of here. Only one way that I can think of, so I start to think about that. I look for a weapon but I know that I will have to be sure. Confident and sure. No turning back and no hesitation. It will have to be a knife. I use knives for the vegetables. If I'm careful, I will be able to hide the kitchen knife under my mat but if Saul finds it or if I fail, it will be the end of me. I am sure of it.

Some nights, Saul drinks beer. He went down the mountain last week and I was so happy. I thought he would be gone for days. He would have to be gone for days. It's a long way down the mountain but he was gone for only two nights. How did he manage that? And he came back with beer. Filled the big rucksack with beer and brought it back after just two nights. The ripping started as soon as he got back.

I am careful and I watch because I want to survive. I am going to survive. I lie on my mat and listen to him drinking next door. I hear him taking the bottle top off and throwing it into the bin. A dull metallic ding. Not like a text coming in on the phone. That's a ping. This is a ding. The length of ripping depends on how much he drinks. If it's a lot, he rips for longer. But afterwards, he goes to lie down next door and sleeps. If it's not much, the ripping is quicker and then he gets up and goes. Paces around the house. I will have to learn how much beer is enough to make him sleep. That will be the time.

I'm keeping count of my body cycles. It's nearly time for my blood and it comes. I am grateful for it. Saul leaves me alone for three days. Then it's worse, but I have the three days and three nights free of him. I bleed a lot of the time from the ripping but my monthly blood is different and Saul knows it, too. He starts to count as well and he knows when it's coming. He checks. Then he goes down the mountain and I have three days alone. And three nights. The tv is still there and sometimes Saul asks if I want to watch it with him but I shake my head and stay alone in my room. He doesn't insist. When he's gone to the city, I switch it on and look at the world. It's still there. Everybody still the same. Their lives are going on as normal. Nobody knows that I'm shackled in the mountains. But I will be free of him. I will do it. One day, I will be free.

The best time is the day after he comes back. That's when he relaxes and drinks a lot. After my next blood, I'll do it. That will be the time, so I wait. The pumpkins are growing and the kaukau. Getting big and fat ready for eating. Sometimes Saul brings coconuts from the city and sago, but I prefer the vegetables and fruits that grow up here. I cook green leaves. Layla taught me that our bodies need green leaves. Layla taught me nearly everything I know. Google taught me the rest but there's no teacher now. No Layla. No google.

In the early days, my ankles bled and got infected. Saul put disinfectant on them and wrapped torn sheets around my legs. But then he put the shackles back on top of the bandages. Eventually, my ankles healed and hardened. I can cope with the shackles now but my legs ache from walking like this. They never stop hurting. I will hide the knife under the mat while Saul's away. He checks the kitchen drawer but he's looking to see if I've kept it clean. He doesn't count the knives.

Things go according to plan. Saul waits for my blood, then he goes down the mountain. I put the knife under the mat. The small knife. I daren't hide one of the large knives. It would show. He would miss it. Saul comes back and starts to drink. All as usual. The second day, he drinks a lot so I go to lie down and I listen to the bottle tops dinging into the bin. One and wait. Not long then it's two and wait. Three and wait. Four. I keep listening. It can get to seven but it should be at least six. It needs to be six. I hear him get up. He's coming early. I'll have to make a decision whether to risk it tonight or whether to wait. I think I'll wait. Four is not enough to make him sleep. I know.

He comes. Rips me apart. He's 'driving them out.' Afterwards, he speaks.

'Sit up, Aulani,' he says. 'Sit up.'

His voice is quiet and soft. What's coming now?

'Hold out your hands.'

I watch while Saul reaches under the mat and takes out my knife. Holds it up and waves it about. I've sharpened it. He almost smiles but not quite and then slowly and carefully pressing deep, he cuts both my palms so there is now a cross in each hand. The old cut from the beginning. And the new one. I try to send my soul out of my body but the pain won't let me. The pain is big and I scream. Saul slaps my face and laughs, walks away.

I look at my hands. I've failed but he didn't kill me. I'll never be able to use a knife on him now, but the pain in my hands grows my hatred so big that I know I'll find another way. It will be me or him. Next time, one of us will die.

Time passes. My hands begin to heal and I wait for my blood but it doesn't come. Have I counted properly? I'm sure I have. I always count. I look forward to the time when Saul will be gone from me. My three days of heaven. That's what it feels like when he's gone. I don't mind the shackles or the cleaning or anything. Just that he's gone makes me happy. But the blood doesn't come and Saul knows. He counts, too and checks me day after day. No blood. He knows what has happened. He has left a part of himself inside me. A new life and sometimes I love it and want it. Hormones, Layla told me. Mothers love their babies because of hormones. Is that all? I asked and she would look at me and smile. But sometimes I hate this new child because he's half Saul and I don't care about the part that is half me. (So the hormones don't always work, do they?)

Saul increases my food. Gives me more fish. He says nothing but he wants this child. My work remains the same but he doesn't go down the mountain. He rips me every day and 'drives them out'. That doesn't change. Surely, he will have to go down sometime. He will need beer. And food. The kind of food we can't grow. He will have to sell the new wooden animals and the new table he has made. He will have to go.

I am right. Saul does go and now I sit in the garden and think. It's hard to think when he's here because I have to watch what he's doing and take care so that I'm not beaten. Now he's gone. I can sit and think. There must be a way. I start to weed. It's a mindless task that's good for thinking.

My garden is like the house. It has to be. Clean. No weeds. Perfect. And even with Saul gone, I do the circle. It's become a habit. I don't know why it has to be done but I've started to believe that it's important. One day, I'll understand. Slowly, I start to make a plan.

5

One day of Saul in the city is already gone. The time is going and all the time I'm sick. Not just in the morning. Layla told me about this. She said the sickness comes just in the morning in the first three months, but no, it's all the time. My stomach is flat. No outward sign of this child but he's there. Or she is.

When Saul comes back, I'm ready. Once again, I wait for the second day and lie on the mat and listen. Ding that's one. Then the second. Three. And I wait. Maybe he's stopped and today will not be the day. Four. Five. Silence. I hope that he doesn't stop drinking now because five is too soon. Ding. That's six. It should be enough. Seven. I wait and he comes.

Rips me apart, drives them out and gets up and goes. Soon he is snoring. I force myself to wait some more. If I fail this time, I will die. The child and me. It's crazy but some of the time I love this child. Most of the time, not always. Concentrate, Aulani. Steady, I tell myself. I'm going to try. I get up with as little noise as possible but I can't be completely quiet. You can hear me when I move because of the shackles, but his snoring is louder than the sound of my feet. I pause and wait between every step. I am heading for the living room. That's where Saul sleeps. His mat is rolled out on the floor.

In the doorway, I stop and look at him. He is huge and beautiful. Even I can see how lovely he is. His skin shines. His muscles are firm and ripple when he moves. His hair is like hard black wool. Tiny curls so close together you can't see them. Like a springy mat. When I was little, I used to sit on his knee and try and twist my fingers into the curls but I couldn't. I tried with a pencil and he liked it when I played with his hair.

I move towards the table one step at a time. I shuffle. One step and pause. Stop and wait. Listen. Another step. I shuffle. Pause. Wait and listen. I'm hurrying too much. Impatient. It's a long way to the table and I'm breathing hard. I get there. Reach down to pull the tablecloth to one side and it's there. I see it. The big stone that I've brought inside. It wasn't easy. I bend and pull it out. Slowly. One small move. It makes a noise. Stop. Wait and listen. Suddenly the snoring stops and my heart beats so loudly, I'm surprised that it doesn't wake him up. I'm surprised that I don't explode. I wait. The snoring starts again. And stops. And starts. Continues.

I bend down and pick up the stone. It's heavy but I've practised and I'm strong. I look again at his beauty and raise the stone as high as I can and then I let it go and watch it fall.

Saul cries out. Opens his eyes and looks at me. Moves.

It's got to be done again. I lift the stone once more. Higher than last time and I drop it. Right on target. Crack. His head.

Saul moans and reaches for my legs but I've moved. One last time. My arms are breaking. My legs are aching but I'm not sick. Not now. One last time. Throw this time. It drops and I fall after it.

He's still. I roll off him and move away.

Now for the second stone. I brought two. It's not over yet. The small rock is there under the table. Small, jagged, hard. Perfect. I reach for it. Pick it up and raise my arm and I look at him but my arm falls, sinks back down and I put the rock back. Can't do it. Time to stop.

The key. I must look for the key. My ankles are breaking, hurting worse than usual. I look down at my feet. The key is the only way to get my shackles off. It's round his neck on a piece of plaited string. That's where it always is. I bend down and push my finger under the string and pull. It comes away but there is no key. It must have dropped off somewhere. Don't panic I tell myself. Go slow, but I can't. I need the key and I see it. It's embedded in his flesh. I stop and try to breathe. My body is not mine, it's shaking and gulping. Legs hurt but the rest of me is numb. I watch myself shaking and hear my breath pulling, in and out, in and out, but I'm not here. Not in my body. I've got to come back. Got to finish this thing.

Just a glint of silver sticking out of the wound on his chest. I reach for it and get it but it's wet with blood and it slips through my fingers. I'm shaking. Try again. This time I get it and pull, but it won't come out. I'll have to hold it with something. His shirt. I pull at his shirt but it won't reach to put around the key. It's stuck. Mostly the shirt is underneath him. Slow down. Think. I turn back to the table and pull at the tablecloth. Hold one end and carefully grip the end of the key with it and pull. Yes, it's out. I've got it.

Such a small thing. A little key. Looks like nothing much. I clutch it with one hand and hold on to the table with the other. Like a life raft in a storm but no storm. Just me and the table and Saul on the floor. Something howls outside and I jump, let go of the table but the hand with the key stays closed. As I sink to the floor, I've still got it.

It's there in my hand. There is a lock on each shackle, so I go for the right one because it's easier to reach. Try to push the key into the small hole in the lock but my hand is shaking so badly, it won't go in. Breathe. Slow down and breathe. Try again. Nearly got it. Don't rush. Nearly there, Aulani. I keep on talking to myself, giving myself instructions.

This time I hold the key carefully and push it slowly into the lock. The first part goes in but then it stops. It won't go all the way in. I take the key out and look at it. It's bent. That's why it won't go in. The smaller stone, the rock, is next to me and I pick it up and hit the key with it several times but no luck. I'll have to go down the mountain in shackles. I'll keep the key and try again but until it can be straightened, it won't go into the lock. Did I bend it? Was it when I dropped the stone? I don't think so, but why do I even ask myself these questions? I giggle. I'm losing control of my mind. I reach for the table leg and pull myself up again. Shackles still on. I'll have to manage.

I've prepared. I have my bilum ready but not much in it. I can't carry much. In any case, the laptop is gone and that's what was heaviest last time. Haven't seen it for ages. I think Saul sold it. He never used one and didn't like seeing Layla and me with it, watching movies, googling things, laughing. It made him feel stupid she said. Better not use it when Saul's around. Now the laptop is gone. (But she was right. It's a bad thing to make people feel stupid. Funny to be thinking about that now.)

I've prepared. The broom is ready and I get it and swipe at the top shelf. My phone is on charge. Always on charge but it hasn't rung for months. Not since before my blood stopped. I swipe and I miss. Try again. Miss. Don't get desperate. Slow down, Aulani. He's dead so there's time. Once again, I swipe, and my phone flies off the shelf and falls on to Saul. He groans.

Not dead.

I've got to do it again. I've got to. I reach for the stone but can't lift it. How did I manage before? Can't raise it off the ground. I pick up the little rock instead. It will have to do and I smash it hard onto his legs. His face is already broken. I lean over him and hammer hard at his legs. Hard as I can and I fall with the rock. Fall on top of him. I roll off and reach again for the rock. I smash and I smash and I hear the bones break. And stop.

My phone is between his arm and his body and I reach to get it. I hold my hand in front of his mouth. No breath. All gone.

It's dark so I can't go yet and I'm still in shackles. There are snakes. But I must go. Can't stay here. First of all, I ring Layla. Oh Layla, where are you? I need you. Please, Layla, answer me. I ring and ring but nothing. I text. Nothing. And again. Nothing. Slowly I move. Out of the house, down the steps, along the path and I step out of the circle. Shuffle one step. Then another. I've got water and pumpkin, some kaukau like last time. So long ago. The light is still on in the house. Kerosene lamp still burning. In front of me, pitch black.

I turn back. Will have to wait until morning. I will go and sit beside him and check that he is dead. I shuffle back and step into the circle. Pick up the broom and half-heartedly jab at the earth. Slowly I shuffle towards the house. Towards the light. I'm leaving the darkness behind me. But the light in the house hides a greater darkness. Up the steps. Can hardly move my legs. I shuffle inside. Stand and look. He's on the floor. Of course he's on the floor.

I can't bury him, but I would like to. I can't move him, but I get a sheet and cover him over. It's the least I can do. This time I sit on the stool that he made - the one with the birds - and I look at the shape of him under the sheet. I didn't want to kill him but I had to. I am sorry for everything. For all that we have done to each other, the good and the bad. Sorry that we ever crossed paths. He has shackled me and torn me apart but maybe I was his to break because once he rescued me and I think of that.

I fetch water and drink. I sit and I look. The broken body lies there.

Torturer.

I feel relief. Emotion all drained out. Nothing left. I am not guilty of this man's death. It is he who is guilty. Or destiny. And so my thoughts run on and on, round and round. There is no end. There are no answers.

I get up and shuffle into the bathroom to wash my hands. For the last time, I go to lie on the mat next door and I sleep.

6

The birdsong wakes me up. Always loud. Blue sky. Sunshine. As usual. Nothing else as usual.

My arms ache and I remember the stone and the killing. That is the first thing, then I look at my phone and pick it up. It works but Layla doesn't answer. I text. Can't say much in a text.

'Saul dead. Help me. Auli.'

I shall need the charger before I go. I'll have to find a way to climb up and unplug it. Even in my bedroom, I can smell the body. It's not Saul. He's gone. It's just his body. But no, according to Layla he's still here. His spirit won't leave the house until the third day after death. That's what she taught me about what happens when a person dies. It was one of the life lessons. I shall have to leave the house open and break the circle. So that Saul's spirit can leave.

It's time I went. The sickness is back and the spasms of retching keep coming. I force myself to eat a piece of kaukau and it helps. I drink. I try three times to get the key into the hole so I can unlock the shackle but it's the same as last night. It won't work. Then I have a brainwave. Try the other one, the one on my left ankle. Push in slowly. Click. A miracle. Turn. A miracle. I take it off. Only one shackle and it's time to leave.

I'm so pleased that I keep trying to walk normally and keep falling over. My legs won't walk like they used to do. The muscles will only let me do tiny steps just like when the shackles were on. I think my brain has learned just how far my leg can move without making me fall over and the message has stuck. I keep trying to move my leg further and wider and I fall down again and again, but I don't care. I can stretch my legs. They are mine. My body is mine with no-one to break me. I am alone and I start to sing. Then I remember that I am a killer and I stop and think about it. And there is a child coming.

The child is there whether I like it or not. In another life lesson, Layla taught me that you can get rid of a child in the womb if you are quick. But you need help and I haven't got any so the child will have to stay and I shall have to be strong. I stand as straight as I can and I open my mouth and croak out loud. An old song that Layla taught me. I go around the house and check that all the louvres are wide open. Then I go to get the charger. Somehow I manage to climb up and unplug it, but it takes ages.

I walk outside and stand still on the verandah. Sit down for a minute on the little bench and breathe deep. I can't stay here. I've got to go so I prop the house door open with the stone that we keep in the corner next to the bench. Slowly and carefully, I shuffle down the steps and along the path. I put down my bilum and I go all the way round the circle and take care to break it all the way round. Then I pick up my bilum and I go. Don't look back.

***

All day I have been walking (if you can call my peculiar movement walking) and the light is changing. I am slow and I hear the crickets start to chirp. Night is coming. I am feeling sick and I think of the child. Saul's child. What will

Layla think of that? I get out my phone and check it again. Same as before. No message. I text again.

'Coming down the mountain. Can you help me? Auli'

Time to make a fire. Harder than last time because I ache and keep stopping to retch but nothing comes out. I need to eat something. I need to rest. I was going to eat pumpkin and kaukau but I find an avocado tree with ripe fruit beneath it, some rotten and half-eaten but some that are fine. Saul never liked avocados. He told me that our people don't eat them, but he was wrong. Layla liked them and she taught me how to put salt and eat. We ate a lot of them, the two of us, mostly when Saul wasn't there. He didn't like us to do things that excluded him, but he wasn't cross about the avocados. He was happy to see us eat. Saul used to be kind and loving.

Stop. I don't want to think about him but my mind has a mind of its own. Ha ha. I need to shut some doors inside my head to keep myself safe and sane. I think about the avocados instead. I've brought salt with me just a little, not much, twisted into some paper and then dropped into a little freezer bag, so I sit down and cut open an avocado. Sprinkle salt and slowly eat. Try to empty my mind but can't do it. Thoughts come like waves of the sea. The sea I have not yet seen. Only on television. Thoughts go their own way all over the place.

Before I ran away to find my birth mother, Saul and Layla had begun to argue. When I was small, there was never a cross word. Not to each other. Not to me. They worked and I played and sometimes I worked, too. Play working. Planting kaukau. Pulling weeds. Sweeping the floor. Sweeping the circle. But the circle was never play work. That was serious. The circle was always serious and the first time Saul beat me, it was for that.

I had run through the circle to go and gather firewood in the bush and I had forgotten to brush it afterwards.

'You left a hole, Aulani,' he shouted and I was going to argue but he took me round the back of the house to the shed and he beat me. Afterwards, I could not stand. 'Go into the garden and work,' he said quietly, voice like ice, hard and cutting. 'And never forget this.'

I walked bent to my kaukau patch. Couldn't straighten. I crouched over the plants looking down and my tears dropped into the raised beds of earth where my plants grew. I looked over to where Layla was working and I saw her look at me but she didn't come over, didn't come to bring comfort. Instead, she got up and followed Saul into the house. The punishment worked. After that, I never forgot the circle even when I was excited about something or couldn't wait to do something or get to somewhere.

Many times I asked about it, why the circle was important. It wasn't even a real circle, just a broad ring of cleared dirt that encircled the whole property. Packed down hard and swept clean. Difficult to manage when it rained. (We used a rake when the earth was wet and a broom when it was dry). I was baffled by the beating. Had not intended to be naughty. Couldn't see how what I'd done was bad in any way. I thought Saul was unfair and Layla, too, because she had supported him but I dare not disobey.

Eventually, I asked Layla, 'Do all houses have a circle?'
'No,' she replied.
'Then why do we?'
'To keep us safe.'

'If they don't need one, why do we?'

It was the right question because it didn't get an answer. I had found the thing to ask and now I know part of it. We are different, but I don't know why. Or how.

I tried listening to Saul and Layla when they talked, but they didn't say much and when they talked, it was mostly about the dinner or the garden or about the work that had to be done the next day. But it changed when they argued. Then they talked about other things. I spent months trying to hear what they were saying in their arguments, and gradually I understood some of it (or I thought I did).

Saul was becoming afraid of Layla. It took a long time before I could believe this, but I'm sure it was true. He accused her of having special powers. Of trying to control him. Of passing her powers to me. That was the worst part. That was what made him angriest. She was spoiling me, he said, she loved me too much and it would have to stop. I was not to become like her. I thought about that a lot. More than anything I wanted to be like Layla. And Saul loved her so why wouldn't he want me to be like her? And what did the rest of it mean?

Once when I was in bed, they had been arguing for hours speaking with raised voices, very unusual. Saul was angry and he shouted twice, 'You're dangerous, Layla. You're dangerous.'

I heard her sob and then something that I couldn't hear, but then I heard her voice again, speaking quietly and her voice was clear, 'I'll have to go, Saul, won't I?'

With difficulty, I stop the thoughts. It's hard to get up because I'm weary but I need more firewood. What I've got will not last the night and it's dangerous without a fire. There are snakes. Too high here for Papuan Blacks but there are plenty of others and some pythons. Layla said she saw someone die of snakebite. Two days and the man was gone. It would be less for a woman or a child. Every time I hear a rustle, I grow tense and I peer into the darkening undergrowth. Sometimes I see an eye. I think I see an eye and then it is gone again. Sometimes I see Saul's face and his eyes looking straight at me. With kindness.

In the morning, I wake and check my phone. I'm in a little clearing and the trees are tall but the light shines through, glancing off the leaves and dancing around the place where I sit. The birds are singing and the sound echoes. I check my phone. Battery - seventy-five per cent. No messages. Where are you, Layla? And then I remember that Layla rang and rang me after I came back, but I was shackled so I couldn't answer. Would Layla think that I didn't want to speak to her anymore? I hope not, but how could she know what was happening? She might think that I'd found my birth mother. She wouldn't understand why I didn't reply.

I eat and drink and set off as soon as I can. I've got to keep going and my legs hurt worse than yesterday. I can hardly walk and my right foot with the shackle is heavy. Before long, I sort of drag it behind me. Can't seem to lift it off the ground. My foot keeps getting tangled in roots, although the track is clear most of the time.

On the fourth day, I am nearly dead and can hardly move. Surely I must be down soon. I grit my teeth and try to forget the sickness in my stomach and the pain in my legs and feet. Have to keep moving somehow or I'll die here. And the baby, too. Not sure I want the baby, but I don't have a choice. Put inside my body without my agreement and now I can't get it out. It's not me or him. It's both of us together, live or die.

It takes seven days. On the seventh morning, I eat the last of the kaukau and I drink water. Then I crawl and keep on crawling. Can't stand now. There is still no message from Layla but every morning and every evening I have texted her. My hands are now as painful as my feet and then I see it. The road. The blessed road. It's close but I'm not sure I can make it. I stop, exhausted. I'm going to ring the police. They're the ones who can get this other shackle off my foot, but I hesitate.

I've thought this through before. Ringing the police is dangerous. I've just killed a man. They won't know that, but they will ask questions. Where have I come from? How did I get like this? What has happened to me? I'll have to tell them that Saul and Layla ran off and abandoned me. That they left the key for me on the table, but that I could only get one shackle off. Would the police go and look for them? I think it's unlikely and I could give them the name of Saul's place which is a long way away. If they looked there, they wouldn't find him. Would they go up the mountain to Keroko to check? It seems unlikely. They would have to walk. There is no road for cars. No airstrip for planes. Would it be worth it? Seems unlikely. All the way down the mountain I've thought about this, but I thought that Layla would reply. I have hoped hoped hoped that Layla would reply. I have prayed, although I don't have a religion. Layla taught me about religions in the life classes. I look again at the phone. I ring her again. The phone rings and rings ... and rings. No reply.

There is no choice. I dial the number for the police. I ring and ring. The sound goes on and on. I give up but can't move. One more time. The phone rings and rings. I know it's the right number. Layla gave it to me long ago.

'Hello. Can I help you?'

'I'm near the road. I'm sick. Please come.'

'Which road?' somebody asks.

'I've come down the mountain from Keroko. Nearly reached the road....'

7

High up on the wall, there is one small window with no louvres, only flywire. That's what I see when I open my eyes. I'm lying on the floor on a dirty mat in what must be a police cell. I look at my ankles. The shackles have gone. The one that was still there on my right ankle has been removed, but I don't remember it happening. Don't remember anything. My stomach is convulsing. I look for somewhere to be sick. There's a bowl on a wooden bench. It will have to do. I retch but nothing comes and I lie down again. I look around for my bilum, my phone, but they're gone. I drag myself up and feel my legs. No shackles but still can't walk. I hobble to the door.

'Hello,' I call. 'Hello. Is there anybody there?'

Two eyes appear in the slit in the door and a voice speaks.

'What do you want?'

'I'm thirsty,' I say, and then, 'What am I doing in here?'

'You rang us,' the voice replies, 'so we came to get you.'

'Yes, but I rang for help. Not to be locked up. Why am I locked up?'

'It's just while we check you out,' the voice says. 'And you were unconscious. It's for your own protection. You needed to recover. You couldn't go anywhere.' I have to admit that there is some truth in this.

'Can I have my bilum and my phone?' I ask. 'Where are they?'

'They're safe,' he replies. 'Locked up. I can't give them to you. You'll get them when you leave.'

'And when will that be?' I ask beginning to feel anxious. How on earth am I going to get out of this place?

'As soon as we've checked you out,' he replies and his eyes smile through the slit in the door.

'And how will you do that?'

'Ask you some questions about yourself and check that everything is in order. Then you'll be able to go.'

'Can't you do it now?' I ask.

'No, of course not. I'm not the one who will do it. Inspector Boa will talk to you tomorrow. It's Sunday today,'

'Oh,' I say. I had no idea what day it was. 'Will you fetch me some water?' I ask and hear what sounds like OK.

In a few minutes, I hear footsteps, something being put on the floor and then the sound of the bolt sliding across. The door opens and a young policeman stands and looks at me. More a boy than a man. Not much older than me probably, but tall. He picks up the tray and carries it into my cell.

'Here you are,' he says, putting it on the bench. I look at the tray and see a white enamel bowl with a chipped blue rim, a white plastic fork and a bottle of water. 'It's good,' he says pointing to the rice in the bowl. 'It's got fish in it.'

'Thank you,' I say and he watches as I sit on the mat and start to eat. He's right. It tastes good. The rice is cold but it doesn't matter. It's cooked in coconut like they do on the coast and there are pieces of fish.

'It's the same food that we had,' he goes on. 'Inspector Boa's wife brought it in, and I saved you some.'

'Thank you,' I say again. 'It's good,' and I feel myself warming towards this young man. One of Layla's life lessons flashes into my brain. *Don't trust anyone*, she told me, *especially the ones who seem to be kind*. But I ignore it. How can I live if I'm suspicious of everyone?

'What's your name?' I ask, but before he replies, I remember that I had once trusted Saul and look how that turned out.

'Constable Goasa,' he replies and then relaxes. 'My name is Joel,' he adds. 'What's yours?'

'Aulani,' I say.

'Aulani what?' he asks. 'What's your family name?'

'Kevau,' I reply. 'I'm Aulani Kevau.' It's a name I remember from a news programme. I've never had a family name and I realise that I don't know the family name of either Layla or Saul. Or whether they have the same name. I'll have to think this through before the questioning.

'That's strange,' he says. 'Where are you from?' I wonder what is strange about the name that I've chosen but don't ask.

'Up in the mountains,' I reply. 'A small place in the mountains in Central Province. Keroko.' I should ask him where he is from but I am so busy trying to work out my own answers that I forget. These are the first questions, I realise. Sooner than I thought and I should have been prepared. I need time to think.

'I need to go to the toilet,' I tell him, 'and I need to wash.' He brings me a bucket and goes away. Tells me to call when I've finished and I feel embarrassed, but I have no choice. When I've finished, he takes away the bucket and brings me a bowl and a jug of water so I wash as best I can. I thank him and tell him that I need to rest. It's not true and I like his company but I can't risk any more questions until I've thought of some answers. I like Joel. He doesn't seem like a policeman. He looks a little like Layla, not at all like Saul and that is a relief. I'm trying to lock Saul out of my mind, but he keeps reappearing. Looking kind and that's the worst part.

All night long, I keep on waking and the tiny space is almost as bright as day with the moonlight shining in. I can't sleep because I keep seeing Saul's face. Over and over again in my mind, I lift the stone and drop it. Sometimes it hits, sometimes it misses. And I'm too hot all the time and sticky. It's much hotter down here than up in the mountains. I keep on going over my answers to the questions I think they will ask and I'm nervous. My answers might not work. Even the name I chose seems to be wrong. Why did Joel find it strange? Too late to change it now. My stomach is heaving again and I reach for the bowl and retch. Hard to prepare myself for questioning with this thing inside me churning my stomach around. Saul has gone but he's left the child behind. His child and my child. No separation. I shiver despite the heat and sleep at last.

In the morning, it's the birdsong that wakes me, even in here. I've figured out the name problem. If we've all got the same name, 'Kevau' wouldn't work because it isn't a North Solomons' name. But how would Joel know that Saul came from the North Solomons? It must be something else. I remember a North Solomons name I saw in *The Post Courier*. It was Kroening. I'm sure it was Kroening. Saul can be Saul Kroening and they'll just have to accept that Layla and myself are Kevau. Maybe that is still wrong, but I can't change it now. Before I have time to do any more thinking, Joel arrives and brings me the bucket and the jug. I can have these first and then he'll bring me breakfast he says. The breakfast is a piece of sago which I don't much like because I'm not used to it, but it settles my stomach and the hot sweet tea tastes good. I've hardly finished eating when Joel comes back and says that Inspector Boa is waiting for me and that he will take me to see him.

Joel notices that I shuffle and hobble after him as he walks down the corridor. He knocks on a light green door.

'Come in,' I hear from inside. Quite a high voice for a man but when I go in, I see that Inspector Boa is not small as I expected but a big man. He doesn't smile.

'Sit down,' he orders.

I sit.

'We have a few questions for you so that we can check your story before we let you go.'

What I want to do is ask why he needs to check my story, but I understand that I have to be submissive. God knows I've had plenty of practice and once again Saul's face appears before me, but I push it away. I nod and look down. Once again, Layla taught me how to behave like this in life lessons. She said that we lived differently from everyone else in our country, but that I had to learn how to behave like other girls. This submissive thing was one of the lessons.

'What is your name?'

'Aulani Kevau,' I almost whisper.

'Speak up, girl,' he commands.

'Aulani Kevau,' I say again a bit louder. I notice that his shirt has a faint dirty mark just underneath the collar as though someone has rubbed at it with a wet cloth but the mark wouldn't come off. Can't take my eyes off it.

'And where do you live?'

45

'Keroko,' I answer. No help for it. I said it on the phone, I think.

'And why were you shackled?'

'I was being punished,' I say, and hesitate but I see that Inspector Boa is waiting for me to explain. He wants more. Joel is sitting in the corner taking notes and he looks up at me. His eyes are kind. *Don't trust anyone*, Layla told me. *Don't trust anyone*. It doesn't matter, I think. I've got to say something. 'For running away,' I murmur and notice that Inspector Boa smiles at last but not at me. He smiles over at Joel as though saying something like *There, I told you so*. I can see he's decided I'm a bad girl. This is not going well.

'And what happened to you after that?' the Inspector asks.

'My guardians ran away and left me,' I say and don't speak further. I am sure that the less I say the better.

'Who were your guardians?'

'Saul Kroening.'

'Yes, and who was your mother?'

'Not my mother,' I say. 'But like my mother.'

'Yes,' Inspector Boa says getting impatient. His fingers are tapping on the desk in front of him and he keeps glancing over at Joel. 'What is her name?'

'Layla,' I reply.

'Layla what?' The Inspector's voice is beginning to sound angry.

'Layla Kevau,' I say, hoping this will be all right and I see the Inspector look over once more to where Joel is sitting, but Joel has his head down, writing away as though his life depended on it.

'And where do you think they went?' the Inspector asks.

'I'm not sure,' I say, 'but I think they were going to Saul's place,' and add hopefully, 'Buka, North Solomons.'

'Are you sure they were both going there?' the Inspector asks.

'I think so,' I say.

'And why did they leave you behind?'

'Because they were angry with me for running away.' I had rehearsed this part in my mind. 'They left me the key for the shackles. It was on the table but it was bent and I could only unlock one of them.' That's it. I haven't thought of anything else. I had hoped it would be enough. But it isn't.

'Why would they leave their home?' the Inspector persists, and I see that what I have thought of is not nearly enough. The Inspector is suspicious. He thinks my story doesn't make sense. But why does he care? I think it's because he doesn't like me. It's almost as though he's afraid of me, but I know that can't be true.

'I don't know,' I say. 'I don't know why they ran away.'

That's it. I am dismissed and led back to the cell, still stumbling and failing to get my legs to stretch out and walk like other people walk. Like I once used to walk. It hasn't gone well but, surely, once they check in Bougainville and find no Saul and no Layla, they will let me go. What would be the point of keeping me longer? My secret fear, of course, the fear I hardly dare admit to myself is that they might send someone to Keroko to check things out up there. If that happens, I am finished.

All day, I lie alone in my cell and it gets hotter and hotter. I think I am going to melt in the heat and a film of sweat coats my body. My blouse and laplap are wet and drops of sweat trickle down my face, into my hair. The back of my neck is wet. There is water to drink but I retch all day and my legs have pains like hot irons. Fire from both sides. Inside my body and out. And fear. I need to know what is happening but know instinctively that Joel will not speak to me while Inspector Boa is there. In fact, Joel is gone all afternoon and another man comes to bring me the bucket and some water, but he doesn't speak to me. Does it all in silence. I listen hard and think I hear Inspector Boa going and someone else arriving. I hope that it is Joel, but I don't know.

At last, it is evening but still hot and two eyes appear in my door. It is Joel and I feel a big relief. I am about to speak to him when he brings my supper into the cell but he looks at me and shakes his head. I understand that someone is still there, and I don't speak.

'Thank you,' I say and that is all.

Later, when he comes to collect my bowl, I can see that he has relaxed.

'They've gone,' he tells me and asks, 'How are you, Au-lani?'

'What's going to happen?' I ask. 'Are you going to let me go?'

Joel shakes his head and my spirits sink. Can't believe that my spirits can sink but they do.

'What's going to happen?' I ask again.

'They've sent a man up to Keroko to check your story,' he tells me and just in time, I remember Layla's words. *Don't trust anyone.* Don't tell him anything I tell myself and try hard to pretend that everything is all right and that it's all fine. 'He'll be back in two or three days time,' Joel says. 'He'll be quick. He knows the mountain. You should be able to go when he comes back.'

'That's good,' I say and manage to smile. 'Are you on duty again tomorrow?' I ask.

'No,' he says,' I'm off until Wednesday afternoon.'

I can tell that he likes me but there's no more to say so he takes my bowl and leaves me to sleep.

8

No sleep comes. Only the night noises and the moonlight. Bright like last night. I have to make a plan. I'm not retching any more but I hardly notice with the heat and the pain and the desperation in my mind. I notice cockroaches running about all over the floor. They must have been there before and I wonder why I didn't notice them earlier. But I don't care. I've got to make a plan. I've got to make a plan. I've got to make a plan. But oh my dear, I can't think of one.

I think of Layla. That's what she would say - oh, my dear, oh my dear - so maybe if I think of Layla, I can find a way out. Layla always knew what to do. Have I come to the end? Do I give up now? And if they find out that I've killed Saul, what will happen next? I know that I shall be killed, but I don't know how. Maybe Saul's relatives will come and kill me. Stop it, I think. His wantoks have not been interested in him for years. Why should they care now? But I know things don't work like that. There's pride and revenge and it's all about those feelings. Payback. Logic doesn't enter into it. Calm down and think. Put the feelings to one side. That's what Layla would say.

I lie in the half-dark with the moon lighting up the cell and I try to do this. There is one solution. I will have to ask Joel to let me escape. He likes me. But does he like me enough? What would happen to him if he let me escape? I don't think I would be worth it. Whatever I might promise wouldn't be worth it. He would lose his job. But it's the only chance I've got. As I send my mind round in the same circles over and over again, I see Saul's face looking at me. And all the time, he is smiling. It is still hot, but at last, I sleep.

Wednesday arrives. The day of reckoning when the man will return if he's as quick as Joel said he would be. I'm feeling sick again. The baby is pulling my stomach apart from the inside. The father is pulling my mind apart with his everlasting smile and I'm dying to go to the toilet.

'Hello,' I shout. 'Can you help me? I need the toilet.'

It's like torture while I wait for the slow slow steps of the duty officer who brings the bucket. I think I won't be able to hold on, but I do. When the body needs like that, it drives out everything else but as soon as I'm relieved, the anxiety returns. I ask to wash and the man brings water and a bowl. It helps a little. After that, he brings me food and water to drink. It's corn and once again, my stomach settles after the food.

I'm beginning to feel better. The retching is not so bad and not so frequent. At least, I'll be able to fully concentrate on being killed I think and laugh. Layla says that you should always laugh. However bad things are, it will help to laugh. Help your body and your mind. But you mustn't let others see you laughing or they will hurt you more and worse than before. How does Layla know all these things? And why did she teach me all this?

The day gets hotter but passes faster than yesterday and the day before. It's because I'm afraid. I listen to one man go and another arrive. Someone brings my evening meal. It isn't Joel but I heard him speaking so I know he's back. He's out there in the office where they sit together and do their work. I saw the place when I went for my questioning.

Every so often, I hear his voice. Why doesn't he come? I think that he's waiting for the other policeman to leave. I'm lucky that I've got Joel to guard me in the evenings. Lucky? Yes. Layla says we should value every good thing, however small. Always value every good thing she said. I remember all her teaching and the life lessons most of all. I must have been listening. There'll be plenty of the bad stuff she told me. What bad stuff I used to think?

At last, It happens. The other man goes and shortly after that, Joel comes to my cell. First of all, he brings me the bucket and the jug and the bowl for washing and I'm grateful. Still embarrassed, but grateful. Then he takes them away.

'Will you come back?' I ask him and he nods. I hardly dare to look at him because I know that the man who went to Keroko has come back. I heard them talking late this afternoon but I couldn't hear what they were saying. Joel will know by now that I am a killer but it doesn't show in his face. I hope he will listen to me. I hope that he will understand why I did it, but from all that Layla told me, he won't. Nobody will sympathise with a woman, although she never talked specifically about a woman having to kill anybody. Just spoke in general about things that people did and about attitudes towards women. And she taught me how girls and women should behave if they want to survive. We lived in such isolation that I had to learn everything from her.

When Joel comes back, he comes in and closes the door. Sits down on the bench while I sit on the mat.

'What happened?' I ask. 'What did the man say when he came back from Keroko?' I can't bear it any longer. I just have to ask and I have to hear him say it.

'It was a mess,' Joel says and looks at me. 'The whole house was a mess. Torn apart. Bits of bedsheets and table-cloth. Some books torn apart. Everything as you said. (No, I never said anything about a mess.) Your guardians have gone.'

I look at him and wait for the next part but it doesn't come and he doesn't look shocked. Perhaps there's been a miracle. Layla taught me about those, too. They crop up every so often, but you can't rely on them. I shall have to keep on pretending.

'I'm free to go then,' I say and it's then that I really see his face. It's full of something. Not shock. It's anxiety. Fear. My left foot starts twitching and I try to keep it still. I look at him.

'No,' he says. 'You've got to stay here. They're going to charge you, Aulani.'

My foot bumps harder against the mat. I look at it as though it doesn't belong to me. Can't control it.

'What with?'

'Stealing.'

I almost laugh. What does he mean 'stealing'? My foot is still twitching.

'They found the money in your bilum,' he says, wrapped up in the bag with the salt. They say you must have stolen it.'

'They left it for me,' I snap. 'It was on the table with the key for the shackles.' I'm surprised at how fast I've replied and how angrily. Almost as though it were true.

I see Joel hesitate before he replies. 'It doesn't matter,' he says. 'They're going to keep you, Aulani. They won't let you go.'

'Why not?' I ask and at last my foot slows down.

'They think you're a witch.'

'What?' I shoot back. 'That's crazy. How could I be? They don't exist,' but I see straight away that my last statement was a mistake. I remember Layla telling me about witches. Not much but a bit. Everybody believes in black magic she told me. People get killed for it.

'You know that's not true,' Joel says slowly, dropping his eyes like a girl. 'You know they exist. Everybody knows. In my own village some years ago, a woman killed a young boy. Sanguma. The boy was my father's little brother.'

'What happened to her?' I asked.

'I don't know,' he says. 'It was before I was born. But I know she escaped.'

'Why do they think I'm a witch?' I ask.

'It's because you were shackled,' he says and points to the scars around my ankles, bands of thick white skin that mark my legs. 'Long time shackled, not just for a couple of days. That means you were dangerous.'

I don't know what to say. A miracle happens. No Saul in the house, but now this. Joel gets up and goes out and I sit up on the mat and lean against the bench. I've got to get out. I know from Joel's face and I know from the things that Layla told me that if they keep thinking that I'm a witch, they will kill me. Or worse. I stand up and shuffle to the door.

'Joel,' I call. 'Joel, come back,' but he doesn't come. 'Joel, I'm thirsty. Can I have some water?' He doesn't answer, doesn't come. There is no sound at all.

Night comes. Moonlight. The night is like day. Not dark but long. Never-ending. Every so often, I call for Joel. When morning comes, it will be too late. He will be gone.

9

The interview room looks different now. Pale green walls. Painted plasterboard. The same, I suppose. Didn't really look at it last time. There's a ceiling fan and it wobbles as it turns. Hope it won't fall. Hope it will. Hope it won't. Inspector Boa is wearing the same shirt with the same mark. Not washed. Maybe his wife has left him. She would have washed it. Should have washed it. Women wash the shirts even though they do other work as well like jobs in offices and shops. And they work in the garden but still do the washing and the cooking and the childcare. So many things I know even though I have not been part of that life. That ordinary life.

'How much did you take?' This is the second time he has asked the same thing.

I give the same reply. 'I don't know,' I say. 'The money was on the table with the key.'

'You didn't say that yesterday,' he says, triumphant. One point to him.

'It didn't seem important.'

'You mentioned the key,' he reminds me.

'Yes,' I say and I don't have to remember to be submissive, to look down. It's all I can manage. I'm afraid and trying hard to hold on. To think clearly and give the best answers.

'Why did you mention the key and not the money if they were together side by side on the table?'

'The key was important,' I say. 'To get the shackles off and it was bent. Only one came off.' If it hadn't been for the bent key, I think, I wouldn't be here at all. Wouldn't have phoned them up. If I'd known what would happen, I wouldn't have phoned them anyway. If only I'd known.

'And why were you shackled?' he asks. The killer question. The one to which he's sure he knows the answer.

I don't reply.

'Why were you shackled?' he asks again, louder and harsher, more insistent.

'I ran away,' I tell him softly.

'Write that down,' he instructs a policeman I haven't seen before, who is sitting in the corner where Joel sat last time. The man has a big scar down his cheek. 'Ran away. Lazy. Wouldn't work.'

'No,' I say.

'Be quiet,' he orders sharply. 'It's not your turn to speak.' Boa turns again to the man in the corner. Scarface. 'Disobedient,' he adds. 'Write that down. You heard her, didn't you?'

There's a silence while Scarface writes it down and Boa flips through his papers. The fan whirrs and wobbles. Finally, he looks up.

'You are charged with stealing,' he tells me and nods to Scarface who is still in the corner sitting down. 'Take her back to the cell.'

My legs hurt. I fall on the way back because Scarface grabs my arm and hurries me along. I can't walk fast. My legs still won't move properly. When we get to the cell door, he opens it and pushes me inside. Hard. I fall on the mat and you can see the marks from his fingers where they've pressed into my arm. Three red marks dipped into my skin. Nothing compared to the shackles, I think. Or the ripping. I can feel nervous laughter rising within me but I keep it down. It will make things worse. Everything will make things worse for me.

The day passes quickly racing towards its end and then the next day and the next one. How many days do I have left? Joel doesn't come. Bucket. Jug. Food. Water. Lie down. Sometimes retching. Not so much now. Hot. Sweaty. Skin is damp. Lie down. Sit down. Stand up. Think. Don't think. No way out. Joel doesn't come and Joel doesn't come and Joel doesn't come.

***

'Hello,' I hear. 'Hello, Aulani. Are you thirsty?'

At last. It's Joel. Nobody calls my name. Only Joel. My heart leaps with hope and I try to push it back but it won't go down. It's the evening. He opens the door and comes in.

'They've all gone,' he says and sits down on the bench.

I look at him but don't speak.

'I had a couple of days off,' he tells me. 'I went to the village.'

'Oh,' I say and am quiet again. Don't know what to say but I've got to think of something.

'What was your guardian's name?' he asks.

'Saul,' I say. ' Kroening. Saul Kroening.'

'No,' he says. 'Your mother. What was her name?'

'Layla,' I tell him, 'but she's not my first mother. Layla's my guardian, my second mother.'

'It was her,' he says and stops to look at me. I hear the note in his voice, the anxiety.

'What do you mean?' I ask.

'Layla,' he replies. 'She's the one who killed my father's little brother. She was married to Saul and he took her and escaped.'

'No,' I say. 'Layla would never kill anyone,' and I stop as my mind fills with the knowledge that I, too, would never kill anyone. But I did.

'But she did,' he tells me. 'Layla is a witch.'

'Did you tell them?' I ask. I mean did he tell Inspector Boa and the others. He knows who I mean.

'No,' he says. 'It was they who told me and that's why I went to my village to find out. And it's true.'

'I didn't know,' I say but I suppose I did know. That's why Saul became afraid of her. He loved her but he believed she was dangerous. I remember his words. *You're dangerous, Layla, you're dangerous.*

Joel holds out his hand to me. Wants me to sit beside him on the bench, but I don't take it. Don't take his hand. I mustn't trust him. *Don't trust anyone*, Layla told me. *Don't trust anyone.* But he's my only chance. I go to sit with him and let him touch me. We sit close and closer. We lie down together and he's gentle. It's not a ripping, it's a wave, an ocean wave of pleasure in my lonely life.

The days pass and I count them. With my nail I scratch a mark at the bottom of the wall behind the bench. One small mark for each day. It's hot, but every day I walk up and down in the small room forcing my legs to stretch out and walk. I'm shuffling less. In the evenings, Joel comes and we talk a little and we lie together.

'Is there a date for the court?' I ask him, day after day.

'No,' he says. 'No date,' and he explains that it always takes a long time.

'Why so long?'

'Usually, it's because we want to keep the girls,' he tells me and blushes.

'What for?' I ask but I already know.

'We have them over the bench,' he tells me.

'All of you?'

'Yes,' he replies but he doesn't look ashamed. It's normal for that to happen. No shame.

'Then why am I different?' I ask and that's when his face changes.

'They're afraid of you,' he says. 'Your court date will be quicker because they don't want to keep you here.' I understand. There's nothing I can say to him. I've tried.

I know what I have to do. I wait and wait and when I have counted five weeks, I tell him. It's exactly five weeks since I came here to live in this small prison with the high window, the heat and the gentle Joel.

'I'm seven days late,' I tell him. 'My blood hasn't come,' and I see that he's pleased. It's impossible, but he wants this child that he thinks is his. He doesn't even know that he's not the first one. He's experienced but he knows nothing. Feels like I'm ancient and he's just a boy, but I'm sixteen and he is twenty. It was my birthday before I came down the mountain and I'm old enough for most things but Joel at twenty should have a wife by now, especially as he's got a good job. Maybe he already has one. Or two. I haven't asked.

'What shall we do?' he asks and I almost laugh. How can he ask me that? But then I think and say what I need to say.

'Let me go,' I say. 'Let me escape and we can meet later somewhere safe.'

He shakes his head. 'I'd lose my job,' he says. 'I can't do that.'

I bite back the words that fill my mouth. Anger. Entreaties. Explanations. I choke on them and swallow them down. They will make things worse. I reach into myself for patience. It's the hardest thing, but I find it. I will have to wait.

One night he comes and I can see there's a change.

'What's happened?' I ask.

'No date for the court,' he says. 'There won't be one.' He pauses and he's fighting with himself. Should he tell me and betray his colleagues? I watch his face. I'm silent.

'They're going to kill you,' he tells me. 'No torture. We're the police, they said, not some primitive village men. We'll just kill her and there will be an end to it.'

'How?' I ask.

'They're going to burn the police station,' Joel replies.

'When?' I ask.

There's another pause. Joel wants to trust me and sometimes he does, but sometimes he doesn't.

'Tomorrow night,' he replies.

'Then you've got to let me go,' I say. No more time for patience, waiting, being careful. Who knows what the right thing is to say or the wrong thing. My words pour out. 'Give me my bilum, Joel and my phone. Let me go.' I watch his face. I think he loves me but there are other things that matter. 'You can't burn your child to death. Your son.'

I think this is the tipping point. Not me. His unborn son.

'I'll lose my job,' he says. 'I can't do it.'

'No,' I say.. 'Tell them that I made you do it. I'm a witch, remember. You had no choice. I cast a spell. Now, Joel. I'm going to make you do it. Make you let me go.'

Fear fills his face and I see that his colleagues and the people in his village have filled him up with their stories about me. Their beliefs and fears about Layla and me.

'It's not true,' I tell him one last time. 'I can't make you do anything, Joel. I can't make anybody do anything. I've got no powers at all,' but I can see that my words are not reaching his brain and he doesn't reply.

Joel goes away, and it is silent. He comes back. Doesn't touch me. Hands me my bilum. 'The phone is inside,' he says. 'My number is in the phone. Ring me, Aulani.'

I walk through the door of my cell down the corridor into the big room where people come in. And I step outside.

10

It is night and it's dark. I am on the run and I don't know where to go. I look around me. I can't see anybody in the street. On the run? That's a joke, I can hardly walk. I set off down the street and see the dirt, the rubbish, the green discarded husks of betel nut and the red stains of the juice covering the bottom of the walls of every store. It's where the walls meet the pavement. It's where people have spat. There's been a lot of spitting. Layla used to chew a lot. Her mouth was always red and her teeth. Saul didn't chew because he said that beer was better, but Layla pulled a face and said he wasn't a proper PNG man if he didn't chew. She made me try it, but I didn't like the taste and she didn't insist. It was supposed to make you feel good but I didn't get that far.

I stumble and nearly trip over some legs as I notice a man lying in a doorway, but he doesn't move or speak and I pass by as quickly as I can. Saul said it was dangerous in the city. For a man he said. No man should walk alone at night. For a girl, I asked? Impossible! What would happen to her I wanted to know? But he wouldn't say. I look around. The place is deserted. No-one around. No body or soul. At least I have a chance, I think. Better than being burnt alive in the police station. Would they have done it? Joel thought so. I want to stop and look at my phone, but I don't. It's too dark to see and I can't risk stopping for more than a minute. I have to keep on walking.

No idea where I'm going. The street is dusty and it's still hot. My feet are used to having earth beneath them, not the hard grey concrete (is it concrete?) of the streets and I feel the little stones start to dig in. My feet are not hard enough for the city. After a few steps, I have to stop and pull a piece of broken glass from my right foot. It bleeds a bit but soon the blood and dust mix together. My foot is all right after I've pulled the glass out. Broken cans are more dangerous but they're easier to avoid. Many people don't wear shoes so nobody will notice me for that although, at the moment, there's no-one to notice anything. That's good and I'm walking better than I did. All the work I did on my legs and the exercise, backwards and forwards in the cell, has helped a lot.

I need somewhere private to sit down and think about what to do and where to go but can't see anywhere. A car drives past, slows down but then continues on. A relief. It's not until my body relaxes again that I realise how tense I am. But the car is coming back. This time it slows down and stops beside me. I walk past.

'Get in the car,' somebody yells at me. 'You need a lift, little girl.'

I don't reply. I keep on walking. Am going as fast as I can but still, I'm slow. Damn my legs. I used to be fast. Out of the corner of my eye, I see the car drive past again then stop a little way in front of me. A man gets out. The car seems to be full of men, I see faces hanging out of the windows. Leering. The man walks towards me and I wonder what to do. Can't turn and run. Can't walk past. I've got no weapon. A knife but it's deep in the bilum if it's even still there. No stone. No roach poison that some girls carry to spray into men's eyes. I've heard about that and wonder if it works. Wish I had some. Face him. That's what Layla said. Always face your enemy then you've got a chance, but what chance is there? I've got no defence. I stop. There's no way I'm going to get past him. I stop and watch him approaching but I don't turn round. I look him straight in the eye. He's not hurrying, coming slow. Smiling at me. It is time to speak.

'Watch me,' I say and I put my bilum on the ground and lift my arms high in the air and turn around slowly, all the way round. 'Don't touch me or I'll make your child die.' I'm speaking quietly but he can hear me. The place is quiet. I see him hesitate and almost stop. 'Your son,' I say and then for good measure, I add, 'and your brother, too. They will both die.' I have no idea if he has a son or a brother. I'm just hoping on that.

He stops and stares at me. We are both still and staring at each other.

'What did you do with your arms?' he asks me.

'You know what I did,' I say and I see that he's thinking that perhaps he does know. Perhaps he does. 'It's the circle of safety,' I say. 'How else could I walk down the street in the night?'

I am afraid of him and the faces hanging out of the car but I meet his eye and pretend to be calm. Still and calm. Pretend that I can do anything with the power of my thoughts. The power of my will. That I have special powers and that I can do to him whatever I like.

'Come closer,' I invite and this time I've won. His eyes show his fear and he turns and walks, breaks into a run. Back to the car, jumps in, can't get in fast enough and they've gone.

I can't believe it. I made it up and it worked. I made him afraid and he went. Ran! Maybe I do have special powers. How else would it happen? How else would I be able to make him run away from me like that? But I do know. I know about fear, and I know that my power is not real so I don't want to chance it again. Soon I'll have people coming after me because I've admitted it as I did just now. I said I was a witch.

I hurry as fast as I can with my damaged legs to the end of the street and turn left into a totally different kind of road. No stores. No pavement. It's dark and there's not much light from the sky. Perhaps it's going to rain. I walk along the side of the road past hedges and driveways, past houses that are all lit up. The third house I come to is dark so this is the one. I breathe with relief and pray that it's empty. Completely empty. I walk into the drive. My right foot is beginning to drag again even though there's no shackle there now. It's as though my brain is stuck in the past and continues to feel what has already gone. There is no sound from the house and no light. A miracle I think. A place of safety for the night from men and from snakes. I go under the house and almost collapse on to the ground.

There's a sink here on a raised slab of concrete so I get up again and step on to it to reach for the tap. Water gushes really loud. I turn it off as quickly as I can but no-one comes so I try again. Turn it just a little bit and drink and wash. I need the toilet so I have to go in the garden. There's a hibiscus hedge but too low. Looks as though it's been cut down recently so there's nowhere to hide but there's no moon or starlight. Must be cloudy and the house is dark so I go into the garden, crouch down near the hedge and hope for the best. No-one comes. Then I go back and sit under

65

the house. Someone might come back later, I think. There's space for a car in the drive. The people who live here might have all gone out for the evening. But that seems unlikely. What about the children? And the women? Wouldn't they have stayed behind? Maybe there are children asleep upstairs in the house but somehow I'm sure that there aren't. It's too quiet. Not a sound from inside.

I see that there's a bulb and a light switch under the house but I daren't put it on. I search in my bilum in the dark and I feel my phone. Hallelujah! I mouth it under my breath. That's what Saul used to say. It came from the songs he used to sing as a kid. Religious songs, I think. What does it mean I asked him. It means Hallelujah, he replied and grinned. It's an expression of joy, Layla said, but I already knew. You could tell from Saul's face. The phone is off so I switch it on, but it's dead. The battery must be flat. Either that or it's broken but at least it's still there. Let's hope it's the battery and nothing worse, but there's nothing I can do about it at the moment. At the moment? Do I think that soon my life will be back to normal sliding along in a happy fashion? Complete with phone charging facilities. Like it used to do when I was small.

The second thing I feel for is the freezer bag to see if my money is still there. And yes, it is and the salt, too. I've got the phone (even though dead) and I've got some money. Tomorrow, I'll get food and try again to find Layla. For now, I need to sleep. I lie down on the concrete with the bilum under my head and wonder whether to do the circle of safety to keep the snakes away. Does it work with snakes? My brain is going soft. Obviously, it doesn't work. I've made it up. But I still do it. Make the circle shape with my hand and turn around. It can't hurt, can it?

11

The cold has crawled into my bones and I wake up early. I used to have a watch but Saul took it from me a long time ago and it never came back. From the light, I can see that it's early and the birds are only just beginning to sing. I must go to the toilet before there's anyone around. My right leg cramps as I straighten it out and pull myself up to stand by the sink. There are clothes pegs here in a plastic container on the draining board. I could do some washing. Ha ha. And then. If only. An intense longing for a normal, ordinary life floods through me as I gaze at the clothes pegs.

I'm surprised at how much colder and harder the concrete is than a wooden floor. Wood is soft but I never knew it till I tried the concrete. I raise each leg in turn a little way off the ground and stretch my foot out. One after the other. Over and over to make them move. My legs hurt from the walking but they are getting better. Not nearly as painful as they used to be, but my stomach is growling. I'm beginning to feel hungry. In the police station, I got regular food and it wasn't bad. Good even. Sometimes delicious. I like the rice cooked in coconut that you get down here. I sit down on the raised slab next to the sink and get my phone out now that I can see it. I was right. The battery is totally dead. No joy there until I've found somewhere to charge it up. (What an optimist I am, expecting to find somewhere to charge my phone, but hope is stubborn. Keeps on rising, despite all the bad experiences that should cause it to die.

I locate my purse and take it out of the freezer bag to put it near the top of the bilum. I am hungry so I'm going to have to find a market. Or a store. Market would be better because it's cheaper I think, although I can't cook anything. Hmmm. I'll have to see what there is.

To tell the truth, I've never been to a market. There isn't one in Keroko. Isn't anything in Keroko. Only us. Not even us anymore. Nothing left. But I've seen markets on tv and I've read about them in the *Post Courier*. Surprising how many news items happen in market places. Hope I've got enough money. No idea how much things cost. Here I go again, thinking I'll find a market and get some food. What do I do then, I wonder? I have no idea. I've got to find Layla but I don't know how. I can't even contact Joel because my phone won't work. Once again, I go through the people I know in this world to see if I can expect any help. There's Saul. Dead. Layla. Gone. Joel. No idea. Don't know where he lives. He never told me and I didn't ask. He thought we could phone each other. Keep in contact that way. Ha ha. I make a mental note to stop myself saying ha ha because it isn't helpful. It's like a hollow laugh and I can do without it.

I look around to check that no-one is looking, take off my laplap, shake it out and then put it on again. Badly creased and dirty. My water bottle is still in the bilum so I fill it from the tap and set off. I'm going to look for a market. Or a store. I'm not going back the way I came because of the police station. The men might see me on their way to work. I'll have to be careful on the road in case they drive past and notice me. Perhaps I could use my spare laplap to put round my head as a disguise but I dismiss this idea.

First, I wouldn't be able to walk without it falling off. Second, everybody would look at me because nobody wears a laplap like that (and especially the police would look because they're always suspicious). And third, it would make me hot. I walk to the end of the drive and look up the road. Plenty of cars now, driving up and down. Just have to pray that the policemen have already gone past or that they don't go to work this way. Soon they will be at work and Joel will have to tell them what happened. I hope he's all right.

I need Layla and I need my phone charging up, but first things first. I need food. I'm starving. Hunger makes me walk as fast as I can and my legs don't feel too bad. Sometimes I can walk like I used to do, but then my legs seem to switch back into shackled mode and the muscles contract and hurt and make me take little tiny steps all over again. The road is long and straight and I can't see the end of it. Nobody else is walking along and I keep close to the side with my head down most of the time.

I walk for hours. Feels like days but must be hours before I get to a roundabout, change roads but nothing else changes. Everything looks the same. The hedges, the houses, the driveways. I sit down and rest for a while and drink some water, but I have to get up and carry on. Another roundabout and a left turn and suddenly hallelujah. There are plenty of people walking about including some women with bilums. I pass a store and hesitate. Just a little bit further I think. I'll turn around and come back if I don't find a market soon. Then I see it down a little track. Market stalls and lots of people. Hallelujah, I think once more. I'm getting to be a praise-be-to-the-Lord sort of person, but really I'm not. I didn't go to church and Layla didn't teach me much about that. I don't believe in a Lord or a God. There are enough bosses in this world without reaching for an extra one.

I've done it. I've found it and I've reached the market area where I'm looking at some nuts set out neatly in little clumps ready for sale, but I'm forgetting to be careful. I take my eyes off the nuts and have a quick look around when suddenly I see Inspector Boa without his uniform. He's walking along with another man and a woman is following behind him carrying a bilum. Oh my God. Where can I hide? (Saul said I shouldn't say *Oh my God* because God would strike me down dead, but it isn't true. I've been saying it under my breath for years.) It doesn't seem real about Saul. I can't believe that it was Saul who shackled me and cut me. That it was Saul who raped me. And I can't believe that he's dead. That I've killed him. All this flashes through my mind while I'm watching Inspector Boa.

I was going to buy some pandanus nuts but I don't have time. I go to hide behind some bougainvillaea bushes. I'm keeping my eye fixed on Inspector Boa to see where he goes when suddenly someone grabs me from behind and puts their hand over my mouth. My heart does more than jump, but it's not Inspector Boa. I try to turn to see who it is.

'Oh my dear,' a voice speaks behind me.

'Layla!' I look at her and tears spring to my eyes.

'No,' she says. 'Not now, Auli. We've got to go.' It's my Layla. My real mother but she's already moving away. 'Be careful,' she whispers. 'Say nothing. Watch where I go and follow behind.' But she moves too fast. I can't keep up and soon I've lost her.

12

Layla comes back to look for me. She doesn't want to lose me.

'You have to hurry, Auli,' she says. 'We have to get out of sight.'

'I can't go any faster,' I say and point to the marks on my ankles. 'I'll tell you later.'

She slows down a bit after that and eventually, we turn off the main road into the University campus, then turn again, and once more and we've arrived. Layla leads me into a house full of women and children all of them talking and shouting at once.

'This is my niece, Agnes' she introduces me. (Agnes? Oh well.) 'Come on, Aggie,' she says, turning back to speak to me. Put your bilum on the veranda and come into the garden. You can tell me about Nasili and March.' (Nasili and March?) I do as she says and follow her into the garden. We go to one end and sit down on the grass.

'Act normal,' she whispers as we both sit down.

'I am normal,' I reply and she smiles. That old Layla smile and my heart melts and I want to throw myself into her arms. But I hold on and we start to talk.

'Where are we?' I ask in a low voice and she tells me that we're on the university campus (I know that - I saw the sign) and that this is her friend, Shantelle's house but she is not Layla. Here, she is not Layla. Only her friend knows that she is Layla and her friend won't tell. 'Then who are you?' I ask. I've got a hundred questions.

'I'm Rosa,' she says. 'I was at college together with Shantelle. That part is true. I'm from Madang, she says. Don't forget, Agnes. I'm Rosa and I'm from Madang.'

'Rosa,' I repeat. 'And I'm Agnes.' Layla nods.

'I'm on the run,' I tell her. 'Have to stay in hiding. Can I stay here with you?'

'Yes, I think so,' Layla says. 'Back in a minute.' She walks off towards the house and comes back a few minutes later. 'Yes,' she confirms. 'You can stay here for now.'

The 'for now' echoes through my brain, but it's better than nothing. I can't complain.

'Will you put my phone on charge?' I ask, fetching my phone and the charger out of the bilum. Layla nods, gets up and once again goes into the house.

'Why didn't you answer me?' I ask her. I rang so many times and sent so many texts.

'I didn't get them,' Layla replies. 'I wiped your number off my phone a long time ago. It wasn't safe.' She sees my face and understands. 'For you,' she explains. 'It wasn't safe for you.' I still don't know what she means.

It's late and it's time to cook so we have to go and help prepare the food. Neither of us brought back any food from the market and I say I am sorry. It's all right, they tell me. You can get some tomorrow. We'll need more tomorrow. Layla looks at me and I know she'll come with me. Not safe for either of us but we will get a chance to talk. I still don't understand why Layla ran away but she'll tell me when she can.

We cook and we eat and there's no opportunity to talk to each other. Just being near to Layla is a pleasure almost more than I can bear. It's like coming home after so long. But we haven't got a home. We're both in hiding and I'm waiting to hear Layla's story. The men of the house come back while we are cooking and they eat first. I don't get to meet them and that's a relief. Too many questions and I don't have any answers.

After we've served the men, we sit down to eat ourselves. We've done the cooking underneath the house but we sit down on the lawn to eat. I don't say much and Layla tells them I'm shy. It's easier like that so I don't have to answer questions. They smile and hug me and ask me when I'm getting married so I go quiet again and they laugh. They tell me it will be all right with the man - - when I get married that is and they laugh some more. What has Layla told them?

We sit and talk for hours and there's plenty of buai to chew, but I'm no good at that and worry about it a bit but Layla tells them I've got a bad stomach. They don't look convinced but the moment passes and mostly I sit and listen. Layla chews enough for both of us and her mouth gets red like theirs just like it did when she chewed at home. I don't mind the lips or the spitting red juice all over the grass, it's the red teeth I don't like but now I'm changing my mind. She's beautiful. Layla is beautiful. Even with red teeth.

For hours they all tell stories and then it's time to go to bed. Telling stories is what the Aussies call gossiping but gossiping sounds bad and telling stories sounds good even though it's the same thing. Or nearly the same thing. I've never lived with other people so it's my first time for this. I know about these things because Layla taught me in the life lessons but I had no idea at the time how useful those lessons would be. That they would help me to fit in and keep me safe.

At last, it's time for bed and I'm tired but still tense. Can't stop worrying about saying the wrong thing. About the way the girls look at me sometimes. About the police looking for me and what I'm going to do when my time here runs out. I'm given a mat in the room with the other girls and I think I won't sleep, but I do. Layla isn't here. She'll see me in the morning she says. They're still telling stories when we are lying down, but I pretend I'm asleep and soon I am, and I don't wake up until the next day.

It's my stomach that wakes me this time. I'm used to the rice and coconut that we ate last night because it was the same kind of food that they gave me at the police station but there was something else in the food here. Some kind of leaves that I'm not used to but I don't think it's that. It's the baby again making me sick. I'm sure of it. I get up and go outside so I don't disturb the others. It's still very early, not quite light. A man is sitting on the steps outside. He's smoking and he looks at me and gets up to let me past. Instantly I feel afraid. What if he's a policeman? He might be. He seems OK and laughs when he sees that I'm nervous of him. Thinks it's just because I'm a young girl that I'm like this. I drink from the tap and go back inside.

It's still early when Layla says she's ready. We've eaten and washed and I'm relieved that I don't have to spend time with the girls. Even though they're nice. We're your cousin sisters they tell me and we've never met you before. What are you doing here? Where is your place? Who did you come with? So many questions that I can't answer and I'm worried about arousing their suspicions. I can't be shy forever. Not so shy that I can barely speak.

Layla and I are both silent as we set off from the house.

'Follow me, Auli,' she says, 'and walk as fast as you can. We can talk later.'

I try to keep up but it's hard and she stops to wait for me lots of times. My legs are aching and tense. They've gone backwards since yesterday. It was easier then but however hard I try, I can't seem to get faster.

'Where are we going?' I ask.

'To the market,' she answers. 'But first of all, we're going to sit in a garden and talk.'

Soon we get to the place she means and I see that there are benches and high hedges full of hibiscus and no-one else there. We sit down and I try to stop the torrent of questions that has been building up in my head.

'Why did we have to walk so fast?' I ask as I sink on to the bench and bend down to rub my aching legs.

'So we have more time to talk,' she says, ' and so there is less chance of anyone seeing us on the road.' Layla has questions, too, so we try to start with hers but before I tell her all that has happened, I can't help asking a question of my own.

'Did you leave because of me?' I ask her.

'Yes,' she says, 'but not for the reasons you think.'

'How do you know what I think?' I ask and she laughs.

'I always know what you think, little Auli,' she says and she hugs me close so that I start to weep. It's been so long.

'So why did you leave?' I ask again.

Layla sighs and looks at me and answers my question with a question.

'How much do you know?' she asks. 'About what happened before Saul took me to Keroko?'

'I think they accused you of sorcery,' I say, 'and it was Saul who helped you to escape.'

Layla nods.

'And do you have special powers?' I ask.

'No,' she says and then adds, 'Or maybe.'

What does that mean? Two answers. Not the same.

'I'll tell you another time,' she says.

'Did you kill a child?' I ask and I can see that she's hurt that I even ask.

She shakes her head. 'Of course not,' she says. 'How could I?'

'But I killed Saul,' I blurt out and I see the shock in her eyes. She didn't know. Maybe she won't love me now. She waits for me to go on.

'After you'd gone,' I tell her. 'Saul changed. He shackled me. He fastened my ankles together with metal cuffs. He cut my hands. I was his prisoner and I couldn't escape. So one day I killed him.' I don't want to tell her about the baby so I can't tell her about the rape. I don't understand why I can't bring myself to tell her these things, but I can't.

'How did you do it?' Layla asks.

'With rocks. I dropped rocks on him while he slept.' It feels unreal even to me. I can't believe that I did it. Layla doesn't speak and I add the final thing. 'And I opened the circle, Layla. Before I left I opened the circle and when the police went to look, his body was gone.' I watch as she turns away and I see that she's sobbing, her shoulders heaving but she's trying to stop. 'I'm sorry,' I say. 'I'm so sorry, Layla. I had to do it. There was no other way.'

I ask myself if it's true. Is that what anyone else would have done? I don't know. These are questions I can't answer. Layla's shoulders are shaking. I've never seen her cry before. She's strong. Always she has been strong.

'I'm sorry, Layla,' I say it over and over again. 'I'm sorry. I'm so very sorry.'

Maybe I should go. I've lost them both now. Both my parents. Saul and Layla.

'Should I go?' I ask. 'Do you want me to go?'

And Layla turns and takes me in her arms.

'I'm crying for Saul,' she says, 'I loved him, Auli. I've always loved him,' and she holds me closer and tries to control the tears but the sobs still come, 'and I'm crying for what he did to you.' She tries to stop. 'Most of all,' she says, 'I'm crying for myself. I don't know what I'll do without him in the world.' And then she becomes calm again. The sobs stop at last. We hold each other and rock from side to side. 'And for what has happened to us, for what has become of us,' she whispers, 'I'm crying for what we have each become.'

Later, I will remember what she says but now I say nothing and we sit in the garden and drink water. I keep picking hibiscus flowers to put in our hair. It is a long time since we did that. Layla's hair is the same as mine. Big and soft. The bright red flowers stay easily. We put them behind our ears and they look pretty. There's a lot more to say. A lot more questions but it's enough for now. We can't manage any more. Not now. We are thinking of Saul. Each in our own way.

'Just one more thing,' I say, 'that you need to know, Layla,' and it's almost more than I can say. There has been too much to tell. There is still too much to tell but this Layla needs to know now. She looks up. 'The police are looking for me. They think I have special powers. Like you. They think that I practise sanguma. That I'm a witch.'

'How did they get you?' she asks.

'I rang them,' I said. 'I needed help and there was no-one else to ring.'

Layla says nothing and I carry on.

'One of the policemen was kind. He told me what his colleagues were planning and helped me to escape. He said they were afraid of me and even he, Layla, even he looked afraid. I saw it in his eyes. They were going to burn me, but he helped me to escape. He was kind. His name is Joel. His number is in my phone.'

Without pause for even a second, Layla replies, 'Don't trust him, Auli. You can't trust him. You are in his debt,' she pauses. 'One day you will have to pay back.'

13

It is time for us to go or we won't get to the market. We need to buy food and take it back to the house. It's hot and my legs hurt. They've been bad all day today. Before we leave the garden, we take the hibiscus flowers out of our hair and drink from the same bottle. We hug each other close before changing into Rosa and Agnes, aunty and niece, close, but not like Layla and Auli are to each other.

We keep close to the side of the road and to each other. If anyone's looking, they'll be looking for one woman, not two. That's what we hope. I am a woman now. My girlhood is gone. I look like a girl, but I'm not. I'm a woman. Almost a mother. Already a killer. Considered a witch. A thought passes by and catches me with the full force of its longing. To be a child again. A baby. To be held and fed and cared for. Held close and rocked. I toss it away and it's gone like seeds in the wind and I walk on. I would like to stride but my legs still won't do that although every day they are stretching wider. It's a good job I think because they'll need to go wide when the baby comes out. What will that be like I ask myself but once again the thought is gone. I have to think of the present. Concentrate on this moment or there will be no time coming for babies or for anything. No future at all.

It's a long way to the market but after what seems like hours, Layla turns to me and says that we're nearly there and I recognise the place from yesterday. There are more people around now, especially women. Maybe it's because it's earlier in the day.

'What are we going to buy?' I ask, 'and who will buy what? Where shall we wait for each other?'

'I'll buy the fish,' Layla tells me. 'And some buai, lime and mustard. You won't know how to choose.' She's right. I haven't got a clue about how to buy fish or the mustard and lime for the buai.

'You can get the pandanus, bananas and some cabbage.'

'What about coconut?' I ask remembering the taste of the rice and feeling the ache in my wrist from scraping the coconut last night.

'Already plenty,' Layla replies. 'No need.'

'How much should I pay?' I ask, thinking that we should have discussed all this earlier and I see that Layla has forgotten that I don't know how to do this.

'Pay what they ask,' she instructs me. 'It won't work twice but it will work once. They'll wait for next time to ask for more.'

'And where shall we meet?'

This is my last question. I'm still muttering pandanus, bananas, cabbage under my breath so I don't forget. I've never been shopping before.

'Where the track comes into the market,' she says. 'Under the tree.'

'It's full of people,' I comment as I look over to where she's pointing.

'Exactly,' she says. 'A crowded area is always the best place to meet.'

'How many bananas, pandanus and cabbage?' I ask, but she's already moving off and I see her struggle not to snap at me.

'Whatever you think, Auli' she replies so I give up and set off with my purse and my bilum (which is already nearly full) and no idea at all of how much I'm buying of anything or what I should pay.

I manage the bananas or think I have. Did she mean eating bananas or cooking bananas? Or both. To be safe, I buy both and discover that I can hardly bear the weight when they're loaded into my bilum on top of everything else. I'll get the pandanus next or the bilum will be too heavy to hold. Don't think I'll manage the cabbage. I go to the same stall as yesterday and remember that it was here that I saw Inspector Boa and his wife. I hover behind a bush and watch the crowd. There's no Boa in sight and I giggle a bit at his name. I think it's safe to go to the stall and buy the pandanus.

The nuts are laid out in little bunches on the grass and a woman sits behind them waiting to sell. That's all she has. Just the pandanus. Nothing else. Not even any other kind of nuts. I'm about to make my choice when I catch sight of somebody in the crowd. A face that I never wanted to see again but I might have imagined it. I look again and he's gone. Peer hard into the crowd of faces. Even look behind me but Scarface is nowhere in sight. He was the one who made me fall over and who pushed me hard. Worse than that, he smiled every time Boa said something unpleasant to me. Maybe it wasn't him. He can't be the only person around with a scar on his face. I decide which three piles of pandanus I'm going to buy and hand over the money. The woman smiles at me. Half her teeth are gone and her mouth is red with juice but her smile is warm. I am handing her the money when I feel a hand on my shoulder and I fall forward on to the nuts.

There's an immediate outcry from behind me as people shout at the man for pushing me forward on to the nuts. It is a mark of great disrespect to move someone's wares or to step over them. I learned it in life lessons and there was a news report once about a fight breaking out in Lae when someone had stepped over a market seller's piles of kaukau. I don't waste a moment. I get up as fast as I can, ignoring the pain in my ankle, and turn to face him but he's gone. Scarface has gone. If that's who it was. I need to disappear. Maybe Layla was right about the crowd being the best place for safety. I'm not sure though. A policeman versus a young girl in a dirty meri blouse? No contest.

I've got a problem. My bilum is too heavy to carry so I dump all the bananas bar two and put them on the grass next to the nuts. The woman is looking alternately amazed then pleased as she nods and smiles at me. She thinks I'm giving the bananas as an apology for falling on the nuts. The pandanus are light so I stuff them down the side of the bilum next to my clothes and I move off, trying to look behind me as well as in front while I walk. It's difficult but I do keep trying. I'm heading for the exit and I'm not going to stop under the tree.

It looks as though a crowd is gathering near the track that leads back to the street so I slow down and wonder what to do. I can't see Scarface, and the people in the crowd seem to be mainly women. They're getting agitated and starting to chant. The main languages here are Tok Pisin and Motu but I can't tell what they're saying. Doesn't sound like anything I know. I wonder where Layla is and hope that she's safe. I decide to go back to see if I can find another way out because I'll never get through the crowd in front of me, but I turn around only to find a denser crowd behind me. I'm hemmed in and both groups are walking towards me with men leading the way waving sticks. One or two are holding stones but it's mainly sticks and while I'm wondering what to do the thought goes through my mind that they can't stone me because there aren't enough stones around here. Takes a second to think that. I know now what they're chanting. It's my name.

'Aulani. Aulani. Aulani. Aulani.' It must have been Scarface. He must be leading the crowd but I can't see him.

I stop and put my bilum on the ground and lift my hands into the air like last night. It's the only thing I can try. Slowly I turn around while the crowd stops and watches. They are round me in a circle now. Silent. Watching my every move. When I finish my turn I am facing the crowd in front of the exit, the people who are blocking the track to the street. I look at them, the ones who are furthest forward and stare straight into their eyes.

'You will move,' I say, 'and let me through,' I pause and they hesitate, 'or your children will die.' I pause again, and add, 'I know who they are and I will kill them.'

Still, nobody moves and I wonder what to do next. Without thinking or making a decision, I bend down, pick up my bilum and start to move forward. And I keep on looking at them, sweeping my eyes around the circle, meeting the gaze of as many as I can but they are moving now, backing off, faster and faster, starting to fall over each other. A child yells and it's like a signal. They run without looking back, pushing each other to get away and my way is clear. Slowly and steadily (I can't manage it any other way because my legs are hurting so much, but only I know this), I move towards the track and then towards the street.

The place is almost deserted when I get to the road. A couple of men in the distance and no cars at all. I trudge on with the bilum wrapped around my head and cutting in. The top of my back and my shoulder and neck muscles strain with the weight, but I keep going until I come to the long road that I walked down yesterday. Was it only yesterday? Was it the day before? I look around but no-one is following and I get to the house where I slept before. It still looks empty and I turn into the drive. I wonder if I've got a guardian angel after all. Layla told me about them, too. In life lessons.

14

There is a loud ringing and I jump up in fear before bur-
rowing into my bilum to find the phone. It stops just as I
get it out. It's Layla. Thank God she's safe. I was just going
to ring her. I'm about to ring back but the phone rings
again and this time it's Joel. He's programmed his contact
details so that his name comes up when the phone rings. I
stare at it as though he's going to appear in person but of
course, he isn't. He doesn't. He's not here. I wonder if he
knows about what happened at the marketplace this afternoon. Does he know what Scarface tried to do? I don't pick
up. Almost as soon as it stops, it starts again and it's Joel
again. I sit holding it in my hand waiting for it to stop so I
can ring Layla. It feels as though he must know where I am
but, of course, he doesn't.

Eventually, the phone is quiet and I try ringing Layla.
She picks up immediately.

'Auli?'

'Yes.'

'Are you safe?'

'Yes. Are you?'

'Yes.' We sigh in unison. I can hear her sigh trembling
out of the speaker.

'Where are you?' she asks and I try to explain and I ask
where she is.

'I'm back at the market,' she says. 'I wanted to make
sure that they hadn't got you. That you weren't still there.'

'Did you see what happened?' I ask.

'Yes,' she says. 'You were good, Auli. More than good, but we can't go back to the house.'

I suppose she's right. We can't go back.

'Then where shall we go?' I ask and there's a long silent space before she answers, 'Keroko, Auli. We'll have to go to Keroko. There isn't anywhere else.'

I don't like the thought of this, but I suppose she's right. There isn't anywhere else we can go.

'I can think of two problems,' I say.

'Only two,' Layla shoots back. 'Then you aren't trying, Auli.'

I laugh. Layla always managed to make me laugh and she's not forgotten how to do it.

'How do we get there?' I ask her. 'I haven't got a clue where I am ... or how to get there ... or how to tell you where I am.'

'Ok,' she says. 'That's one.'

'And how do we live once we're there? I haven't got much money, have you?'

'No, I haven't,' Layla admits, 'and money by itself won't solve the problem. One of us will have to come down the mountain to buy food.'

'There must be a way we could manage up there,' I say. 'What about a pig? We could take a pig with us and then we'd have meat.'

'We'll solve the food problem later,' Layla says sounding confident. 'First of all, let's get ourselves there.' My whole body shudders as I remember the sight of Saul's body lying on the floor. How was it possible that the police didn't find it?

'And how will we do that?' I ask.

'You'll have to tell me where you are, Auli, and I'll come and find you. Then we'll go together.'

I nod, but then smile realising that she can't see me. 'I'm nodding,' I tell her.

'Ok,' she says, 'and now think back to when you left the market. Which way did you go?' I do my best to remember and tell her as clearly as I can.

'Stay where you are,' she says. 'I'll try and find you. Can you put something in the driveway so that I know when I've found the house?'

'Yes,' I say. 'I'll put some stones in the middle of the drive. I'll do it now.'

I gather the stones and take them to the driveway entrance next to the road. It's easy to get them because there are plenty of good-sized edging stones along the flower-beds. Lumps of soft earth fall on to the hard driveway as I dislodge the stones that keep the border soil in place. It doesn't take long to gather a pile of stones to mark the house. I place them in a circle. Then I go to sit under the house and drink water.

The tap sounds loud just like before but nobody comes and after the third time, I don't worry so much and let the water run for longer. I hear some dogs start to bark but it's not because of the water and I eat a banana. I'm very hungry but I manage to save the other one for Layla. I wonder if she'll find the house. I've built quite a large stone circle in the middle of the driveway. She's bound to see it if she gets this far. For a second, I wonder what I'm going to do if she doesn't get here, but I push the thought away and get the pandanus nuts out. I could eat all of them. Oh, my dear. I put them away and get them out again. Perhaps I could eat half of them, but no, I put them away again to save for when Layla gets here. It might be a long time before we get more food.

There are all kinds of things I can't allow myself to think about to do with going back to Keroko. The worst one is the fear of seeing Saul's body and worse than that. Layla seeing Saul's body. I still can't understand why the police didn't find him. Maybe they didn't go. Perhaps the man they sent there lied because he was lazy and didn't go all the way to Keroko. This seems the most likely explanation.

I wish I'd got a watch. I've no idea what time it is or how long I've been sitting here waiting for Layla. Hoping that she'll somehow find the place. I decide to have a look on my phone to see what time it is but I can't keep doing that because of the need to preserve the battery. She hasn't rung or texted. As this thought is going through my mind, my phone rings. I pick it up and am about to answer when I see that once again it's Joel. What does he want? What can I say? I can't tell him where I am or where we are going, so I don't answer. There's no point. I'm sorry that I can't answer. I like Joel. He was kind and nice to lie with in the evenings. Layla says I shouldn't trust him, but she might be wrong.

***

I'm asleep when Layla comes and she puts her hand over my mouth to stop me from crying out.

'Where have you been?' I ask.

'On the way,' she replies.

'Why so long?'

'Had to see somebody. Get food,' she replies and it's true. Her bilum weighs a ton. It's full of food but I don't know how we're going to carry it up the mountain.

'It's too heavy,' I tell her but she shakes her head.

'We'll manage,' she says and smiles at me. (We? There's no way I can lift that thing, and I certainly can't carry it up the mountainside.) She's got two mats in there and gives me one to lie on. I'm grateful because the concrete is cold and very hard. I settle myself down, thinking we can talk about things tomorrow but she tells me, no, ten minutes rest and then we've got to go.

'No, Layla,' I say. 'I can't go now. I'm tired. My legs hurt. I need to sleep.'

She doesn't reply. Just looks at me and waits for me to start packing up. It's mother Layla back again in teacher mode, telling me what to do. No choice, I suppose.

'Can we eat?' I ask. 'I'm hungry.'

'Later,' she says. 'Not now. Come on, Auli. Get a move on.' Within a few minutes, I'm on my feet and following her out of the drive. On to the road. There are no cars now, only very occasionally and we hide from the lights. The trick is to stop moving as soon as we hear a car coming, or a truck. We have to stay absolutely still and it seems to work. Nothing stops and each time we breathe again.

We walk for hours and my legs ache badly. Layla won't stop and she speeds up as the light comes into the sky and the first birds start to sing.

'Come on, Auli, hurry up,' she says. 'You've got to hurry up.' She knows I'm in pain but she keeps saying that we've got to leave the road. We need to reach the mountain track and start to go up.

'I can't,' I say as I stumble along. 'I can't go any faster, Layla.'

'You can,' she says. 'You must.'

And somehow I do.

We don't stop until we're half an hour into the mountain and then I collapse. I can't move one more step, I really can't.

'All right,' she says and gives me a mat, but I'm too weary to get on to it so she pushes and pulls me until I'm lying on the mat and covers me with a laplap. Then I sleep.

The crickets wake me up when it's getting dark and I know that I've slept all day. I hope we're not going to walk through the night and am relieved when Layla says no, we won't do that. She makes a fire and lights it. We're going to stay here and rest. Tomorrow, we'll start to walk again. I watch her place the stones and get the kaukau and fish to cook in the fire. The smell of the food mixes in with the smell of the smoke and I never knew I could feel this hungry. I look into the fire and see only two small kaukau, two small corns and two small fish.

'Is that all we've got?' I ask, staring at the small food. I'm going crazy with the smell.

'No,' she says, 'but it's all that we're going to eat today.'

'I'll swap you a fish for a kaukau,' I offer, thinking that the kaukau is much bigger than the fish.

'No,' she says. 'We won't do that,' and she fetches big leaves for us to use as plates. 'Here you are,' she says, 'you greedy girl. Eat it slowly and it will be enough.'

I try. I look at Layla and see her taking very small bites so I do the same. I don't want to have finished mine while she's still eating.

'Drink a lot,' she says tossing me the plastic water bottle that's half full. 'The water will fill you up.' There's a waterfall only a few steps away right next to the track so we can drink our fill.

It's time I told her, I think. If she knows about the baby, I might get more food.

'I'm pregnant,' I announce and watch her face. 'Joel had sex with me in the police station.'

'Did he rape you?' she asks.

I hesitate. It would look better for me if I said that he did. And it's completely believable. But I can't say it.

'No,' I reply. 'I was lonely. I liked it.'

'I knew it,' Layla says after a pause.

'Knew what?' I asked.

'That you were pregnant,' she said, and then adds, 'but I thought you'd been with Saul.' She comes over to where I'm sitting and puts both arms around me and her tears fall as she smiles and laughs. 'I'm glad,' she says. 'I'm glad for you, Auli, and I'm glad for me, too.'

I don't speak, but she can see the question in my eyes. Why is she glad?

'I couldn't bear to think that you were carrying Saul's child,' she says. 'I've wanted Saul's child for most of my life. Ever since I married him. It's what I wanted most in the whole world.'

I look at her. I hug her back and eat the rest of the kaukau without noticing.

15

There are two more nights on the mountain and the bags are heavy. Layla carries most but I'm still slow and she's still quick. There's a change. Layla was always kind but now she's kinder. Waits for me more patiently. Asks if I'm feeling sick. Gives me the best fish and the biggest kaukau. She sings sometimes and tells me to join in. It's too hard to sing while I'm struggling up and up but after we've eaten when we sit by the fire, I sing, too. She taught me all the songs I know and sometimes we sing in harmony remembering the old tunes and the way we used to do them. But as Layla gets lighter, I get heavier.

It's the thought of Saul. It was easier not to think about him when I was somewhere else, but the closer we get to home, the heavier I feel. As though I can't force myself to keep going. I don't want to get there. I'm afraid of what we'll find. Don't know how Layla will react. I think about it. Would I still have killed him if he hadn't raped me? If it was only the shackles. Only the shackles? Yes, I think I would. In the early days, whenever he ripped me, he would mutter things like 'I'm getting you clean, Aulani. I'm driving them out.' I never asked him what he was driving out. I didn't know that he thought there were spirits inside me. I didn't ask. I didn't speak at all. Later, he said nothing but he drove into me with a force that tried to rip me apart. That was how it felt, as though I was being torn apart. I shudder and carry on climbing. Slower and slower.

'Come on, Auli,' Layla calls to me. 'It's not far now.'

'My legs hurt,' I tell her. 'Sorry, Layla.'

We're nearly there and it starts to rain. Layla calls some more. Tells me to hurry up or we'll be soaked. I'm already soaked I tell her. I nearly say that she can go without me, but no. I want to be there when she arrives. I want us to arrive together. I need to know what there is and what we shall both see.

I stand and look at the avocado tree that grows near our house. It's huge. I know it well and I'm back in the place of my childhood that I thought I had left for good. The three stones that we put under the tree - one for each of us - are still there. Covered in ferns and roots but still there. Things grow quickly here. Everything seeds, takes root. There are bushes and branches, leaves everywhere and green gushes out of the earth, wild and lush. Man-made things get covered over. Soon gone. I breathe in and smell the place. Even from here, the scent of jasmine that grows by the window at the back of the house reaches my nostrils. I can't see it but the heady scent mixes with the leaves, the heavy undergrowth. I love it. Everything fresh and sweet. No hint of death.

'The circle has been broken. We'll have to mend it,' Layla says as we stand together at the edge of our garden, at the place where we leave the track and turn right on to the little path that leads to our house. I stand with her and I nod. 'I didn't think I'd be coming back,' she says, and I nod again.

'Neither did I.'

Layla steps over the circle that is no longer there and I remember the saying about old habits dying hard. Suddenly I feel like giggling. It must be hysteria and I swallow it back as I follow her up the path. The garden has become overgrown even in such a relatively short time but I hardly notice it. I'm looking at the house. Layla starts to climb the steps up to the veranda and I see that they're dirty and look neglected. The whole place looks neglected. The house door is closed so maybe the policeman did come here. I know I left it open. Layla pulls the door back and steps inside. There is no lock. We didn't need one because there was always one of us in the house and nobody around anyway. I've got as far as the veranda. My feet won't move. I can't go in.

'Come on, Auli, where are you?' Layla calls. 'We'll have to clear up. It's a terrible mess in here.'

I still can't move so I sit down on the bench. I've already put my bilum down next to the steps. Layla comes out and sits next to me.

'Aren't you coming in?' she asks and then she's quiet. She must know something of what I'm feeling. 'You'll have to tell me,' she says and I look at her.

'Tell you what?'

'Where you put him,' she says. 'How did you move his body'

I shake my head. 'No,' I say. 'I didn't move him. He was too heavy.'

After a while, I get up and go inside, leave Layla sitting on the bench. I think I need to go in by myself. I walk into the living room and look on the floor. He's not there. There's a mess. Bits of torn sheet and tablecloth. Chewed up mat. An enamel mug on the floor. Saul's mug. I walk into the other rooms and the shower. There's animal shit everywhere. Shit of various kinds. Mouse. Rat. Something bigger. A boar? Nothing left of Saul. Nothing at all.

'He's gone,' I say.

It's getting dark and too late to clean the house or get the generator going. Layla lights a lamp and we sweep the veranda and lie down there for the night. We lie in silence, each separate, contained in our own thoughts.

**

For a whole week we sweep and scrub and clean. In a corner of the shower room, I find bits of Saul's watch. The face and a small bit of the strap. Chewed. He never took it off. Not even at night. He used to boast that it was waterproof but I don't know if he kept it on when he washed. Nothing else. I can see that Layla doesn't believe me that I didn't move him, but surely she can understand that he was too heavy. I couldn't have moved him even if I had wanted to. I think that sometimes she believes me and sometimes she doesn't. There's no smell she says. If Saul's body had been left here, the whole house would have smelled of it. How does she know that? But she stops asking about him and we clean until our fingers hurt from the bleach and then we work in the garden.

'How are we going to manage for money?' I ask one evening as we sit on the veranda after we've eaten. 'How much have you got left?

'There is some hidden,' she tells me. 'We used to hide it behind the shed. It will still be there.'

'Who were you hiding it from?' I ask and Layla laughs.

'From ourselves,' she says. 'We used to pretend that it wasn't there so that we didn't spend too much. There might have come a time when Saul couldn't carve and we would need it.'

'And who's going to go down to the city to get food?' I ask.

'I will, Auli,' Layla says. 'Don't worry. I'll keep you safe.'

I feel ashamed because she's lost Saul. I killed him and she has to look at me knowing that. I ask if it's hard for her knowing that I killed him and she says that it is.

'I know with my mind,' she tells me, 'that you had to do it, Auli. But I wasn't here and I remember him in different ways. I remember him saving me. And loving me. And staying with me even though it was dangerous, and he had to give up everything else and give up everyone else. It was a big thing.'

'I can understand that,' I say. I tell her that me, too, I remember Saul as he used to be and it doesn't seem real what he did to me. But it was. The scars on my hands show it. The scars on my ankles show it. They will always be there, although I have to admit that the pain in my legs has almost gone. Every so often, Layla asks me about Saul and the shackles and eventually, she tells me her own story.

'Did he tell you where he got them from?' she asks one day when we're out in the garden. I know she means the shackles.

'No,' I say.

'They were meant for me,' Layla says and goes on. 'In the village, when they said I was a witch, they put me in shackles. Somebody in the village had been to Australia and brought them back from there. I don't know why he got them but they were used on me. When Saul helped me escape, he brought the shackles with us and he kept the key.' She pauses and stares at the earth pulling weed after weed and tossing them on to a pile on the path. 'The shackles were a symbol of my freedom. We loved them.'

'I never saw them,' I say. 'I didn't know you had any.'

'No,' she says. 'We didn't want to burden you. We were going to tell you when you were older.'

'Like the meaning of the circle?' I ask. 'Why have you put it back, Layla? Why have you started sweeping it again?'

'It's to keep us safe,' she says and grins at me.

I raise my eyebrows and wait for her to go on.

'We know it means nothing,' she says and pauses. 'But if anyone comes, Auli, it will mean something to them. They will know that it's the circle of safety and they won't step across.'

'But there's nobody here,' I say.

'Someone may come,' Layla tells me. 'So we have to be ready.'

16

Nobody comes. We work hard to get new vegetables growing, starting early each day before it gets hot. It is a good thing that Layla has brought pumpkin seeds and kaukau for planting. No wonder the bilums were so heavy and yet all I did was complain. All I thought about while going up the mountain was finding Saul.

'Where did you get them from?' I ask. 'All these seeds. And the cabbage seedlings and the pineapple.'

'From my friend,' she says. 'From Shantelle, where we stayed. She's good to me. Always good to me.'

'What did you tell her?' I ask. 'About where I'd gone and where you were going.'

'I said you'd gone home. Felt homesick and gone home.' I watch as she makes raised beds ready for more pumpkin seeds. Layla works fast. 'And I told her I was going into hiding again. She knows what happened and that's why she gave me the seeds.'

'Does she know that we're here?' I ask. 'You said that we shouldn't trust anybody.'

'No,' Layla replies. 'Only that we're somewhere in the mountains.'

A few minutes later, she asks me about Joel. Is he still ringing? And am I tempted to reply?

'Yes,' I say. 'I'm tempted, but you told me not to respond. I like Joel but there's no future is there?'

'The future is in your belly,' she says, glancing at my bump which is getting big now. 'But you're right. It's better he doesn't know.' She stops and straightens up. 'And he's a policeman,' she says pulling a face.

'So what,' I snap. 'He saved me, Layla.' And I realise that it's true. So much has happened that I've hardly thought about Joel. But if he hadn't let me escape... An image of the police station burning ... with me trapped inside, of the fire reaching my clothes, my skin... I've heard that being burned is unbearable. Painful beyond imagining. Burned alive. Like Joan of Arc. Except she turned into a saint afterwards. I shiver. No point in being a dead saint. Better to be a live sinner.

'Has he been in touch?' she asks again and he has but I shake my head. If she's going to pull faces about him and make disparaging remarks, I'm not telling her about Joel. What's wrong with being a policeman anyway?

Mostly, we work without speaking. It's in the evenings after the crickets have stopped and the light has gone, after we've eaten and cleared away that we sit outside and talk a little. We sit in the dark with just the light from the moon and the stars. The kerosene lamp is only good in the house. If you carry it outside, the light attracts every type of flying thing, especially mosquitoes. It's good to sit here and as time passes, we think less about Saul. It wasn't often that he sat outside with us. The veranda was our place, not his. Usually, he was inside the house watching tv. We haven't managed to get it to work again yet because we've been busy with everything else.

It's light outside tonight. I look up and see the moon surrounded by some black space and then the stars. Thousands of them filling the sky. There are hibiscus bushes right next to the veranda and after looking up, I look down. I lean over and stare at the foliage but even though it's such a light night, you can't see the colours. The bright red flowers nestling among the green leaves are a memory, just dark shapes now, but the jasmine grows higher and the little white flowers are clear to see, little stars that I can reach out and touch. I breathe in the scent and think of the garden in the city where Layla took me to talk and we put flowers in our hair. We haven't had time for any of that since we've been back home. Home. That's a big word.

One evening, Layla starts telling me about her village and what happened to her. It is Joel's village, too, I remember. It's Joel's place she's talking about but she doesn't know him. She left before he was born. It was a good place to be, she tells me and her face lights up with the memories. Her voice sharpens and lifts. It was where she grew up and where she lived until she went to train as a teacher. Even after she started work and married Saul, she went back a lot. Saul had a store in Boroko and sold carvings, masks and tables and that's where they lived, but Layla's father was old and sick and her mother needed help so she spent a lot of time in the village.

'So why did they say you were a witch?' I ask. 'Why you, Layla?'

'There was a man,' she says and her face darkens. 'He wanted my father's land. Kept asking him to sell, but my father wouldn't.' Layla turns and looks at me. 'So that's why, Auli. That's why it was me.'

I still don't understand so Layla continues.

'His son died,' she goes on. 'His small son and after that, he went mad. He used his son's death as an excuse to get the land. Told the village I was a witch. Said it was me who killed his son. They tortured me,' she says and looks at her hands and I see them twisting. 'That's how the man could get my father's land. My father would have to pay compensation on my behalf. They took his land as payment for the dead child.'

'And did you?' I ask. 'Did you admit it, Layla?'

For a long time, she is silent and I think our talk has finished, but then she speaks again. I can hardly hear her.

'They put hot rods in my body, Auli. You can't imagine.' Layla gets up and goes inside leaving me to sit and stare at the sky and then down again into the bushes below.

The next day we finish the planting and Layla says we should have a rest. She will try and get the tv going and we can watch a movie. I am lazy all afternoon and spend the time reading through my old books. Children's books so they only last a few minutes. I skim through them and start to feel irritable. I find myself longing for my laptop. I could get stories on my laptop as well as news and movies. I look again along the top shelf. Saul's shelf. But there is nothing there. No laptop. Some lumps of dust that we must have missed when we were cleaning.

'Have we got enough money for a laptop?' I ask her hopefully as I stand in the doorway and watch Layla as she bends over the table where the tv lies with its back off.

'What!,' she says, 'You must be joking. We've hardly got enough money for food. And we already need to fetch some more.'

'How soon?' I ask and she turns to look at me.

'Now,' she says. 'Tomorrow.'

'So will you go down the mountain?' I ask her. The baby is kicking and I don't want her to go. I'm scared of this being inside me waiting to fight its way out. What if it's like Saul? Huge and aggressive. What if Saul's spirit has gone into the baby and I'm carrying him around inside me? How will I manage? Who can I ask for help?

Layla says she's surprised that my bump is so big but that everybody is different. Some women have big bumps. Some have small ones. And it might be twins, she says.

Oh my God, I think. One is bad enough. Pray God there aren't two little monsters in there. That's what it feels like now. A monster. The kicking never stops and my stomach rises first on one side and then on the other.

'I don't want it,' I blurt out to her. 'I don't want it, Layla.' Then she walks over and slaps me hard on the face and tells me to get out of her sight.

I go to lie down and I hear her start to cook. She's underneath the house, banging the pot and everything else down there. And I think she's crying.

I get up and go to help her. We chop in silence and drop the vegetables into the pot.

'I'm frightened,' I say. 'When you go to fetch food, I'll be here by myself.' She looks at me but her face is hard. 'The baby might come while you're gone,' I whisper.

'Of course, he won't,' she says. 'You've got at least another month left. Maybe two' and her voice gets quieter. 'And don't you ever complain again about having a child!'

I listen and I understand. But it doesn't help. I'm still afraid and I'm beginning to hate this being inside me.

After we've eaten, Layla puts down her bowl and tells me that she's going in the morning. She spends all evening messing about with the tv and trying to get it to work. Hardly speaks to me as she keeps poking the back of it. The tv is laid out on the table but the connections are on a board so there's nothing she can screw or unscrew. Layla is angry. I know that it's me she'd like to be jabbing and hitting but she leaves me alone and concentrates on the tv. After pulling bits and poking and scraping at the back with her screwdriver, she plugs it in and surprise. It's alive. Definitely better than before. There are grey flickering lines all over the screen as well as a harsh white noise.

'Take this,' she tells me and hands me the aerial. 'Now hold it up high.'

I try.

'No, not there. Left a bit. Higher.' The lines on the screen move more frantically than before. 'We've nearly got it,' she says. 'Move back a bit. Stop. Higher.'

This feels more like ordering me about than mending the tv but I do as she says.

'I can't hold it up any longer,' I tell her and put the aerial down on the table and the tv springs into sudden life. A picture, sound. Somebody talking. We stand and look at it mesmerised. If we move, it might disappear but then Layla does move slightly and the whole thing dies. Black screen. No lines, no crackles. Dead.

'It's buggered,' Layla announces. 'You shouldn't have moved.'

I'm speechless as I watch her pick up the hammer and raise her arm. 'It's completely buggered,' she says and hesitates.

'Well, it will be if you smash it with that,' I say and she starts to laugh.

17

The next morning Layla sets off straight after breakfast. She tells me what to do while she's away and tells me not to worry. She's back to normal this morning and she hugs me before she goes, but things are different between us since I killed Saul. We're more equal. Not so much mother and daughter. She loves me less.

'Remember you can always phone me,' she says. 'Or text.'

'Be careful,' I say. It's not safe for me, but it's not safe for Layla either.

'I will,' she says. 'Don't worry, Auli.' I watch her walk down the path and, after stepping over the circle, she turns and waves. 'Don't forget to sweep,' she says.

'I won't,' I shout to her and stand on the veranda waving long after she has disappeared down the track.

There's work to be done. I've got to weed round the cabbage seedlings and I need to sweep the house, but first of all, I'm going to look at my phone. I need to turn the sound on. I've had it off for weeks so that Layla doesn't hear the ping when a text comes in. It's Joel. He's been texting a lot. He keeps telling me that he loves me. And he asks about the baby. I've texted back a couple of times, but I haven't told him where we are. I have a look but there's no new message. It's been four days since he texted. Maybe he's found a new girlfriend.

Is that what I am, I wonder? A girlfriend carrying his baby? Part of me is surprised that he keeps in touch. He will never be able to ask me to marry him and he knows it. But part of me is not surprised at all. I know, like all women know when it happens, that Joel is in love with me. I know my power and it is nothing to do with witchcraft. He can't keep away. I peer again at the phone. I suppose I'm enjoying the messages of love and the fact that he wants to see me. I don't love him but I like him a lot and I'm grateful. He is kind. He has saved my life, and, as Layla says, I owe him.

I go into the garden to start work. Better to work outside first so that I can go inside when the sun gets hot and I've hardly started when the phone rings. My heart jumps and I look but it's not Joel. It's Layla.

'What are you doing?' she asks.

'I'm in the garden,' I tell her. 'Weeding the cabbages.'

'That's good,' she says. 'I wanted to remind you to sweep the circle.'

'Of course, I will,' I reply. 'It's my next task.'

'That's no good,' she says. 'It has to be your first task, Auli. Every day, it has to be your first task and your last one at night. To keep the house safe.'

'OK,' I tell her. 'I'll do it now, tonight and first thing to-morrow. Before anything else at all.'

'All right,' she says, then asks me how the baby is and I tell her fine. What else can I say?

'Where are you?' I ask.

'Nearly half-way down,' she replies. 'Take care, Auli. I'll ring tomorrow.' I say goodbye and am about to hang up when she says it one last time. 'Don't forget to look after the circle, Auli.'

I put the phone down on the banana leaf that I've fetched so that I can put it down without it getting dirty and I look at the sky. Looks like rain and I feel the first drops start to fall. Big ones splashing on to my face and arms. It will be good for the garden, but I had better go in. I'll clean inside until the rain stops. Then I'll sweep the circle and get back to the weeding. I hate housework and wish I had a book to read. I miss my lessons. It seems like years since Layla gave me exercises to do and research projects. I used to feel like a normal girl with a future. I'm not a girl anymore. I remind myself that I'm a woman. With a baby inside. Layla said that the baby was my future.

I start cleaning the house and try to make myself do it properly but it looks clean already. Maybe it will be all right until tomorrow. The rain is beating hard on the roof and I like hearing the rain. Or maybe I can leave the cleaning for a couple of days and do it just before Layla gets back. I stand in the doorway and look out through the downpour. I see the earth sucking in the rain like a great thirsty animal.

I go back inside and sit at the table. The baby keeps moving and I'm getting very heavy. How big is this child? It's strange being here without Layla. I remember the times from before when I was here alone and how good it felt when Saul was gone. Even though I was shackled. Now I don't want to be here alone. I want Layla back as quickly as possible. I think about our conversation and how I complained to her and what she said. That I was lucky.

Well, I don't feel lucky, but I suppose it's all relative. That's what Layla used to say in the past. *It's all relative* and I would say it, too, but she told me to beware. It's a cliche she said and so we discussed what a cliche was. She said that those sayings that we like become used so much that their truth wears out. They stop you thinking she said.

'Truth can't wear out,' I argued as I sat there playing with my laptop while Layla marked my exercises.

'Yes, it can,' she said. 'Think about it, Auli.'

I did think about it but I still don't know what she meant. But yes, everything is relative and one thing is always compared to another. I am lucky not to be shackled or dead but as each of these fates float by into the past, they become less real and I'm left with what I have now. What I am now, and I contemplate that and compare it with what I would like to be.

I ponder the what-ifs. If Layla hadn't been accused of witchcraft and tortured, she would have been able to have her own babies and I wouldn't have been rescued and brought here. If Saul hadn't loved her and saved her, he wouldn't be dead. A heavy thought. Just think, Saul did two good things - he rescued Layla and he rescued me but getting involved with us got him killed. Well, sort of. I'm getting my thoughts twisted up now. I'm sure there should be straighter lines between one thing and another and not so many of them. When I had the laptop, I used to look up 'destiny' on google. I looked up 'fate', too, because they were more or less the same thing, but there were no answers. Definitions for both said that it was outside a person's control. I asked Layla if she believed in destiny and she answered.

'No, Auli. You make your own fate.'

Well, I'm not sure about that.

I go into the garden, carefully treading down the slippy steps and go to carry on weeding. The ground is wet from the rain and the dirt goes under my fingernails. The sun is out again and I stare at drops of water shining on the leaves. I spread out the banana leaf once more and put my phone down on it. With a bit of luck, I should finish this bed before lunchtime.

***

In the early afternoon of the second day, I'm sitting on the veranda having a rest and my phone rings.

'I'm down,' she says. It's Layla telling me that she's back in the city. 'Are you OK?'

'Yes,' I tell her, 'I'm fine.' And I ask how she is, but we don't speak for long. It's dangerous down there and she wants to finish quickly. She'll buy food and matches and come back as soon as she can. She's going to stay one night at her friend's and start back tomorrow. She rings off and the world is cut off. No, I tell myself, the world is here. I've got to stop sitting and thinking. Stop longing for this and that. Get on with something. It's quiet here but it's not silent. Maybe we could get a dog, I think. I'd like a dog. Would be better than a baby. This little monster kicking and kicking. Never goes to sleep. He's always awake.

I hear a noise and instantly, I'm on high alert. Trembling and scared. No-one comes here. Who is it?

'Aulani,' I hear a shout. 'Aulani, are you there?'

It's Saul's brothers, I think. Who else could it be? They've found the place. They've come for payback.

'Aulani,' I hear again, louder now and closer. 'Are you there?'

I'm still on the veranda. I should have hidden in the house. Too late now. I look to the end of the path and see someone standing just outside the circle.

18

It's Joel but is he alone? He's seen me. He's waving and calling my name.

'Aulani,' he's calling. 'Aulani, it's me. Come and let me in.'

What does he mean? Come and let him in? There is no gate. He can walk up the path. And then I remember. He will think that he can't cross the circle. Slowly I go down the steps and walk down the path towards him.

'Joel,' I say and look at him. So tall and thin. Didn't remember. Sweet smile. Big hair. Looks a bit like Layla but I suppose he would do. He's from the same village. He's one of Layla's wantoks. I stop and look at him, still a few feet away. 'Are you alone?' I ask.

'Of course,' he replies. 'I've come to see you.'

'How do I know?' I ask and he understands. He knows about the danger.

'I promise,' he says and he knows that a promise is not enough and I know that it's not enough, but it's all there is.

I walk to the end of the path with the broom and I sweep a space.

'You can come in,' I say and he steps on to the path. I sweep again to close the circle and feel amazed that he doesn't know. That he can't see that this is merely a charade, an empty act. Can't see that it's just some earth that I'm sweeping backwards and forwards with my broom. But I can't tell him. Layla's right. We need the circle. He follows me to the house and up the steps.

'Are you alone?' he asks.

'Yes,' I say. 'Only me here.' I'm not sure whether to tell him about Layla. He looks around and then looks back at me. Stares at my bump and smiles.

'My son's in there,' he says.

We need to talk. There's a lot to say but no place to start. We go to lie down on my mat and I lie on my side. I want him and he's gentle, and afterwards, we lie together and talk. He fetches water and we drink. He smokes and asks if I want a cigarette. I shake my head. I've never smoked and didn't know that Joel did. I smelled the smoke on him sometimes when we were in the police station but I thought it was from the others.

'I didn't know you smoked.'

No,' he replies. 'It was too dangerous to smoke when we were together before. Boa would have smelled it. He would have been suspicious.' And Scarface I think to myself but don't mention him. I've never talked to Joel about Scarface.

'I suppose so,' I say, then ask him, 'How long are you staying?'

'One night,' he replies. 'I have to go back tomorrow. Have to get back for work.'

'How did you know I was here?'

'I guessed,' he says, 'not many places for you to go in the city. It would be dangerous for you there so I was sure you would have left.'

'Are they still looking for me?' I ask.

'Don't think so,' he says. 'Not actively.' He stops and looks at me. Puts out his hand and strokes my belly where the little monster is kicking away. Touches him lovingly. 'But if they see you.....' We are both quiet for a minute and he strokes again where the child is moving. 'He's big, isn't he?' he says, and I nod. 'In two months time, he'll be born,' Joel says. 'I've worked it out.'

He's tired after his trek up the mountain. He came up quickly and he's not used to climbing. His legs ache so he lies down to rest while I go and cook. There's not much food but I do my best. It's pumpkin and pumpkin with half a tin of fish. It's all we have but it tastes good with a little salt. After we've eaten, he chews.

'Do you want some?' he asks and is surprised when I refuse. Layla is right. I should have tried harder to learn with the buai. It's a social thing.

There is so much to say, but mainly we lie together and stroke each other without speaking. Joel says he will come again as often as he can and next time he will bring some food. I am to text him a list of things. Anything, he says, anything I want. I am relieved that he is going before Layla comes back and wonder if they will meet on the mountain. If he is going to come again to visit, I shall have to say something about her but there is hardly any time. And I don't know how to begin.

I tell him at breakfast before he goes.

'I am alone now but I live here with Layla,' I blurt unable to find an easy way in.

'That's a relief,' he says and he looks at me and grins. 'I saw the mat in the living room,' he says. 'The one on the shelf and wondered who that was for.' He pauses for a moment, 'Did Layla come back without him?' He empties his mouth. 'Saul, I mean.'

'Yes,' I say. 'Saul never came back. Only Layla.'

Joel finishes eating and passes his bowl for some more. He wants more tea, too, but there's no sugar and no tinned milk. He pulls a face and switches to water.

'I'll bring sugar,' he says,' when I come again. And some milk.'

I tell him that Layla has gone to buy food in the city and that she'll be coming back up the mountain soon. It should be today so he'll meet her on the way and I see the fear come into his eyes. What can I say to him I wonder? I can't tell him that Layla can't do magic, that she has no special powers and neither do I. I think about it.

'I'll text her,' I tell him. 'And then you'll be safe. Layla only uses magic when she's in danger. She's a good person. She's my mama.'

'But she admitted it,' he says. 'She admitted to killing the boy. I went to have a look and I saw what she'd signed.'

'They tortured her,' I tell him, but he shakes his head. He doesn't believe it.

There is no more time to talk. He has to go. Before he leaves, I text Layla as promised.

'When are you coming back?' I text. 'Have you set off?'

'Not yet,' she replies. 'Have been delayed. Two more days here. Coming back on Wednesday.'

'Are you all right?' I text.

'Fine,' she replies. 'Are you?'

'Fine, too. See you wed. xx'

'Xxx'

'She's not coming back until Wednesday,' I tell Joel so you won't meet her this time. He looks relieved and says he has to go. I go with him to the end of the path to let him out of the circle and he hugs me.

'I love you, Auli,' he whispers and I know he means it. He is brave to come here.

***

Layla is not pleased when I tell her about Joel. She is angry.

'We are not safe now,' she tells me. 'Sooner or later he will talk. Others will come.'

'But he loves me,' I protest.

'Makes it worse,' she says. 'Love is the most dangerous thing.'

She blames me for his coming and won't listen when I explain that I didn't tell him where we were.

'You replied to his texts,' she says as she wipes the sweat from her forehead. She's digging new beds and the earth is hard. 'That was encouragement enough.' Then she adds, 'And you knew it, Aulani. You knew he would come.' It isn't a question and I suppose she is right. I am tired of Layla always being right. I tell her this and at last, I get a smile.

I'm heavy now and I lumber about. Like a bear, I think, although I have never seen a bear. Not a real one. My feelings shoot all over the place and sometimes I'm high but mostly, I'm crawling along the bottom of the world. Uncomfortable and scared of what's coming. Whatever I feel like, I'm careful not to moan to Layla. It will be over soon, I think, and this baby will be out. I lie on my mat at night unable to get comfortable or sleep and I wonder what the child will look like. I spend hours wondering what colour he will be. I'm afraid that he will be dark like Saul and then Layla will know. She will instantly know that the baby is not Joel's. And Joel, too, will know. And then I fantasise that the baby will be light-skinned like Joel and that everyone will believe that he is the father. He might even want to take his son to the village. I might be able to give him away and be free at last. Oh happy day.

At other times, I'm filled with a fierce love for this creature I can't see and I am sure that I will cope with anything that comes and will do anything in the world in order to protect him.

The time drags on and on.

Three weeks after Layla comes back from the city and just before she goes down again, my child is born. She's a girl and a surprise in every direction. Her skin is lighter than mine! I name her Jenn.

'Come and see,' I text to Joel. 'Your daughter is born. She was born early but she's beautiful and her name is Jenn.'

How could I ever have thought of giving her away? She is gorgeous. Small and perfect. I can't take my eyes off her. I hold her all the time and carry her around with me. Layla makes a special bilum so she can hang outside from the tree branch and rock while I work. Rockabye baby, I think to myself but not like the nursery rhyme. My Jenn will not fall down.

It's supposed to bring bad luck to name a child so soon after birth. It's in case the child dies, but I don't care. She won't die. I am sure of it and her name is Jenn. Jenn is a short version of Jennifer which comes from Guinevere. It means 'my fair one' and she is beautiful. She has to be Jenn.

One week later, Joel arrives loaded down with food and gifts. It's the first time that he and Layla have met each other and I see how cautious they both are of the other, but the house is full of the joy of Jenn and we all feel it. Once again, I let Joel into the circle and I see that Layla watches and approves. He steps in and puts everything down on the path.

'Where is she?' he asks and I bring her to him. The way he looks at her and holds her fingers makes me love him. He takes her in his arms and carries her into the house. I see how he supports her head and holds her gently. He tells me he's had plenty of practice with all his nieces and nephews in the village. He can't stop smiling. He is the perfect father.

'Mi Papa blo yu,' he tells her and then again in Motu. Finally, 'I'm your daddy, Jenny girl,' he says.

'It's Jenn,' I tell him but he shakes his head.

'She's my Jenny girl.'

There is so much food. We had almost run out, but Joel has brought plenty. Rice and coconut, fish, too, so we eat the food of Layla's childhood and plenty of it. We eat and we drink and there is beer for us all. I pull a face when I taste it but I drink it, too, and even Jenn, no doubt will get a little when I feed her.

Once again, Joel can't stay long.

'I'll be back,' he says as we let him out of the circle. He turns and waves and is quickly gone.

'Do you like him?' I ask and even Layla has to say that yes, she does, but her wary look is never far away.

19

We settle into a routine and it's the best time you can imagine. We work and we eat and Jenn grows fast and learns to smile and to push herself up on her arms. And Layla plays with her and carries her about almost as much as I do.

'She's better than you were,' Layla says, teasing me. 'You cried most of the time. Not like this one. This one smiles and laughs.' And it's true. Jenn is a happy baby and it spreads. The happiness spreads. Only occasionally do I catch myself longing to read and to study, to leave this place and seek another future. It is a time of delight.

One day, when Layla comes back from the city, she brings me a present. She's wrapped it up in leaves and there are so many, I wonder if I'll ever get to what's in the middle.

'What is it?' I ask.

'It's the world, Auli,' she tells me. 'I've brought you the world. I can see you've been missing it.' I hold it in my hand and feel the weight. 'Be careful,' she tells me. 'It's fragile,' and she watches as I remove the wrappings.

I gasp.

'Layla!' I say. 'Layla!'

It's a laptop. A Toshiba. Powerful. Silver. I can't believe my eyes.

'It's used,' she says, 'but I've had it checked. It's a good one.'

'We'll share it,' I say and she nods.

'Yes, of course,' Layla says, 'of course, we will, but it's still yours, Auli. I got it for you.'

I'm so overwhelmed that I have to sit down and then I just stare at it.

'Come on, then,' Layla says. 'Let's plug it in. Put your hotspot on, Auli.'

I get my phone and switch on the hotspot. Hope it still works with the pay-as-you-go. We haven't used it for ages. Years. Not since the time of Saul. I push his face out of my mind and we plug it in. Wait while the battery charges up. For about ten minutes, Layla and I sit on the mat together and stare at its beauty and then it's on. It works. It's perfect.

I hug her and thank her and Layla is pleased. She knows that this is what I've wanted more than anything. But I don't know how she found the money. I ask and she says that it didn't cost much. Her friend got it cheap in a going-finish sale. I half believe her but am still not sure. When she goes to the city, she goes for longer now than she used to do. Always stays two or three nights before she comes back. I ask her why but she shrugs and says it's to spend some time with her friend.

The time passes and Jenn grows. Soon she is one year old and she's already talking saying one or two words. Joel comes to visit and thinks she's a genius and each time it's pleasant when he's here. He never stays long and we don't quarrel, don't really talk much at all. We try to avoid discussing things and most of all we avoid the future. Thoughts of it, talk of it, but we know that it won't stay hidden forever. Sooner or later we'll have to face it and talk about things. But I don't know what we'll say.

He and Layla like each other but keep their distance. Joel is afraid of her and Layla knows that it has to stay like that. The same applies to me and it keeps us apart. My lies keep us apart. In spite of these things, I enjoy Joel's visits and Jenn adores her papa.

Before we get to talking, Joel and I, something happens. Joel sends a text.

'Leave now,' he texts. 'Saul's brothers are coming. Police told them Keroko.'

I show it to Layla and she says we must go.

'What about the circle?' I ask.

'It won't work,' she says. 'They will see it and know we are here. They will burn the place. They will burn us out.'

'OK,' I say. 'We'll leave tomorrow.'

'No,' Layla says. 'We've got the big torch. We'll leave to-night.'.

We take Jenn and the laptop, some food, matches and water, two mats and sleeping bags. And spare batteries but they're heavy. It's almost too much.

'We'll walk until dawn,' Layla says. 'Then we'll sleep for two hours and carry on. We need to get down the mountain before the brothers come up.'

'It's not safe to walk in the night,' I say. 'Not with Jenn.'

'It's not safe to stay here,' Layla replies.

I text Joel.

'When are they leaving?' I ask.

'Don't know,' he replies. 'Leave now. Not safe.'

Once again, I show Layla but she's already standing at the door.

'This is the second time,' I tell her and I don't need to say the rest.

'I know,' she says. 'He's a good man, Auli.'

***

I don't know how we made it. About halfway down, we threw away our food. It was too heavy and the batteries were more important. Jenn got so heavy that I considered putting her in the bilum and pulling her along like that but of course, it wasn't possible. We took it in turns to carry her and I could feel that she sensed our fear, but she was quiet. She didn't cry. We had short breaks and each of us slept for one hour only. The other was on guard.

It took two days and we managed with only some scratches and a bruised knee. It was dark when we got to the road below the track and that was a help. The darkness. We got to Shantelle's house in the middle of the night. She was waiting for us with food and made a joke of it the next morning. Told the girls we were in training for a walkathon event to raise money. We slept all day while Shantelle looked after Jenn.

It is evening when I awake and there are three texts from Joel.

First one - 'They've set off. Are you safe?'

Second one - 'Are you safe?'

Third one - 'Where are you?'

I show Layla.

'Don't tell him,' she says. 'Someone might look at his phone.'

I decide to wait for him to ring and half an hour later, he does.

'Are you safe?' he asks.

'Yes,' I reply.

'And Jenn?' he asks.

'She's fine,' I say and I hear him sigh.

'Where are you?'

'I can't tell you,' I say and I hear him sigh again. He doesn't know it, but we must be quite near to each other because Joel stays at his uncle's house on the uni campus. It's too far to drive from the village each morning to get to work. The campus isn't that big. We're bound to bump into each other sooner or later because we'll have to leave the house sometimes. If we don't, Shantelle's family will become suspicious. In any case, we shall need food. And money.

'Wherever you are, it's not safe,' he says. 'Saul's brothers know Layla and sooner or later, they will find her. They think she killed Saul. They say he would never simply disappear.'

'That's not true,' I say. 'Saul disappeared when he rescued Layla and they didn't look for him then.'

'No, but it's different now.'

'Why is that?'

'They assumed he was safe with Layla even though they didn't know where he was. Now they know he's missing because the police have asked about him. They've come to find him. They say they won't stop until they've found him. Or until they've found Layla.'

'Oh,' I say and it's my turn to sigh.

'Ask Layla where he is,' Joel tells me. 'She must know where he is and we can send the brothers after him.'

'She doesn't know,' I say but I realise I've spoken too fast. 'But I'll ask her again,' I pause. 'She said that they quarrelled and she came back to look for me. She doesn't know where he went.'

'Where were they when they quarrelled?' Joel asks and I have to admit that I don't know. I can tell from his voice that he doesn't believe what I'm saying. He doesn't trust Layla. I can almost hear his thoughts wondering if it's true that Layla killed Saul.

'No, she didn't kill him,' I say responding to the question he hasn't asked and I put the phone down.

I go to find Layla and she's under the house chopping vegetables.

'Will you come with me?' I ask and the two girls who are down here chopping with her look up in surprise. 'I need your help with Jenn,' I say and they start to laugh. Layla gestures to the mat spread out a little way past the sink and I see that Jenn is lying there asleep. Oh, bugger. Bugger and shit.

'Go with her, Rosa,' the girls say and they are smiling at me now, 'We'll keep an eye on Jenn.'

I walk with Layla to the end of the garden to where we used to sit at the corner of the lawn.

'I've spoken to Joel,' I tell her and explain why he said that it wasn't safe for us to stay here, especially her. 'What are we going to do?'

For the first time, I see Layla falter and hesitate. My mama who is always so sure and confident. Who always knows what to do and where to go. Who has worked hard to keep us safe. She slumps forward and looks worn out. She carried twice as much as I did down the mountain. She always has and I've taken it for granted. She's my mama. But she's getting older and life is wearing her out.

'I know what to do,' I say and she looks up at me, waiting for me to go on. 'We'll have to go to Australia,' I say. 'They won't find us there.'

'We can't do that,' she says. 'We'd need money and we haven't got passports.'

'I'll ask Joel,' I say. 'He'll have to help.' And I wait for her dismissal. Her argument. Her alternative way forward. But it doesn't come.

'All right,' she says. 'Go and talk to him.'

I try not to show my shock as we walk back across the lawn and Layla returns to her chopping.

'Is it man trouble?' the girls giggle as we get back to the kitchen area under the house. They've noticed that I don't appear to have a husband.

'It might be,' Rosa replies and they laugh some more as I escape back into the house.

I can't phone Joel from inside. Even if I'm quiet, people will hear. Instead, I go back out and walk around the garden looking for a place where I think I can talk without anyone hearing. Everywhere is too close.

'I'm going for a walk,' I call out to Rosa/Layla. 'Back soon.'

'Don't go far,' she shouts.

20

I walk for a while and sit down under a tree. I need the shade. It's much hotter down here than up in the mountains and I need to adjust. People walk past but only occasionally and nobody looks surprised that I'm sitting here by myself under the tree. They can see that I'm trying to phone so they probably all think the same as Shantelle's girls. I'm talking to my boyfriend. Secretly.

Well, the 'secretly' bit is right.

'Joel,' I say when he picks up. 'I'm sorry I put the phone down. I was upset.'

'It's all right,' he says and then goes quiet. 'How is Jenn?' he says while I'm trying to figure out how to ask for his help. He's always asking about her. Every five minutes.

'She's fine,' I say and half-smile into the phone. 'Still fine. Just like she was fifteen minutes ago. How are you, Joel? Are you at your uncle's?'

'Yes,' he says. 'I'm at his house on the uni campus.'

'I need your help' I say but there's no response. 'Joel, are you still there?'

'Yes,' he says and goes quiet again. How do I say this?

'We need to leave the country,' I say and it sounds dramatic and unreal. 'We need money and passports. Have you any idea how we can get them?' I don't suppose he has so I am surprised when he replies.

'I think so,' he says and I sit under the tree moving my foot from side to side in the dust making patterns. I wait for him to continue. 'The money's the hardest part,' he says. 'How much have you got?'

'I'm not sure,' I say. 'I'll ask Layla and phone you back. How much do we need?'

'I don't know,' he says, 'but I can find out.' He tells me that he knows a forger. A man who can make fake passports. Good ones but they're expensive. 'And then you'll need money for tickets. And money for when you get there. That's a lot. Where are you planning to go?'

'To Melbourne,' I say. 'Layla has a friend in Melbourne.'

'I'll ring you back as soon as I can,' Joel says, 'Got to go now' The phone goes dead before I can say goodbye. Maybe someone came in. I should have texted first to see if it was safe to ring. I must be more careful I tell myself. There's speed and there's care. I must remember to be careful. Slowly I get up and walk back to the house.

The food is ready and Jenn is awake.

'Mama,' she shouts when she sees me. I pick her up and give her a feed. She's pleased to see me, but she hasn't missed me. She's happy down here with the girls. They play with her and marvel at the way she can already say some words. They are teaching her Motu. Layla can speak Motu, of course. It's her first language but she doesn't use it. It's because of Saul she told me. He wasn't a Motu speaker so they always used English or Tok Pisin. At home, we almost always spoke in English. Not normal for a PNG family but my life hasn't been normal by anybody's standards.

I keep my phone close by but Joel doesn't ring back and I get no chance to speak to Layla alone until late in the evening.

'Come for a walk with me, Agnes,' she says. 'I want to hear more about your man troubles.' The girls giggle again and I get up and follow Layla into the garden. I speak quietly. We're not far from everybody else and they're probably dying to know about my man troubles. I tell her what Joel has said and ask how much money we've got.

'Not much,' she says. 'About 250 kina.'

That seems like a lot to me but I don't comment.

'How much do we need?' she asks.

'I don't know,' I say. 'Joel's going to find out and text me back.' I've hardly finished speaking and the phone pings.

'It's expensive,' he texts.

'How much?' I ask.

'Minimum K1,000 each,' I read.

'Impossible,' I reply. 'Can't be that much.'

'Up to K10,000 fine for forgery,' he texts back. 'It's dangerous so passports are expensive.'

I show Layla.

'So that's that,' I say. 'We need three passports. That's K3,000. And we've got K250.'

'Ask if he'll do three for K750' Layla says. 'I think I can get some money from a friend.'

'What friend?' I ask. 'Who will give you money like that?' Layla shakes her head and won't tell me.

'Just do it,' she says. 'Text and ask, Auli. We've got to go. Somehow we've got to go.'

'Would he do three for K750?' I text.

'Don't think so,' Joel replies but I can set up a meeting for you if you like.

'Yes, please,' I text back without asking Layla.

'Ok,' Joel says. 'Will let you know.'

After that, we argue. Layla says that she'll go to meet the forger man but I say that it has to be me. Layla's the one in the biggest danger at the moment and reluctantly, she agrees. I'll have to wait now to hear from Joel.

For the rest of the evening, I sit in a state of unbearable impatience waiting to hear from him but there are no more texts. The girls tease me a little and think that my distracted state is due to man trouble.

'Where's her papa?' they ask me. He must be gorgeous. They're talking about Jenn and how pretty she is. I can see Layla thinking of Joel and it's only in my own mind that the image of Saul rises huge and powerful. Terrifying. He's angry that I've told everyone that Jenn is the daughter of Joel. How can he be angry I think? He's dead. I've got to hold on to my sanity and think things through but my logic doesn't work. Doesn't save me from Saul's face that stares out of bushes and stones, out of walls and pavements, out of grass and leaves and won't let me be.

I sleep badly. Partly it's too hot. Mostly, it's my thoughts chasing each other in wild tangles and then it's my dreams. Nightmares. There is no rest. I come fully awake with a jolt when it's still dark. Jenn is beside me and the room is full of nighttime breathing. Three girls and a woman I don't know. No Shantelle and Layla's gone again. I don't know where she goes at night and it worries me.

After waking up early, I finally go to sleep and get up late. The girls are not so friendly today. I need to do my share of the work so I try to make up for yesterday and for getting up late. Layla is already there with the others preparing food but she looks exhausted. There are no further texts from Joel. I go to work in the garden and at midday, a text arrives.

'3 pm?'

'Yes,' I reply. 'Where?'

Joel texts back and surprisingly suggests the tree where I phoned him from yesterday.

'If I've got the right place, that's where I was yesterday. Did you know?'

'No,' Joel replies, 'but it's a good place. Outside. No-one will hear. People will think you're meeting your boyfriend.'

'Aren't you coming, too?'

'No,' he says. 'Kandin said it has to be just you and him. Or Layla and him.'

'We're Rosa and Agnes down here,' I tell him.

'Too late,' he says. 'You should have told me before.'

'It's me,' I tell him. 'I'm going to the meeting. It's too dangerous for Layla,' and Joel agrees.

'All right,' he says. 'Be there at three.'

'OK,' I reply and realise that I've only got a couple of hours to prepare myself. I go off to tell Layla.

'More toktok?' the girls ask but they're pleased with me again. I've worked hard all morning.

'Yes,' I say and Layla gets up from the circle and we walk across the garden. Three o'clock I tell her and she says that everything depends on me. I've got to get him to agree to three for K750. If I don't, then we can't go. That's the most we can get together.

'Where's the money coming from?' I ask again.

'I've got a friend,' she says. 'Don't ask, Auli. Just do your part.'

Before I go, we discuss two things. The first is money.

'Shall I take the money with me?' I ask Layla.

'No way,' she says. 'You have to get the agreement first. Take the money next time.'

'OK,' I say.

'If you take it now, he might steal it from you,' Layla says. 'We won't give him the money until he's done the passports.'

Privately, I wonder if the forger man will be willing to start on the passports without any up-front payment, but she might be right. I'll have to ask.

'What's the second thing?' I ask.

'Names,' Layla says. 'What names are we going to use?'

'Our real names,' I say. 'The passport lasts for years. I don't want to travel under a false name.' (Agnes springs to mind and I shudder.)

'But we can't use my family name,' Lalya says, 'we'll have to choose something else.'

'What about Keroko?' I suggest but Layla pulls a face and says definitely not.

'We'll be Sogeri,' she says. 'It's where I went to school.'

'I don't agree,' I tell her. 'Everybody knows Sogeri is a place. He'll know it's a false name.'

'No,' she says, 'He won't be sure. Place names can be family names, too. He might think it's false and he might assume our other names are false, too and that will be all to the good. And if anybody finds out and looks for us in Sogeri, then what will they find?' She looks at me and grins.

'Nothing,' I reply and so it's decided. We are going to be the Sogeri family Layla, Jenn and me.

There is no-one under the tree as I approach it just before three. We had another little argument before I set off, but Layla finally agreed to let me go. Joel knows that it's me who is going and has confirmed that I have to go alone. He has told me the name of the man I am going to meet.

Kandin. His name is Kandin, but there is no-one there. Shall I keep going? I decide to go and sit under the tree by myself like I did yesterday. I'm nearly there when a truck drives past with several people on the back. Going too fast. A cloud of dust settles on my hair and I feel annoyed. I want to look good.

It will help, won't it, if I look good? I've changed into my best laplap. It's blue with a pattern of green and yellow leaves. It goes well with my blue meri blouse and my body has gone into a good shape again since Jenn was born. Not the same shape to be sure, but my stomach is nearly flat and I think I look good. What strange thoughts to be having as I approach the tree. I ought to be worrying about leaving the country. Changing our lives. Getting caught. Instead, I'm wondering if the forger man will like me so that I can negotiate a better passport price.

Layla has lent me her watch and I keep looking at the time. I've been waiting nearly ten minutes and no-one has turned up. Is this the place he meant? Have I got the right meeting place? I'm sure that I have. I discussed it with Joel and he confirmed the place. I'm about to get up and walk back home (home?) when a car drives past and stops. A man gets out and walks towards me.

'Hello,' he says and holds out his hand for me to shake. 'I'm Kandin.' I turn to jelly. This is a golden man. Look at his hair (big and soft). And his face (smooth brown skin, wide lips, big smile and laughing eyes). Look at the way his shoulders bulge underneath his tee-shirt which is pure white. I look at his arms and admire the strong rippling muscles. He's not as tall as Joel, but quite a bit taller than me. Not thin like Joel. Kandin is packed full of muscle and every movement is graceful and sexy. He is looking at me, directly into my eyes and I find myself looking directly back. Not down as a PNG girl should.

'Aulani,' I reply, taking his hand and feeling his touch.

'What can I do for you?' he asks as he gestures to me to sit down. We sit next to each other. Not looking at each other now.

'I need three passports,' I tell him.

'Yes,' he says. 'Joel told me. I'll do them for you for a special price of K3,000. That's cheap.'

I'd expected him to ask why I wanted them, but he shows no interest. It's just a business transaction. Or is it? I can feel him looking at me. He wants me. I think he does.

'We've only got K750,' I say. 'Will you do them for K750?'

'Each?' he asks.

'No,' I reply. 'For all three.'

Kandin laughs and gets up.

'Sorry,' he says. 'You don't understand, Aulani. This is a dangerous thing. And difficult. The passports I make are perfect. They work. The paper has to be right. Everything has to be right. And if I get caught....' He is about to go, but I can't let him go.

'Stop,' I say, and he turns to look at me. 'There must be a way you can do them for K750.'

'Well, yes,' he says, 'but you'd have to pay me in a different way.'

Instantly, I understand what he means but instead of dreading it, I find myself wanting him. My face gets hot. I blush and he laughs.

'You might like it,' he says and I am suddenly angry.

'What arrogance,' I say. 'Goodbye, Kandin,' and this time it's my turn to start walking.

'Let me know if you change your mind,' he calls and I half turn and see him smiling. The golden smile.

21

'What happened?' Layla asks as soon as we manage to go and sit in our lawn spot. We know we're attracting attention with our secrets, but it can't be helped.

I tell her what has happened but don't say that I stormed off. I've changed my mind since then. I'm going to go back.

'No, Aulani,' she says. 'I'll go and pay him.'

'You can't,' I say. 'It's too dangerous.' And then I pause and look at her directly. 'I think he wants *me*, Layla.'

I see Layla's hands twisting in her lap. She's still my mama. She doesn't want me to go. She wants to protect me like always and this is a step too far. Oh, I think to myself, if only she knew about Saul. If only she did. But she doesn't. And then I realise where Layla has been getting the money for our food. The money for my present. The money for the passports.

'It's what you've been doing, isn't it,' I say. I'm not asking her, I'm telling her that I know. I look at her and she nods.

'There was no other way,' she says. 'We had no money and we needed food. And now we need passports.' I go to hug her. I understand what she's done. I know it is love. And survival. But mainly, I think, it is love. Layla's love for me.

'Now, it's my turn,' I tell her and feel I have to come clean. 'I like him, Layla. It won't be hard.'

She looks at me and her eyes show pity.

'Oh, Auli,' she says. 'It's not as easy as you think.'

But it will be. I think of Kandin and the prospect of his body. And I think of Saul and how he ripped me and broke me. Layla doesn't know. She will never know. I shudder. Nothing could be worse than that.

'It will be fine,' I say. 'I'll be all right, Layla, and we need the passports. There isn't another way.' Layla doesn't argue further. She can see that I've made up my mind.

'Wait here,' she says and goes into the house. When she comes back, she takes something out of her bag and hands it to me.

'Take these,' she tells me. 'One each night.' I look at what she's handing me and see that it's a pack of tablets in silver paper with the days written on the back where you push them through. 'They're contraceptive pills,' she tells me. 'I was going to give them to you because you go with Joel. At least you won't get pregnant.

'Thank you, Layla,' I say and we go back to the others. After we've eaten, I text Joel.

'Can you set up another meeting for me with Kandin?' I ask. 'Tell him I've got the money.'

'How was it?' Joel asks. 'Will he do it?'

'I think so,' I reply. 'Tell him I'm ready to do a deal and let me know what he says.'

Jenn is already asleep and as usual, we sit together with the girls after we've eaten. I've already had a text. It's tomorrow at ten in the same place but there's no chance to tell Layla. At last, I manage to sit next to her and show her the text. She nods and I put the phone away. She's looking tired but that night when I go to bed, she's gone again. Oh, Layla.

***

I wear my other laplap. I've only got two. I prefer the one I wore yesterday but don't want to wear the same thing twice. I've showered as usual but I've spent time on my hair and last night I put coconut oil on my arms and legs. There was a bottle in the bathroom and Shantelle said I could use it. My skin has been getting dry lately. I look at the silver scars on my ankles and twist to see what they look like round the back of my legs. I don't like to see them. Don't even like to touch them. What will Kandin think of my scars? I see Layla at breakfast and every day she looks worse. This morning I see the worry in her eyes as well as the weariness. And she notices my skin. She knows what I've done. And why.

'I'm going for a walk,' I say. 'Will you keep an eye on Jenn?'

'I can't get near her,' Layla tries to smile. 'The girls carry her about all day long.'

'They try,' I say 'She's always running these days. Doesn't like to be carried anymore. Will you watch her for me, Layla?'

She nods and I set off. I'm still wearing Layla's watch. I'll have to give it back soon.

Like yesterday, there's no-one there when I reach the place. Kandin must make a point of being late for his meetings, but no, his car arrives right on time and stops just past the tree. He gets out and comes towards me. He has a lazy, arrogant walk.

134

'Good morning,' he greets me, holding out his hand like yesterday. I put my hand in his and he holds it just a second longer than necessary. He walks towards the car and holds the door open. I get in.

I don't know what to expect. I'm a little scared but pretend that I'm calm and confident. We leave the campus and he keeps on driving. I don't know the city. I have no idea where we are or where we are heading.

'Where are we going?' I ask and he turns to look at me. Half smiles. Only one hand on the wheel (like they do in the movies).

'You'll see,' he says and puts his foot on the accelerator. We leap forward and I pretend that I'm used to going in cars. Going fast. Pretend that this isn't the first time ever.

He takes me to a huge house behind locked gates. Dogs bark but he shouts at them and they go to lie down. He looks at me once again with that funny half-smile.

'There's a swimming pool,' he says. 'Do you want to cool off?'

'I don't swim,' I tell him and notice his surprise.

I expect him to take me to bed straight away to get it over with, but it's not like that.

'Come and talk to me,' he says. 'Tell me about yourself.'

He couldn't have asked me anything worse. What on earth shall I say? Then I realise that I can tell him lies. Not easy to think up a whole life story on the spur of the moment. I'll have to be careful. He notes my silence and offers me a drink?

'Most people like to talk about themselves,' he says. 'Why have you gone quiet?'

'There's nothing much to tell,' I say.' Why don't you tell me about you?'

135

'Where shall I start?' he asks.

'At the beginning,' I say. 'That's usually the best place.'

'Would you like some orange juice?' he asks instead of telling me anything about himself and I nod. I've eaten millions of oranges (well, thousands or hundreds). There are orange trees in the bush near our house. Lemon trees, too, although I can't see much use for lemons. Oranges, on the other hand, are sweet and I love them, but I've never drunk just the juice. Would think it a waste to throw away the rest of the fruit.

'Yes, please,' I say.

Tastes good but not quite as good as the fruit of the orange.

'Thank you,' I say and look around the room where we're sitting. It's cool. Air-conditioned. Another first for me. The floorboards are polished wood. They shine. I look at the glass with the orange juice. The glass is foggy with cold. Frosted. I draw a line with my finger down the side of the glass and turn it into an A.

'Cooled in the fridge,' he says in explanation. He knows it's all unfamiliar. Knows that this is not my world. Knows that I'm not sure of myself despite my pretence. He knows it by my feet. I have no shoes. Only village girls have no shoes. But I'm not a village girl. I can see him trying to work me out.

'I like you, Aulani,' he says but he doesn't need to. I know that he does, but he's not in my power. Not like Joel is. He can take me or leave me.

We go to a bathroom with a shower like I've not seen before and we stand in the spray together. He soaps my body and sees that I've had a child.

'Boy or girl? he asks.

'Girl,' I tell him.

He looks at my ankles and sees the scars but doesn't comment.

And, in turn, I start to soap him. He's mostly smooth with not much body hair. Golden skin. Firm. Strong. Exciting.

'It's all right,' he says as he sees that I avoid touching certain parts of him, but still, he gently touches parts of me. I can't help feeling shy although I'm still trying hard to keep up my act. We go to the bedroom still wet and I see a bed that is not on the floor. A bed like they have in the movies. We lie on it and it bounces and I have to laugh. Can't stop the giggles that break out uncontrolled. I bounce up and down. It's like a trampoline and he looks at me and smiles. Then he takes me and it's as I imagined. Better than I imagined. He is altogether better than I imagined. I shouldn't like being here with him using my body as payment for passports but I do, and I don't want it to end.

There's more orange juice afterwards and we shower again.

'Shall I give you the names?' I ask.

'The names?'

'For the passports,' I say and he frowns.

'Not yet,' he says. 'There are two more payments, Aulani. Then you can bring me the K750 and I'll start work on the documents.'

'No,' I say. I'm angry. 'That wasn't the deal. We need them quickly. You have to start work on them now.' I stare at him hard like I've learned to do and wait for him to look afraid but no, he looks amused. He doesn't know about my special powers. Or doesn't believe in them. One or the other.

'OK,' he agrees unexpectedly. 'I'll start doing them tonight.' He fetches a piece of paper and a pen and asks me to write down the names for the passports. Looks almost surprised as I write. As though he had expected me to be illiterate. This man needs teaching a lesson, but so far he's been in charge all the way. If this was an American movie, they would say that he was 'calling the shots'. Maybe this language is rising up in my mind because this whole place feels like a movie set. It doesn't feel real. I don't feel real.

He takes the paper, folds it and puts it in his pocket.

'I'll pick you up tomorrow. Same time,' he says. 'I will start work on your passports, but I still expect two more payments.' I nod and follow him out to the car and soon we're back at the tree and I'm walking away.

***

I go each day and after the second day, Kandin tells me that the payments are complete, but I don't stop going. Every day, I'm there by the tree and he arrives on time and he drives me to the house. I don't tell Layla what the situation is. I go with Kandin day after day. I take the money from her and I give it to him. The passports are finished and he hands them over but I ask him to wait. I'll take them soon. We need to leave but I'm caught by the golden boy. He has me in thrall.

One afternoon after we've eaten lunch and just before Kandin is going to drive me back, the dogs start to bark. We go outside to have a look and it's Joel standing at the gate.

He's full of anger. He's in uniform and he's come in a police car. I stand on the veranda and watch as Kandin goes to speak to him, then opens the gate and walks back to me.

'He wants you to go with him,' Kandin tells me, scowling. 'Go to him, Aulani. He thinks I'm keeping you here against your will.' I shake my head. 'Then go and tell him,' Kandin orders, 'but he has to leave. And not come back. A visit from the police is bad for business.'

I remember that Kandin is a forger, a criminal and I can see that he is angry. I walk to the gate and speak to Joel.

'You're crazy,' I tell him. 'I won't get the passports if you behave like this.'

'They're already finished,' Joel shouts in my face. 'Kandin told me last night when I asked him.'

'He's lying,' I whisper and look into Joel's eyes, 'he's going to give them to me tomorrow. But you've got to go or it will be the end of everything.'

'I'll text you,' he says and turns away. He's angrier than I've ever seen him and he doesn't believe me.

22

Kandin tells me to get my bag. It's time to go. He hands me the passports and tells me I should go back to my boyfriend. He won't pick me up tomorrow.

'He's not my boyfriend,' I tell him. 'He's the father of my child.'

'The father of your child!' Kandin asks with a curve of his eyebrow. 'But not your boyfriend. What kind of a girl are you, Aulani? And what kind of trouble are you running from?' Kandin hasn't asked before. He has shown no interest at all in my need for three fake passports.

'I'm a witch,' I shout, uncaring now and wanting to keep him any way I can, but he starts to laugh.

'A witch?' he says. 'So what can you do? Cast a spell? Strike me down? Turn me into a frog?'

'All of them,' I say and try to look fierce.

'Then do it,' he says and I know I can't, and he knows I can't.

'Not today,' I reply. 'I need you to drive me home.'

'Not today,' he mimics. 'Not today. A fine witch you are,' he says. 'Can you only do magic on Sundays? Or when the moon is new?' He's laughing at me and suddenly I start to laugh too.

'That's right,' I say but I can't stop laughing now and I'm swamped with relief. I don't have to pretend and here is a man who is not afraid of me. Who thinks that witchcraft doesn't exist. We go back inside and he fetches a bottle of wine. That's something else I've never had before but I've seen it in the movies. Everybody drinks it in the movies.

'Let's talk,' he says, and he fetches glasses.

'Do you prefer red or white?' he asks and I'm done with the pretence.

'I've no idea,' I reply. 'I've never tried either.'

He fetches white and I don't like it, but I persevere. This is the life I feel I should be leading so I've got to learn how to fit into it. The time flies and Kandin talks. I listen. He's the same age as I am, but he's mixed race. Didn't realise that. His mother is from Melbourne and she comes back tomorrow. (I had wondered why he had such a large house to himself.) It's his parents' house.

'And where's your papa?' I ask.

'In Oxford, England' he says. 'Doing a doctorate.' It's a long story, he'll tell me another time.

'And what about your mother? What does she do?'

'She runs Tara Jewellers in Boroko,' he tells me. 'Do you know it?' But of course I don't and once again, he looks surprised. The more he talks, the more I realise that although he thinks he's a PNG man, we come from different worlds.

'Shall I pick you up tomorrow?' he asks me. 'I can introduce you to my mother. She will be here early. You'll like her.'

I'm not at all sure about this, but I want to keep on seeing Kandin so I have to say yes. I wonder what I could possibly wear and what she will be like. A *waitpela meri*. When the wine is finished, he drives me back to the tree, and somehow, it feels as though a barrier has been broken. Joel's visit has brought us closer together.

At home (home?) things are not good and I fall back to earth with a crash. There is a price to pay for my dalliance with Kandin and when I look into Layla's weary eyes, I feel sick with guilt and know that I deserve every bad thing that happens. I go to look at Jenn to say hello but I've come back so late that she's already asleep. The girls look at me and frown. They don't like me anymore. The teasing has stopped and they hardly speak to me now. I don't blame them. I haven't been working or looking after Jenn but I still come back and eat. They are right to be cross. Layla looks at me and gets up from the grass. Leads the way across the lawn to the place where we go each evening and have our talk.

'We've got to leave,' she says. 'Shantelle wants us out of here as soon as possible. The girls are asking questions about where you go every day and what we're doing here.' I hand her the passports and she gives a sigh of relief. 'At last,' she says. 'I thought you'd never get them.'

'Tomorrow I'll ask Kandin to get the tickets for us,' I say searching madly for an excuse to go there one last time. Layla considers what I've said.

'All right,' she says. 'I was going to ask Shantelle, but I don't think she'll do it anymore. Can you trust him?'

'Yes,' I say but Layla looks doubtful.

'Will you tell him it's urgent?' she asks and I can see that it is.

'Yes,' I say. 'I'll ask for us to leave as soon as possible.'

While we're talking, a text arrives from Joel.

'Meet me at the tree in half an hour,' he texts. 'Bring Jenn and bring her passport.'

I show Layla and she looks anxious.

'Can't do that,' I reply. 'Jenn's asleep.'

'I'm taking her to the village,' Joel texts. 'I'll bring her to Melbourne myself. Will follow you there.'

'Why?' I ask but I already know.

'Because,' he replies and then texts again. 'If you're not there with Jenn, I'll come to the house and get her.'

I show Layla.

'What's happened?' she asks and I tell her about this afternoon.

'What shall I do?'

'You'll have to take her,' Layla says. 'Joel will look after her. It will be all right.'

'I can't bear it,' I say. 'I can't leave for Melbourne without Jenn.'

'You'll have to,' Layla says. 'I think he means it.'

And I do, too. This is a new Joel and I've stepped over a dangerous line. Slowly, I get up and Layla comes with me. We start packing Jenn's things into a bilum and Shantelle asks what we're doing.

'Her papa wants to take her to the village,' I say. 'He's coming for her.'

'Tonight?' Shantelle asks and we nod.

'I'm coming with you,' Layla says.

'It's not safe,' I say but she doesn't care and lifts the sleeping child into her arms. Jenn stirs but doesn't wake. Your daughter's been running around all day, Layla tells me. She's tired. We've nearly run out of time so we set off for the tree.

'Back soon,' we tell Shantelle.

Joel is already waiting and I see him start to relax a little when he sees Jenn.

'I'll bring her to Melbourne,' he tells me.

'Do you promise?' I ask and remember to look at him directly with the fierce look that makes him afraid.

'I promise' he says. 'Where's her passport?'

I hand it over and he looks inside and starts to frown.

'It's wrong,' he says.

'What do you mean, it's wrong?' I ask.

'It's got the wrong name in it. It gives the family name as Sogeri.'

'That's what we decided,' I tell him. 'We decided to name ourselves after Layla's school.'

'It has to be my name,' Joel says. 'Jenn's name is Jenn Goasa. It will have to be changed.' He's angry again and there's nothing I can do. It had not occurred to either me or Layla that Joel would want his family name on the passports. 'I'll do it,' he says. 'I'll get it changed.' He stops and looks at us. 'In any case,' he says, 'how can I travel with a child who has a different name?'

I don't know if Kandin will change the passport for no extra money and say so but Joel frowns some more and says he'll find whatever money is necessary.

'And how will you explain her in the village?' I ask. 'It's not normal for a man to suddenly turn up with a child that nobody knows about.'

'They're already suspicious,' he says. 'I've been disappearing weekends for a long time now. They know that I'm seeing someone.'

'And what will you say' I ask.

'I'll tell them the mother has run away and left me with the child,' he says and I feel my heart tumble and fall, but he's not sorry. Joel's face is set and hard and I'm back in the old familiar place of having no choice. I kiss her and hand her over. My beautiful child.

23

My steps are slow and heavy as we set off back to the house. Layla keeps talking to me, but I barely answer. Don't hear what she's saying. My spirit is with Jenn and I don't want my body walking in the opposite direction. Eventually, Layla's words penetrate the wall of grief I'm wrapped in and I hear what she says. Her voice is urgent and insistent.

'We've got to leave, Auli. Can you get tickets for Sunday? Latest Monday?'

I consider. It's Friday night now. I won't see Kandin until tomorrow. It will already be Saturday.

'I'll try,' I reply and hear Layla's stress pouring out.

'No good, Auli,' she's saying. 'You've got to succeed. Try and fail and it might be the end of us.' She's not exaggerating. I think of Kandin and his laid-back attitude to life and wonder if I can force him to move as quickly as we need. He doesn't even believe in sorcery. Doesn't take it seriously. Hasn't got a clue about the danger we're in. Layla's right. I've got to find a way to make him get those tickets quickly. We're getting close to the end of the line. Shantelle has had enough.

When I set off the next morning, I've got more than my clothes and Kandin's mother on my mind. They don't matter any more. It's the tickets. I've got to get the tickets. I've got to persuade him to get them. Layla's cracking up and Jenn's in the village. My misery must show in my face because Kandin notices immediately and asks me what's wrong. I get in the car and on the way to his house, I explain as clearly as I can. I don't notice where we're going but I'm surprised when he stops the car in a place I don't know. We park under a tree next to a beach and I get out and look at the ocean. It's blue green. Little ripples coming in. Fills the bay and goes on forever and my eyes go with it. It's the Coral Sea. For a minute, I drift and dream. We sit on a bench at a picnic table and stare out at the water. In the distance, I see what look like fish jumping out of the sea. Kandin follows my gaze.

'Dolphins' he tells me. 'They leap like that,' and in an instant, I see my own dolphin, the one Saul made for me. And I see Saul's face. Smiling at me with kindness. I drag myself back.

'Why have we stopped here?' I ask him. 'I thought we were going to see your mother.'

'We are,' he says. 'But you seem full of talk about tickets so I thought we'd better sort it out before we get to the house.'

'Yes,' I say and before I know what I'm saying, I ask Kandin to come with us.

'We've got to go immediately,' I explain. 'We can't stay in the house any longer. Latest Monday. Preferably tomorrow. Why don't you come with us? Just for a while? Can you afford it?'

'Oh yes,' he says and grins. 'I've got plenty of money, Auli, but plenty of work as well. The work has to be done.'

'Oh,' I say and don't know what else to add.

'Joel got in touch last night and wants me to change Jenn's passport. Did you know?' I nod. 'I can't change it,' he says. 'I'll have to make another one. If I come with you, Jenn's passport will have to wait.'

I feel the disappointment but once again, there's no choice. 'Then stay and do the passport,' I say. 'I want Joel to bring her as soon as possible.'

'If you can wait until Monday,' he says. 'I can have it finished by then and we could go together. We could have some fun together in Melbourne. It's more than a year since I was there.'

'You've been before?' I ask.

'Of course,' he replies, 'it's where Chrissie comes from.'

'Chrissie?'

'My mother.'

I should insist that Layla and I go tomorrow, that we don't wait until Monday, but I don't. I fear that if Kandin doesn't come with us when we go, he won't come at all. I agree for us all to go on Monday and Kandin says he'll get tickets for Layla, me and himself. Then we get back into the car and set off to see Chrissie. His mother.

Instantly, I know who she is. As soon as I set eyes on her. And I can see that she remembers me, too. She's the Aussie woman who was there at the hotel. The one with the hard hair and the hard face. The one who looked at my dirty clothes with contempt. The one with the chunky necklace.

'Meet my mother,' Kandin says and turns to smile at me. 'Mum, this is Aulani. I've told you about her.'

'Hello, Aulani,' his mother says with the same forced smile as before. 'I'm Chrissie.' She recognises me, but she's not going to say anything. Now, why is that?

'Hello, Chrissie,' I say. 'Pleased to meet you.' I go to shake hands with her and she suggests that we go and sit poolside. Poolside? Echoes of tv and the unreality of this place rise up around me, but that's where we go with our orange juice in frosted glasses. We go poolside.

We can't think of anything at all to say to each other and Kandin jumps in to fill the awkward spaces. He talks about visits to the Yacht Club and who he saw there, what they're doing and a hundred other things about which I know nothing. And care less. I don't like this woman and wonder how it can be that I'm so deeply attracted to her son while at the same time being repelled by her. More than repelled. It's as though there's some chemical signal between us that makes us hostile. Defies logic and I realise that I don't like anything about her. Don't like the way she looks or dresses or talks. And I don't like the things she says. I'm disappointed. I had expected to like Kandin's mama.

I'm still wearing Layla's watch and after half an hour that feels like at least a year, Kandin stands up and says it's time to go. When we're in the car, I give him all the money I've brought with me. It's for the tickets and he says he'll text me the time to go to the airport. He'll pick us up at the tree and take us. Will we have much luggage he asks? I smile.

'No, not much.'

***

Layla is disappointed that we've got to wait until Monday and hopes that Shantelle won't kick us out before then. But she asks and it turns out to be fine, now that we're definitely going. Am I sure that we are definitely going she asks me? Will Kandin be certain to get the tickets? I nod and she's relieved but almost explodes when I tell her that Kandin is coming with us.

'No,' she says. Layla is beside herself. 'You should have asked me, Auli! He can't come.'

'Why not?' I ask. 'He's going to pick us up and take us to the airport.'

'No,' Layla says. 'Shantelle will take us to the airport. I already asked her. Didn't you think that I would have arranged all that?'

Well, no, I don't suppose I did.

'And we're staying with my friend Carolyn. You did know that.' I nod. I did know that we were going to stay with Carolyn and that Carol was doing her masters in Melbourne. 'He can't stay with us,' Layla goes on. 'There won't be room.'

'Then perhaps I could go and stay with Kandin for a little while,' I suggest and Layla slaps me. It's the first time she's hit me since I complained about being pregnant. She is shaking with frustration and weariness.

'Wake up, Auli! Where's your head?'

I look at her.

'There is Joel and Jenn to worry about. Getting a job, earning some money and getting somewhere to live when we've only got a tourist visa. Surviving in a foreign country. Making preparations for Jenn to arrive. Working out how we're going to care for her. And all you're thinking about is swanning off to have a good time for a few days with some crook.'

She's right. That is exactly what I've been dreaming of. Layla is right. I look at her tired eyes and hold my hand to the side of my face that she just hit.

'I'm sorry,' I say. 'I'll tell him that he can't stay with us. He'll have to get a hotel.' I hesitate. 'But I won't tell him until we're on the plane, Layla. I can't risk having a row with him when we're relying on him to get the tickets.'

Layla relaxes a little.

'OK,' she says. 'Have you heard from Joel?'

I haven't. I text him.

'How's Jenn?' I ask.

'She's fine,' he replies. 'Happy in the village.'

'Kandin says he'll do her new passport by the end of Sunday,' I text. 'When will you bring her?'

'Soon,' Kandin replies. 'Let her have a little holiday first. My mother loves her.'

'OK,' I reply, 'but I want a date, Joel. I need to know when she's coming.' And then I send another one. 'And you. I need to know how long I've got to wait until I can be with you.'

'I'll let you know,' he texts. 'When are you going?'

'Monday,' I tell him. 'We're leaving on Monday.'

'OK,' he says.

'Look after Jenn,' I text. 'Kiss her for me and sort out a date.'

'OK,' he replies and that's it. He sends no love to me but he does love Jenn. He'll keep her safe. And I believe that he'll bring her soon. I look at Layla and see that she can barely stand. She's exhausted.

'I want to go to bed now,' Layla says. 'We're going shopping tomorrow, Auli.'

'Shopping?'

Even though she's exhausted, Layla manages to chuckle.

'Look at your feet,' she says. 'And where is your coat? We can't go to Melbourne with no shoes and no coat. I've got some money, Auli. We'll go and buy some clothes tomorrow. We'll be careful.'

The shopping trip is good and I get my first two pairs of footwear and my first coat. I get a pair of thongs and a pair of sandals. My feet seem to be too wide for most shoes. It's not my scars, it's the shape of my feet. Layla's are the same. We were both looking for shoes, but in the end, we had no choice. Had to buy sandals because that is all we could get to fit. They feel funny on my feet, but Layla says we have to wear them and I know she's right. She's thought of everything. She's worked all day, gone with men at night to get money for both of us while I've been sitting 'poolside' with Kandin. I wonder what she'll think of him.

I go for a walk and manage to speak to Joel instead of the eternal texting. He's stopped being angry and I talk to Jenn. I can't bear the thought of leaving her behind but I've got no choice. It's the story of my life. No choice, no choice. I say the same to Layla and she tells me to stop whingeing.

'Nobody has any choice, Auli,' she says. 'Nobody does.'

What happened to everyone making their own fate, I wonder, but now is not the time to bring it up.

I get a text from Kandin and he tells me we must be at the tree by 7.30 am. If we're not there, we shall miss the plane.

We are there. Of course, we are there. We have one suitcase that Layla found from somewhere (another going-finish sale) and we each have two bilums, one large and one small. Layla keeps worrying about our fake passports (and fake visas). Will they work? I feel so overwhelmed that we are leaving Papua New Guinea and leaving my daughter behind in the village that I have no space in my heart to worry about the passports.

As it turns out, they work fine and soon we're on the plane. Everybody looks as though going on a plane is the most ordinary thing in the world. When we take off, I feel that I'm being torn away from the earth, but I manage not to cry out.

24

It's freezing. My God, it's cold. Our coats seem to make no difference at all. How can people survive in a climate like this! When we get through customs we see that Kandin is met by a driver in a large silver car. He offers to take us with him to his house in West Brunswick.

There's room for all of us, he says, leering at me and speaking with that lazy drawl that sounds almost Australian now he's out of PNG.

'No thank you,' Layla snaps at him. 'We're staying with a friend of mine.'

'Then let me give you lift,' he offers, but before I can say yes please, Layla has butted in again.

'No thanks,' she says. 'We're fine. Bye, Kandin.'

'I'll come and pick you up tomorrow,' he says turning to me. 'I'll ring your local number.' Kandin glances at me and gestures towards Layla with a lift of his eyebrows, but I shrug and set off after Layla.

'OK,' I say turning back towards him as I catch up with her.

I look at her and see that she's shivering like me and feel annoyed. Why wouldn't she let Kandin give us a lift? He's been helpful. He has given both Layla and me new sim cards so that we can use local pay-as-you-go tariffs which will be cheaper. I told Kandin that I couldn't use mine because I need to keep my old phone number so that I can stay in touch with Joel and Jenn. First Kandin suggested that I use Skype but I hadn't heard of it. He wasn't surprised. Says it's not very popular in Australia. (How does he know that?) Then he suggested Whatsapp but I didn't know that either. He told me that it was time I joined the modern world but he did go off and came back with a new phone for me.

'Use this,' he said. 'You can have both phones with you.'

So he's gone but I've got two phones. My old one with the PNG number and this snazzy thing that looks very expensive. Far too expensive to be a second phone I think. I thought at first that it was an iPhone but it isn't. It's a Samsung. Not the latest, he told me, but it would do.

When he's gone, I ask Layla how we're going to get to Carolyn's. Where does she live? She's got a flat in the CBD Layla tells me. Where's that I ask? It's the Central Business District. In the middle of the city. We get a taxi to the address, but Carolyn's not in so we go for a coffee. One coffee costs the price of a pair of shoes but we try not to look surprised. We go back and find that Carolyn is there at last. Her flat is a student studio apartment which means it's got one room that contains everything. The kitchen and a fold-out bed with a shower behind a curtain at the side and a toilet in a cupboard. So there's no space, but Carol makes us welcome and for the first time since we arrived, my body stops shaking and I start to warm up.

While we're eating our evening meal together which is a takeaway pizza that I think tastes like cardboard, I offer to show them my new phone.

'Wait until we've eaten, Auli,' Layla says. 'Then we can have a proper look at it.'

She's telling me to be polite and I take the hint and try to smile in between mouthfuls of chewing the hard thick substance that you have to eat along with the bits of salty meat and melted cheese on top of it. I've had cheese once before and I didn't like it so I don't like either the top or the bottom of this food. Layla seems to be doing much better than me and has accepted a second helping. With determination, I manage a bit better until something really horrible lands in my mouth. Is Carolyn trying to poison me? I spit it out. It's a small black thing with a stone in the middle.

'What's that?' I ask and rush off to get a drink of water. When I come back, they're laughing at me.

'It's an olive, Auli,' Layla tells me. 'They're nice.'

I look to see if she's teasing me, but no, both she and Carol are eating theirs and appear to be enjoying them.

Carol laughs and picks one from the top of her pizza and pops it into her mouth.

'You'll get used to them, Auli,' she says. 'They're the best bits.'

I go and put mine into the bin and get some water from the tap. I'm not going to get on very well in this place if I have to eat stuff like this. There isn't any washing up because we ate out of cardboard boxes so all we have to do with them afterwards is to throw them away. I wash my hands and get more water and Carol asks me to put the kettle on and make some tea. I look at the kettle and wonder where I can put it to heat the water. There's no fire and although I can see her cooker, I don't know how to use it.

'Just plug it in,' she says and Layla comes to show me how it works.

'It's an electric kettle, Auli. Just fill it up and put it on the kettle base.' When she does that a red light comes on and she tells me that the water is heating up. She takes over the tea-making and tells me to get the phone out.

'How do you know all this?' I ask her.

'I've been to Melbourne before,' Layla tells me. 'I came when I was training to be a teacher.' I feel a renewed respect for her. Layla has been everywhere. She had an interesting life before she came to Keroko and spent her life looking after me. I must ask her about it. She's never talked about the past.

For the next twenty minutes, we have a look at the phone Kandin has given me.

'It's expensive,' Carol says. 'He must be rich.'

'He forges passports,' I say, 'so I suppose that's where he gets his money.'

'Be careful, Auli,' she tells me. 'He wouldn't be that rich just from the forgery business. How many people want fake passports?'

'What about the refugees?' I ask and I see Layla look at me hard.

'Yes,' she says. 'And how much money will they have available?'

She's right. I hadn't thought about it.

'Maybe it's from his mother,' I say. 'Their house in Moresby looks big and expensive.'

'Perhaps,' she says, 'but be careful, Auli. Don't trust him.'

25

Layla is always telling me not to trust people and mostly I think she's right. The only person she didn't warn me against was Saul and look what happened there. After we've drunk tea, I take the mat that Carol offers me and lie down at one side of the room. When Layla lies down, too, there won't be room to step on the floor but it's friendly and comfortable. I can't believe that we're safe at last. No-one listening to catch us out. Nobody coming to get us. I've not felt safe since the long-ago time in Keroko when the three of us were happy together. Me, Layla and Saul. Yes, I think as I lie on the mat and pull the doona around my body. Even with the doona, I shiver with the cold, but Layla tells me it's because I'm tired. I'll be warm tomorrow. I hope so.

I'm safe, but I miss Jenn. I miss Keroko and I miss Moresby, the heat and happiness of my own country. Happiness? I didn't know I was happy while I was there, except perhaps sometimes, but this place is cold.

I feel slightly better the next morning. There's no point in whingeing. It's the poms who whinge apparently. The British. At least Jenn seems happy although I spoke to her for about two seconds only because it's expensive from here. Joel says he'll bring her soon. Soon. But still no date! Layla says I shall have to be patient. She says it will give us time to sort things out. This morning she's going off with Carol and I'm staying here because Kandin's coming later on, to pick me up.

'We're going to have a rest today,' Layla says, 'a holiday!'

'So what are you going to do?'

'We're going shopping,' Layla tells me. 'Just window shopping to see what there is. Carol's going to show me around. It's so long since I was here, I've forgotten everything.' She sounds more cheerful than I've heard her for months. Longer than that. Not since I was small. It's like getting a Layla back that I'd forgotten existed. My mama. But not really. This is a new Layla with parts that I don't know.

Carol and Layla leave early, giggling like young girls. After the window shopping, they're going to the Uni where Carol is doing her masters. She's going to introduce Layla to the people on her course and show her the library.

'The library?' I ask, thinking that it won't be much of a sightseeing trip going to the library but Layla's eyes are bright and she's looking young and alive again. She's quite somebody my mama. And she knows about all sorts of things that I'd never imagined.

After they've gone, I stretch out in the room before going to squeeze myself into the shower. Kandin isn't coming until eleven and by that time, I've eaten some bread (not too bad) with jam I found in the cupboard, drunk loads of tea and I'm feeling clean and warm. The sandals I bought before we left look odd with the socks that Carol's given me, but I need them. I've got to put something on to keep warm.

Kandin is half an hour late so I think he's not coming. I text to see if he is on his way and get no reply but at 11.30 precisely, he buzzes the intercom.

'I'm on my way,' I tell him. I don't want him to come up and see Carol's flat.

When I reach the foyer, he's standing there. Immaculate jeans and a leather jacket. His hair is almost blond from the sun. Nice contrast with his smooth brown skin. He's still the golden boy even here in Melbourne. He takes one look at me and starts to laugh.

'What's wrong?' I ask him and he points to my feet.

'You can't go out in those,' he says. 'It's winter. Your toes will freeze to death and when it rains, your socks will get wet. And apart from that.... you look hilarious.'

'Tough,' I say (like they do in the movies - the mere presence of him somehow changes my vocabulary and sends me into film set mode.) 'It's all I've got.'

'Come on then,' he says and I follow him out into the cold, blowy Melbourne day. Layla was wrong. I'm still shivering. He's got a car waiting and I'm surprised. Maybe Layla is right and he is wealthier than he ought to be. But how would I know? His mother is probably rich. Or his father. He has hardly mentioned his father, who must be from Papua New Guinea. I must ask about him.

It's nearly three hours later when we arrive at his house in West Brunswick. It's not as big as the Port Moresby house but it's huge compared to Carol's flat. We've been shopping and Kandin has bought me an enormous amount of clothes. More than any human being could manage to wear in a lifetime. Layla will be cross.

I started off saying no, no, no but then he started buying me things without me trying them on.

'They'll be the wrong sizes if you don't try them on,' he said, 'I'm going to buy them for you anyway so you might as well try them on and get them in the right size.'

So I decided to enjoy it and face Layla's wrath later. I've got all sorts of clothes and I love them. I've got some jeans. I've always wanted some jeans. In the movies, the women look sexiest in jeans in my opinion. Not in those evening gowns with shoulder straps and overflowing breasts. My breasts wouldn't overflow in any case. They're quite small but my bum is big. Sexy, Kandin says and I shake my head but secretly I agree with him. I think I look good in these clothes.

I've got some boots. Two pairs. One shortish pair in red leather with soft creased tops and another pair of long black leg-hugging ones. High heels. I've never worn heels before. They're impossible to walk in but Kandin says I'll manage it soon and I think that if I could manage the shackles, I ought to be able to manage anything, and definitely heels because they make you look elegant. If you can walk in them that is. I'm not sure how I can be thinking these things and laughing when I remember my shackles. (I haven't told Kandin, but he's seen my scars.) I don't laugh for long because my mind soon bumps against memories of Saul and I don't want to go back in that direction.

There is some warm, practical stuff in my shopping bags. Thick tights. Warm, fluffy socks. Three sweaters. One that looks sporty. Plain and bright red but classy-looking. And underwear! I've never seen such sexy bras and matching panties. Feels as though I might be getting ready to appear in a strip club. But I like them. I look good and it's nice. And a three-quarter length belted wool coat. Tweedy looking. And a long anorak. Kandin said I might need it for hiking. Hiking? I know what 'hiking' is but I can't imagine myself ever doing it. Why would you?

It's late afternoon when we get to his place. We had lunch in town so I'm not hungry. We're going for a rest, he says and a drink. I know what kind of rest he means and I'm right. As soon as we get in the house, not five minutes later, we're in bed. Soft and warm. Smooth skin. He's brought our drinks in here and they're on little cabinets at each side of the bed.

'What is it?' I ask when I've had a sip.

'G & T,' he replies. 'Gin and tonic.'

It tastes bitter and the slice of lemon makes it sour but it's wonderfully relaxing after only a few sips. Much better than the beer and the wine we drank in Port Moresby.

'Do you like it?' he asks and I nod.

Kandin falls asleep after we've rolled about on the bed together, but I can't sleep, I'm too excited. I get up and get dressed. I put the jeans on. They're my favourite and I go into the living room to have a look around. The living room is similar to the one in their house in Port Moresby but on my way to the bathroom, I notice a door that's slightly open and I have a quick look inside. It's full of computers. All of them on. They've got screensavers of naked women and some with men and women together in pornographic positions. I don't like what I see. It makes me feel uneasy, suspicious. Layla's right. I need to be careful. I can't trust him.

But we came together from Papua New Guinea, I remind myself. He's my wantok. Well, only half, I suppose. He's mixed race. He's got a mother who's an Aussie. I hear a noise from the bedroom and quickly move away from the computers and go into the bathroom. I don't want him to know that I've been looking into his private room because I don't know what to say. I'll discuss it with Layla later.

'Hurry up, Auli,' he shouts. 'You've been in there for ages.'

'Sorry,' I reply. 'Are you waiting for the bathroom.'

I hear him laugh.

'Of course not,' he says. 'I used the shower room at the back. But I'm missing you, Auli.'

I'm not sure that I like him calling me 'Auli'. Perhaps it's because it feels as though he's taking liberties. Pretending to know me better than he does. (He doesn't know me at all and I'm feeling wary.) He makes some coffee but it's too strong for me, so I ask for tea and we have a hot drink and eat some cake. I start to relax again. Chocolate cake. Tastes delicious. It's got real chocolate pieces that melt in your mouth and he's put dollops of cream on it.

'What work do you do?' I ask him suddenly in the middle of him telling me about a movie he saw recently. He looks at me in surprise.

'You know what work I do,' he replies. 'I forge documents.'

'You must make a lot of money,' I say and he nods.

'Yes, Auli,' he says. 'I do make a lot of money.'

I want to ask him about his mother and father and the rest of his family, but he says he has to take me back. He has to work tonight and has to start soon.

I expect him to say that he'll pick me up tomorrow, but he doesn't. Just says that he'll be in touch and he drops me off with a quick peck on the cheek, leaving me clutching all my shopping.

26

My feet are much wider than most Australian women's feet so it was hard to find the boots. The black ones look gorgeous but they're uncomfortable and I should have left them in the shop. The short red ones, on the other hand, are soft, ankle-length and easy to pull on. It's as though they were made for me and I love them.

I was right about Layla's reaction. She takes one look at all the bags when I walk in and says I'll have to take them back.

'You can't keep them here, Aulani,' she says. 'There's not enough room.' I see I've changed from Auli into Aulani so I know she's cross although I doubt that Carol notices. Layla can be cross while she's smiling. But I always know. For once, however, she's only slightly cross. She's had a lovely day with Carol and as soon as I've taken my coat off, she starts to tell me about it.

Unlike me, they didn't spend long in the shops. They've spent most of the day at the Uni talking to people there. Carol tells me that Layla could be accepted on to a master's course. She's got the qualifications. Her teacher's degree would make her eligible because she graduated with first-class honours.

'Oh Layla,' I say. 'Why didn't you ever tell me? Why didn't you ever talk about these things?'

'Well, I did talk about things, Auli,' she says. 'Don't you remember the lessons? All the lessons we had?'

'I do, but they were lessons for me, weren't they?'

'Yes,' she says. 'But I prepared your lessons, Auli, and I carried on learning.'

So when is she going to start doing the master's course I ask and Layla explains that she can't, it would cost too much money. Other PNG students are sent by the university back home. Nobody could afford the fees or to live here without being sponsored.

'Then why are you so pleased?'

'Because they said they'd have me. In principle, they said, there wouldn't be a problem and even though I can't go, it makes me happy.'

It is at this moment that I resolve to find the money to send Layla on her master's course. I don't know what you do with a master's degree once you've got it, but I don't need to know. The sight of her happiness at the mere thought of being able to do it is enough. My first thought is Kandin but as soon as the possibility occurs to me, I dismiss it. Layla would never accept Kandin's money. And it would be impossible to take it and pretend to Layla that it was mine. I'll have to find another way.

After we've talked about the courses at the university and what Carol is doing for her dissertation, we finally get round to the lowbrow stuff of looking at my shopping. Carolyn is impressed and shares my pleasure at the clothes and the boots, but Layla still keeps muttering and making disapproving noises.

'I'm not giving him sex for these, Layla,' I finally say in frustration. 'I'm going to bed with him because I like him. These are just presents.'

'No such thing as 'just presents',' Layla says. 'You'll pay for them, Auli. Everything comes at a price. The ferryman is always waiting.'

She might be right. We'll have to see but for tonight I'm going to enjoy them and I say so and after that, she relaxes. I go to put the kettle on and make a pot of tea.

'There's something else I need to tell you about,' I say but before I can say anything else, Layla asks about Jenn.

'Did you speak to her today, Auli? How is she? When is Joel bringing her?'

I spoke to them this morning I tell her, but only briefly. It's terribly expensive to phone from here. Jenn seems fine and Joel says the same as before. He'll bring her soon but he hasn't got a date yet.

'We need to find somewhere to live,' Layla says, 'and work out how we've going to earn money. We're illegal, you know. Or we shall be soon. Even now, we've only got tourist visas. Not allowed to work.'

She's right and I've spent a whole day forgetting about these problems. We ask Carol if she's got any ideas but she hasn't. One thing is sure and that is that Jenn won't be able to stay here. This flat is for student accommodation only and people will complain. It will attract attention to us. And in any case, there's not enough room.

We spend the rest of the evening wondering how to solve this problem and then we go to bed. It's not until the next morning after Carol has gone to the Uni that I talk to Layla about the computers that I found in Kandin's house.

'What do you think?' I ask her.

'Sounds as though he's making money from porn,' Layla says. 'You need to be careful, Auli. I don't like him.'

I can understand Layla saying that, but I can't explain why I'm drawn to him the way that I am. I tell her that he pulls me towards him like a magnet and that I can't understand it, but Layla laughs.

'Oh, Auli,' she says, 'You're so naive sometimes. It's sex that pulls you and it's strong. That's why you have to be careful. It's nothing to do with him being 'nice' or a good person. It's clear that he isn't either of those things.'

I remind her that Kandin gave us sim cards and bought me clothes, but she dismisses this. 'It's not because he's good, Auli. It's because he wants something.'

'What could he possibly want that I don't give for free?' I ask. 'I don't have anything that Kandin could possibly want.'

'I hope you're right,' Layla says,' but I don't think you are. You'll find out.'

Then we discuss what we're going to do when Joel and Jenn come, where we'll live and how we'll manage.

'There are only two ways I can think of,' Layla says.

'And what are they?'

'One is prostitution. The other is to look for work in the Queen Victoria market, probably the night market. It's just possible we might be able to find someone who would employ us without papers. But....'

'But what?' I ask.

'Even if we do, it won't pay enough,' she says.

'So it's prostitution then,' I say and Layla looks miserable.

'Not for you, Auli,' Layla says. 'I'm not letting you go and do that.'

'And I'm not letting you,' I reply. 'So we're stuck.'

***

It's three days before I hear from Kandin and when I ask him where he's been, he just says, 'busy' and that's that.

His tone tells me not to ask further. For each of these three days, I've texted Joel, and Jenn is fine but I can't speak to her, it's too expensive. Joel says he's saving up for them to come. No date yet. And since we've got nowhere for them to stay, I don't complain or tell him to hurry up.

'Do you miss me, Auli?' he texts.

'Of course,' I reply.

'What are you doing?' he asks.

'Nothing much,' I reply. 'Waiting.'

'Waiting for what?'

'Waiting for you and Jenn.'

I can almost hear the relief in him after these exchanges, always the same, even though we don't speak.

We email as well and I write empty words about walking around Melbourne and he writes stuff about work, but the emails are not the same as the texts. The texts are urgent and I feel his need as he feels my resistance, but I don't feel I can tell him that he and Jenn can't stay with us where we are.

I miss Jenn and at the same time, I long for Kandin even though increasingly. I don't trust him and sometimes I don't even like him. I don't long for Joel. I keep on trying to work out what I should do.

One afternoon, I'm lying with Kandin in bed. He's relaxed but not sleepy and I try to talk.

'When is your mother coming?' I ask. 'Is she still in Moresby?'

'She isn't coming,' he replies. 'This is my house. My mother doesn't come here.'

'Oh,' I say. 'Then where does she stay?'

'She's got her own house,' he replies

'Then why isn't that your house?' I ask. 'Why don't you both live in the same house?'

'You're wearing me out with your questions, Auli,' he says and offers no more information about either his or his mother's living arrangements.

'Where did you grow up?' I ask.

'Moresby mainly,' he replies and starts to look irritated. 'Why all the questions?'

I can never understand why he doesn't want to talk about his life. Why he always answers in monosyllables. And why he doesn't ask about my life. What I did before I came here. What I'm planning to do next. It's as though our whole relationship happens in the present with no past and no future. It feels weird.

'What about your father?' I ask. 'Where is he?'

'In Oxford, I think,' he says and then adds, 'I don't like him, Auli. And my mother doesn't like him either.'

'Why is that?' I ask and he shrugs and goes silent but then seems to change his mind. He tells me that his father's name is Lucas, who, he says, fell in love with Chrissie, but for her, he was just a passing toy.

'A toy!' I say. 'How can a person be a toy?'

Kandin doesn't answer but keeps on talking. 'I've got a sister he says. Her name is Grace.' He explains that his mother and father fell out over Grace. His sister is older than he is, a couple of years older and after she was born, Chrissie told Lucas that she'd lost the baby. The truth was, Kandin tells me that Chrissie didn't want Grace but she couldn't admit that to Lucas.

'Why not? I ask.

'Because she wouldn't seem like a natural mother. Not a nice person,' Kandin says. 'It's not acceptable for a woman not to want her child so she lied to him.'

'So what happened?'

'Mum sent Grace to live in England with a friend of hers, someone who was going-finish.'

'But your father didn't know?'

'No, not at the time,' Kandin says. 'But after I was born they had row after row. Dad didn't like Chrissie any more and one day when they were shouting at each other, Chrissie told him that Grace wasn't dead after all. That she had been sent to live in Oxford with her friend.'

'And what happened then?'

'Dad went mad. Said she had no right to send his daughter away and lie to him. He was furious.' Kandin drains the rest of his G&T. 'He said he didn't want to see Mum anymore. He would send money for me and I could go and see him but that he didn't want to live with us. He asked Mum to give him the address where she had sent his daughter, but she said she had no idea where Grace was. Anyhow, Dad still decided to go to Oxford.'

'He must be rich,' I say. 'It must be expensive to travel to Oxford.'

'No,' Kandin says and smiles a big lazy smile. 'He's not rich, Auli. It's me who is rich, but he disapproves of me. Dad works at the university. He got a scholarship to do a doctorate in Oxford. He's gone for a couple of years. Might be three. I'm not sure.'

'So did he find Grace?' I ask wanting to get all the ends tied up.

'I don't know,' Kandin says. 'We haven't heard from him.'

I think of something else. 'Why wasn't he around when she was born?' I ask. 'He's not much of a father if he wasn't there when your mother had the baby.'

'Oh, Auli,' he says sighing,' you haven't got a clue. Men don't bother to be around when women give birth.'

'They do,' I argue wondering where I've got my information from on this topic and realise that it must be the movies.

'Some do,' he admits, 'but most are not around. Dad wasn't around.'

'Well, where was he?'

'Here in Melbourne at the Uni doing his master's degree.'

Oh,' I say thinking there's not much more to say about that, but my mind comes back to his mother. 'And what do you think?' I ask. 'What do you think of your mother, Kandin?' I can hear myself sounding angry. I suppose it's because my own mother dumped me.

'I think she had a right not to want the child,' he says and looks hard at me. 'Don't you agree?'

This is such an unusual point of view that I stare at him in disbelief. I can't think of what to say. How could he think such a thing?

'No, I don't,' I say. 'She is unnatural. And what about you? Don't you want to meet your sister?'

'Not particularly,' he replies. 'Why should I? In any case,' he adds, 'I don't think she's there. I think she probably did die.'

'Then why would your mother say such a thing?'

'Just to upset Lucas,' he replies, 'and to get him off her back.'

27

It's all right for a woman not to want a child. That's what Layla and Carolyn say. I can't believe my ears to hear Layla say this after all that she's told me about her wanting babies and not being able to have them and being angry with me for not wanting to be pregnant. Doesn't make sense and I say so.

'Yes, it does,' Layla says. 'It's all about choice. It's about my right to have children so that I am the one to choose whether to have them or not. That right was taken away from me.' (I see Saul's face in my mind and think that I had no choice about getting pregnant, but Layla doesn't know that.)

'But what about not wanting the child after the baby is born?'

Still all right, they say although I can see that Layla understands how I feel about this. Nobody would agree with them, I say but I realise that it's not true. Layla tells me that she knows lots of women who don't want children. Or they don't want to keep on having babies year after year as they are pressured to do by their husbands and other family members.

'I don't want babies, Auli,' Carolyn says and I'm shocked but try not to show it. 'I think that Chrissie was brave to send Grace away.'

'Brave?' I ask.

'Yes,' they tell me and say I should think about it some more. Look at it through Chrissie's eyes. It's easy for Lucas to be angry, they say. Men don't have to care for the children.

'But she had another child,' I remind them. 'And she kept him.' They shrug. Maybe she changed her mind. Perhaps her circumstances changed. It was still fine for Chrissie to behave like that. Lucas might condemn her, but they would not.

What I find most surprising is Kandin's reaction to it all. Not only does he not condemn his mother for what she did, but he seems to have no real interest in finding out whether he's got a sister or not. I look at Layla and get the feeling that she has started liking Kandin more since I told her about his reaction to Chrissie not wanting children. Funny that because it makes me like him less. I've spent a lot of time thinking about mothers and babies because my own mother didn't want me. She threw me out. Literally. According to Layla and Carol - and Kandin - that was fine although we didn't specifically talk about getting rid of babies by throwing them out of windows.

If I think about all this with my head, I agree with them. It is fine. If I think about it with my baby heart, or even with my grown-up heart, it's not all right. I'm angry with my mother. I hate her for it because I wanted her to love me. I wonder where she is now. I still want her to love me and anything less is definitely not all right.

It's getting late, nearly ten o clock so I get up to wash the dishes. We ate late and we've spent the whole evening arguing. We were going to watch tv but we've missed the start of the drama we wanted to see. While I'm filling the bowl and squirting too much washing-up liquid into it, the intercom buzzes. It's Kandin and he sounds excited.

Happy excited. I've got to leave the dishes and go somewhere with him immediately he tells me. He's got something to show me.

Earlier on that evening, I had been telling Layla and Carol that I was getting to dislike him and that I was suspicious of what he was doing with all those porno screensavers. Now I find myself falling over in my haste to put on my coat and boots and rush downstairs. I look up and see Layla and Carol giving each other I-told-you-so looks.

'I'll be back soon,' I shout as I rush out of the door. 'I'll finish the washing up when I get back.'

Kandin is positively awash with happiness and goodwill when I arrive in the foyer to greet him. And he's excited. This is not the Kandin I know. He's usually good-tempered, occasionally not, but almost always laid back, lazy and sort of not caring. Can take it or leave it. Anything and everything. Including people. Including me. The way he walks. The way he smiles. That's how he is, but not today.

'Have you won the lotto?' I ask him as I return his smile. His happiness is infectious.

'No,' he says, 'but I've got something for you, Auli. Come on.' He sets off to the underground parking area and I walk behind, almost have to run. 'Keep up,' he says. 'Come on.'

'What is it?' I ask when we're sitting in the car. 'And where are we going?'

'You'll see,' he says, reminding me of his answer that first day after I met him at the tree and he drove me off to 'somewhere'. It seems ages, but it was not that long ago. I keep my mouth shut after that and soon he starts to talk again. 'It's a present,' he says. 'An apology from me.'

Apology? I think to myself. Kandin doesn't do apologies. And what does he think he has to apologise for?

'What are you apologising for?'

'For not caring about your feelings,' he says.

This is stranger and stranger. I've felt drawn to Kandin from the very start, but he has never shown any interest in my feelings. Mostly, he hasn't noticed them.

'Your feelings about mothers and babies,' he says eventually and I wait for him to explain further. I don't remember ever telling him about being thrown through a window or how I felt about it. 'You're missing Jenn,' he says finally. 'And then I talked about Chrissie (he often calls his mother Chrissie) getting rid of Grace.'

'Oh, I see,' I say but I don't. And I still can't understand why he's so excited. For half a second, I have a surge of hope. Maybe a miracle has happened and he's fetched Jenn to Melbourne. But no, I saw him only a few hours ago. He wouldn't have had time, and in any case, Joel would never have let her travel with Kandin.

Eventually, he stops the car and turns to look at me.

'Are we in West Brunswick?' I ask him. 'We seem to have gone in the same direction we take when we go to your house.'

'Nearly,' he says. 'This is East Brunswick. It's the next neighbourhood. Look out of the window.'

Dutifully, I stare out of the window but it's dark and there doesn't seem to be much to see. Just a street with houses down both sides.

'Number 59,' he says getting out. 'Come on, Auli, hurry up.'

Kandin leads the way to the door which is only a meter from the road. It's a single storey house similar to all the others. He inserts the key and steps inside.

'Here you are,' he says and offers me a bunch of keys. 'Here's your new house, Auli. It's for you and Jenn. And Layla, of course.' I notice that he doesn't mention Joel and it's shameful that in this moment of his gift that it is this that catches my attention. I don't believe it in any case. He must be playing games with me. Houses are phenomenally expensive. I've heard Layla and Carol talking. They used to be cheap here but not anymore. You have to be seriously rich to buy a house in Melbourne in 2017.

'You're joking,' I say putting the keys down on the table in the hallway where we are standing.

'No, Auli,' he says, 'it's not a joke. You told me that you were worrying about where you could live when Jenn came and how you were going to earn money.'

'That was only a couple of days ago,' I say. 'You haven't bought a house in two days.'

'No,' he agrees. 'I already had this house. I was going to sell it because I didn't need it anymore, but then I thought of you and it seemed perfect.' He grabs me, pulls me close and kisses me long and hard (also not typical Kandin behaviour) and then he goes off into the kitchen to get us some drinks.

'Come and have a look at it,' he says. 'It's yours, Auli. For you and Jenn.'

'I can't accept it,' I say but even as I speak, I think that yes, I can. It would be for Jenn. I could accept anything for her. Layla was considering prostitution I remind myself.

Kandin laughs, 'Of course, you can,' he says. 'Think of your daughter.'

'But how will I explain it?' I say. 'Joel wouldn't bring her. He wouldn't let her come if he thought the house had anything to do with you, Kandin.'

'Then don't tell him,' Kandin says. 'I don't want you to tell anyone that the house is from me.'

'Then where would the money have come from?'

'You said it yourself,' he says. 'Lotto.'

I look at this man who just lately I've been liking less and less and realise that I haven't even said thank you. He's standing there, leaning against the bar area in the kitchen. The bar area!

'Are you sure?' I ask him and before he says another word I feel myself blacking out and when I come to, I'm on the bed.

'Are you all right, Auli?' he says. 'I wanted a reaction, but didn't expect quite such a dramatic one.' He's beginning to look more like his old self again, slow and easy with his old manner of couldn't care less. But not quite. He's happy to have given me this house. He's pleased that he's done it.

'I'm fine,' I tell him. 'I'm fine.' I stop and look around the bedroom and back to Kandin who is sitting on the side of the bed. 'I'm grateful,' I tell him. 'More than grateful. How can I thank you, Kandin? What can I do for you?'

'I'll think of something,' he says. and comes to lie beside me.

28

The house has been put in my name - Aulani Sogeri. I've seen it (and kissed the document). I've got a copy of the property title. And we've got an income. Both Layla and I have managed to find jobs in restaurants doing kitchen work. Nobody in the markets would employ us. That's where we tried first but the restaurant work is better. We earn enough to pay the bills and Layla is saving every cent so that she can apply to do her master's degree. Shouldn't take longer than twenty years or so I think. At first, she wasn't happy about Kandin giving me the house but when I pointed out that it was for Jenn, she softened.

'We can't always be legal,' I tell her.

'No,' she says, 'but we can try to be moral.'

I didn't argue with her about that. It's much too big a subject and we don't really know how Kandin makes his money. Not for sure. She's moved into the house with me. That's all that matters. The main problem, however, still remains. The main problem is Jenn. I've told Joel that I won with Lotto and that I've bought a house, but I can tell that he doesn't believe that I've won money like that. He believes me about the house but is suspicious about where the money has come from. And the thing we didn't think of was the speed of it all. How could I have bought a house this quickly? I should have thought it through more carefully but it's too late now. He still says that he'll bring Jenn, but he still won't give me a date. Layla says he doesn't want to bring her because he'll miss her. He'll have to go back because of his job. What about me? I ask. I'm missing her.

I decide that I'll have to go back and get her. If I turn up in person, Joel will surely let me bring her back. It won't be easy, Layla says. Jenn's passport has been changed to Joel's name. I smile. I've still got the old one, I tell her. I asked Kandin to get it for me. Joel had to hand over the Jenn Sogeri passport before he got the Jenn Goasa one. I've got Jenn's other passport. But it's dangerous for you, Layla says. And she's right. It will be dangerous if anyone sees me. And it's dangerous to have to travel again with the forged passport. If anything goes wrong, I'll be in jail. But I'm desperate to get my daughter back so I decide that I'll go, and I'll tell Joel tonight. I text him to say that I want to speak to him and we set a time so that we can talk before I have to leave for work.

All day, I'm on edge about it. Kandin is away somewhere on one of his trips. Won't be back until the weekend. Layla has already started to study (in anticipation of one day being able to join the course). Carol brings her books from the library, and Layla spends all day reading them and making notes. As though her life depends on it. As though her life depends on those things she reads in the books. There's a park nearby and I go there so I can talk to Joel privately. Don't want Layla to hear although I'm not sure why. At seven o'clock exactly I sit on a bench next to the deserted play area and ring him.

'Hey Joel,' I say. 'How are you?'

'I've got something to tell you,' he says before I can tell him that I'm coming to fetch Jenn. His voice is hard and cold and my heart plummets. I can feel a sick feeling in my stomach. Something bad has happened.

'Is she all right?' I ask. 'Is Jenn safe?'

'Perfectly safe,' he replies in a voice that doesn't sound like his. 'But I'm not going to let you see her anymore, Aulani, and I don't want to hear from you again.'

'What!' I say. 'What's happened, Joel? I'm coming to get her.'

'No, you are not,' he replies in the same icy tone. 'If you come to Moresby or anywhere near her, I'll inform my colleagues. You'll be picked up and that will be it.'

'What's happened?' I ask again, but he puts the phone down. The line goes dead and I ring and ring but there's no reply. What's happened? What's made him suddenly change? I'll have to go there. I'll have to find out. I look at my watch and rush back to the house. I need to get to work or I'll lose my job.

'What's happened?' Layla asks as I rush in to get my things.

'Tell you later,' I say and am out of the house on my way to the tram stop. If I'm late or sick, my job is gone. That was made clear at the outset. I can't afford to lose it. It was hard to find work. I get to the tram stop just in time and feel relieved that I haven't just missed one. I work like a robot until 2 am, working in the kitchens and then cleaning up. Catch a taxi home and look for Layla but she's not back yet. I go to bed and lie down. Feel exhausted and lie awake but eventually, my eyes close and I'm gone.

I'm awake at first light. Can't have had more than a couple of hours sleep. Oh Jenn, where are you? I look out of the window. It's spring and the trees are sprouting new growth. Not my beloved eucalyptus trees, of course. Those evergreen giants are down by the creek and they fill the world with the smell that soaks into your clothes so you can take it home with you and sniff it later. But lots of the others. The smaller trees and the bushes. There are hundreds of pale green shoots with the early morning sun shining on them. Today the winter's gone and when I step outside, the air smells fresh. It even feels warm. Well, not cold, let's say. Even in the city, the air smells good. It's not like Keroko of course where the air was like nectar but I never knew it until after I left.

I go outside to check the box for mail and look for my bird friend and there he is. He's a crow with a bad leg who's come to live next to our bins and I always speak to him. I can't help it. He reminds me of Saul so that's what I call him. Softly so Layla doesn't hear.

'Hello, Saulie bird,' I whisper and he cocks his head to one side and then hops closer to me. 'I've got to go away soon,' I tell him. 'Will you miss me?' He hops away behind the bins and I go back into the house. Layla's still in bed and I try again to ring first Joel and then Kandin. I'm trying Kandin in case he's in Moresby. I'm going to ask him to go and see Joel to find out what's happened. Neither of them answer. I ought to leave Layla to sleep. She needs it, but I'm restless. Don't know what to do with myself so I go into her bedroom and sit on the side of the bed and watch her open her eyes.

'What's wrong, Auli?'

'It's Jenn,' I say and before I can manage to say anything else find myself hunched in a sobbing heap. Sitting on the floor with my back against the wardrobe. Layla gets up and leaves the room. Comes back with tea. It's sweet.

'What's happened?' she asks and I tell her that I don't know. Only that Joel said he wouldn't let me see her again.

'I'll have to go, Layla,' I say and I see her shake her head.

'It's not wise, Auli. You might end up in jail. Or dead,' she adds. 'That won't help Jenn.'

'I know, but there's nothing else I can try. I'll have to go.'

Layla fetches more tea and we sit and drink.

'What about getting Kandin to get her for you?' Layla suggests and I'm surprised.

'I thought you didn't like him.'

'He's not too bad,' she replies. 'And I can't think of anything else to suggest.'

Layla is going to the library this morning and meeting Carol for lunch so soon I'm alone in the house. Walking backwards and forwards. Then outside and inside. Go out. Come back in. Backwards and forwards. Even Saulie Bird has disappeared. Maybe he's avoiding me.

Every ten minutes I ring first Joel and then Kandin. But often I can't manage to wait for ten minutes. In the early afternoon, my phone rings at last and I lunge towards it so desperately that I knock it on to the floor.

'Hey Auli,' it's Kandin. 'What's up? I've got about 50 missed calls from you.'

'Kandin,' I say and slowly let out the breath I didn't know I was holding. 'Where are you?'

'Tullamarine,' he says. 'Just landed.'

'Where have you been?'

'Moresby,' he says.

'Damn.'

'You're not making any sense,' he tells me.

'I wanted you to go and see Joel.'

'I've already seen him,' Kandin replies. 'Getting a taxi. Be with you in about twenty minutes.'

I watch the clock and actually it's twenty-five. I've already got a G&T ready for him and even though I don't normally drink in the afternoons, I'm already on to my second. He gives me a hug and a quick kiss before taking off his jacket, but he's my laid-back man, couldn't care less. He's not on edge. It's only me. We sit at the table and I tell him what has happened. I watch his face, and he doesn't look surprised.

'You know what's happened, don't you?'

'I can guess,' he says. 'It's some kids from his village,' he sips at his drink. 'I sold them a few pills and Joel's gone crazy.'

'A few pills?' I ask feeling shocked. 'Do you mean drugs, Kandin?'

'Sure,' he replies. 'Nothing serious. Nothing heavy.'

I don't know what to say. I'd suspected Kandin of making money from porn. But never from drugs.

'And how does that affect Jenn?' I ask without making any comment on the drugs.

'I'm not quite sure,' he tells me. 'But he asked if I still saw you and I said I did. He was angry, Auli. He said that as long as you were associated with me, Jenn was having nothing more to do with you.' He looks at me, smiles and reaches towards me to pull me over, but I push him off. He looks surprised.

'Do you want me to go?' he asks, getting up and reaching for his jacket.

'Yes. No. I don't know,' I say and pour myself a third G&T.

'You won't get through work tonight if you keep drinking like that,' he says and sounds quite prim. I look at his face and can't work it out. He doles out drugs then nags at me for drinking three G&Ts. How can that be? He's right about the drinks, of course.

'Get a grip,' he says. 'You're over-reacting. Just like Joel. He'll have changed his mind by tomorrow.'

'Of course, he won't. He's a policeman, Kandin. And he cares about the kids. And about doing the right thing. I can't believe you've been selling drugs. So now I know where your money comes from. I thought it was porn.'

My anger doesn't touch him. Kandin just laughs which makes me angrier. I pick up my glass and am about to throw it at him when he grabs my arm. In one swift and graceful movement he removes the glass and holds me still.

'Stop it,' he says, 'and listen to what I'm going to tell you. My money doesn't come from either sex or drugs. That's for the low life. The pills were a few I was carrying with me. I sold them for almost nothing as a favour. Recreational drugs. Nothing serious, I told you.'

'What were they?' I interrupt.

'This and that,' he replies. 'Not much, as I said. The kids would hardly have felt the effects.'

I've never taken anything. Layla always told me that drugs were dangerous and in Keroko, I was never in a position to try anything. I know kids take stuff but don't know much about it. I'm out of my depth.

'Go on,' I say. 'Where does all your money come from?'

'I'm a hacker,' he tells me, 'and a good one. I'm a good forger, too, but it doesn't pay enough.'

'What do you hack?'

'Scientific information,' he replies. 'Then I sell it on.'

'Information on what?'

'All sorts,' he says, 'whatever pays well. At the moment, it's mainly neuroscience. Information on how the brain works,' he says. 'On how to manipulate people's belief systems. For people who are doing targeted ads on social media.'

There's a pause while I take this in.

'And they pay you for that?' I ask.

He smiles at me. 'I'm getting big money, Auli. And it's going to get bigger.'

'Where do you get the information?' I ask and I see the triumph on his face.

'Recently,' he says, 'from my father. From Lucas. He always said I wouldn't amount to much, but he does the work and I get the money.' Kandin can't conceal his delight. 'Perfect.'

My mind is reeling. I need time to process all this but my first thought is Jenn.

'I need to get Jenn,' I tell him ignoring everything else. 'I'm going to go to Moresby to get her.'

'That's crazy,' Kandin tells me. 'And stupid. You'll be picked up in no time.'

'I'm going,' I say. 'Whether you like it or not. You've cut me off from my child and I'm going to get her back.' And this time Kandin does start to look angry.

'Not me,' he says. 'I gave you a house to bring her to. I haven't cut you off from anyone. It's Joel, who has done that.' This time Kandin does pick up his jacket and he walks out.

29

Layla doesn't come back before I go to work so when she sees me the next morning, she is amazed. I am blonde.

'You look like a Tolai,' she tells me. 'Fantastic! It suits you, but there is a problem if it's supposed to be a disguise.'

'What's that?' I ask.

'You've still got the same face.'

'Ha ha,' I manage to smile at her and say there's nothing I can do about that, but at least from a distance, I won't look like me. I've been letting my hair grow lately and it's big. At the moment, bigger than Layla's and now it's a bright white halo around my head. I'm not going to comb it, I tell her. I'm going to leave it shaggy.

'Hmmm,' she says. 'The big blonde shaggy look. In Melbourne at least, everyone will certainly notice you coming.'

'I thought of that,' I say. 'But in Moresby, I won't attract attention.'

'You will,' Layla says. 'You look fantastic, Auli. You'll have more men hanging around than you can deal with.'

She's got a point that even when trying to disguise myself, I didn't attempt to make myself look unattractive.

'Maybe I should have gone for the invisible look,' I say, 'but that's what I had before. More or less anyway.' I put the kettle on. 'Before I dyed my hair blonde, I looked like everybody else, but most of all, I looked like me. Now, at least, I don't look like me.'

Then Layla turns serious and asks me when I'm going.

'Tomorrow. I couldn't get a flight today.'

'What about work?'

'I've got a week off and I can still keep my job.'

'Does Kandin know you're going?'

'No, he walked out when I accused him of cutting me off from Jenn.'

'And does Joel know you're going?'

'No, Layla. Only you. You're the only one who knows that I'm going.'

'Do you want me to come with you?'

'Are you mad?'

'No, but you seem to have gone slightly crazy yourself. You probably need me'

'No, I don't.'

Layla grins. 'Let me at least teach you about the village. I assume that's where you'll go to try and get Jenn?'

I nod and for the next two hours, Layla draws me maps and gives me information.

'What do you think Joel's told them about me?' I ask.

'Well, he said he was going to tell them that you'd run off and left the child with him, but he won't have said anything about you being suspected of sorcery. And presumably, he won't have said anything about your connection with me.' Layla looks thoughtful. 'Because if he did, he would risk Jenn being seen as having bad associations. He wouldn't want that.'

'So you think the village people won't know that I'm suspected of witchcraft?'

'I don't think so,' Layla says. 'But I can't be sure, Auli. It's very dangerous.'

'Have you got enough money?' she asks before I set off and doesn't wait for a reply. She hands me an envelope full of money. It's her savings for the course she's dreaming of and I hesitate, but it's for Jenn. I might need it. I kiss her and put it in my bag.

***

It's late when the plane lands at Jackson's airport. About nine pm. Not a good time or a safe time, but my heart rolls over in pleasure as I step into the steamy night air. Even when it's warm in Melbourne or hot, the air is different. I get a taxi. I've got no choice. Hope that Shantelle won't turn me away.

She says she's delighted to see me once she gets over the shock of my transformation into a girl from East New Britain. You look more like a Tolai than a Tolai she tells me.

'Why did you do it?' the girls ask me.

'It was a dare,' I tell them. 'A bit of fun.'

They find some food for me and it tastes like heaven. Like coming home. Rice cooked in coconut with some fish. It seems so long ago that I was here, but it's not. I remember when I lived in Keroko that I preferred kaukau and pumpkin to this coastal food, but I've changed my mind. It tastes like manna. After eating, I don't have to clear up. The girls do that for me and I go with Shantelle to sit at the other side of the lawn. Where Layla and I used to go and sit.

'How is Layla?' Shantelle asks me.

'She's fine,' I tell her. 'She's got a job and sees Carolyn most days. Layla's saving up to do a master's course.' I feel guilty as I pass on this information and remember that I'm carrying most of what she's saved. I've hardly got any money apart from that because I bought an open return. It was more expensive, but I knew I might have to leave quickly and I didn't know which day it would be. And I might need money for Jenn. She ought to be able to travel free on my lap. That's what they told me. But you never know. I've got Layla's money just in case. I hope that I can give it back to her without taking any out.

'And why have you come back, Auli - or should I call you Agnes so that we remember?'

'I've come for Jenn,' I tell her. 'Joel says he won't let me see her anymore, but she needs me, Shantelle. And I need her.'

Early the next morning, I set off for the village. I remember Layla's words when I get whistled at and shouted after over and over again. Maybe going blonde was not such a good idea. I get a bus to the village. It's a rickety old PMV and it seems to take forever, but actually, it takes less than a couple of hours (this time thing again, like elastic how it stretches and shrinks). Will Jenn remember me? I start to worry. She's only little and I've been gone for more than three months.

I get off and walk with some women who have been to the market. Tell them I'm going to see my aunty. I'm lucky. Two of the village men are married to Tolais so they assume that's who I'm going to visit. I'm relieved when they turn off and point me in the right direction for the houses where the Tolai women live. So far so good. I've been lucky. And then I see her. I see Jenn. She's playing under a tree next to the gardens. I go towards her and call her name.

'Mama,' she shouts but then looks uncertain. 'Mama hair..' I run towards her and pick her up. Hold her tight.

'Yes,' I tell her. 'Mama's dyed her hair.' I pick her up and hold her tight and she laughs and wants to go down.

'Mama hair,' she shouts and points over and over again at my hair. 'Mama hair.'

'Yes,' I tell her again. 'Mama's dyed her hair. Come on, Jenny girl. I'm taking you to see your aunty. Aunty Shantelle. Do you remember her?' Jenn doesn't look very sure, but I pick her up and start walking back towards the PMV stop. Walking as fast as I can. There's another bus due in a few minutes. I walk and I pray. Look around but don't see anybody. We get to the place where the PMV stops and I put her down.

There's nobody else waiting for the bus and I thank the God in whom I don't believe. Suddenly I remember Saul. He went to missionary school and talked a lot about Christianity. I look at his daughter and pick her up ready for the bus coming. I'm the only one who knows that Saul is her father. Not Joel. Not Layla. Not Jenn. What would Saul say? But there's no time to think about that now.

'Going on the bus,' I tell her. 'We're going on the bus to Aunty's house.'

We get on and I manage to find a seat. It's crowded inside but we're the only people getting on here. The bus sets off. I've done it. I've got Jenn. I hug her and she keeps saying, 'Mama hair. Mama hair.' I try to distract her and point at things out of the window but she keeps coming back to 'Mama hair, Mama hair.' There's an old woman sitting next to me who keeps smiling at her. She's got no teeth at all, her mouth is bright red from buai juice and she starts joining in with Jenn and pointing at my hair. 'Mama hair,' the old woman says together with Jenn. 'Mama hair,' she says again and cackles louder and louder each time.

There's not much traffic on the road but the windows are wide open and all the dust flies in. With a bit of luck, my hair will be so dusty soon that Jenn won't notice that it's blonde. It will be grey. That's the colour my hair usually goes when covered in dust, but now it's blonde it seems to be staying light. Not going grey as usual. There's nothing I can do. But suddenly there's a worse problem. A massive problem. There's a police car driving behind the bus.

I watch it overtake and think it is going to drive off but it drops back and now it's following us. It must be Joel. They must have told him that Jenn had disappeared. I can't believe how fast this has happened. Incredible. But he can't be totally sure that Jenn is on the bus. Or me. If he were sure, he would stop the bus and take us off. At least I think he would.

What am I going to do? Surely I haven't got this far to fail now. It sinks in that it's not just that I won't get to take Jenn back with me. If it is Joel in the police car, then I'll soon be locked up. And after that, dead. Burnt. They won't hang around a second time. Once they've got me, that will be it. I'm a dead woman sitting on a bus. A dead woman with her daughter I remind myself. What am I going to do? The only thing I can think of is to leave Jenn on the bus, get off and make a run for it. I'll get off at the market so there'll be plenty of people around. It might be possible to get away. Joel's first thought will be to find Jenn. So this is what I decide to do. I sit on the bus holding my daughter, loving her, feeling the smooth skin of her sturdy legs and looking at her laughing eyes. I try to sound cheerful.

'Aunty Shantelle,' Jenn manages to say, or something that sounds very much like it.

'Yes,' I say, 'We're going to see Aunty Shantelle.'

'Aunty Shantelle,' the toothless old crone next to me repeats and laughs. At any other time, I'd laugh with her and think how nice she was but at this moment I wish her dead.

'Aunty Shantelle,' Jenn says again. This is a great game. At least it's slightly better than 'Mama hair.'

The trip out to the village took a lifetime but it seems that the trip back is taking no time at all. We are arriving at the market in the blink of an eyelid. I keep looking and see that the police car is still close behind. The bus stops and what I ought to do is to leave Jenn on the seat and go and get off the bus, but I don't. I pick Jenn up and walk with her to get off the bus. She's still saying 'Aunty Shantelle. Aunty Shantelle.' As I get off the bus, Jenn suddenly shouts even louder.

'Papa!,' she shouts at the top of her voice. 'Papa!'

Someone tries to trip me up and out of the corner of my eye, I see Scarface looking thrilled to see me. Joel grabs Jenn from my arms and as I get up, I see him trip Scarface as he lunges after me. I don't wait to see more. I'm gone into the crowd and away. I don't look around and am surprised that I arrive at Shantelle's, breathless, bruised and dusty but in one piece. She takes one look at me and she knows.

'Go and have a shower,' she says. 'Take this.'

'What is it?' I ask. 'It's black hair dye,' she tells me. 'I use it for my grey hair. You have to spray it on. Get rid of your blonde hair and be quick.' She passes me a clean laplap and meri blouse and has somehow managed to get a ute waiting for me when I come out of the shower. 'He'll take you to the airport,' she tells me. 'Go.'

30

'Well, Auli,' Layla says to me as I walk in the door, 'you look like a witch!'

She already knows what has happened. I told her on the phone but I must have forgotten to tell her about the second dose of hair dye. In spite of everything, we hug each other and collapse in a giggling heap. Hysteria rises as I don't have to hold on anymore.

'Go and have a look in the mirror,' she says and I go. She follows me into the bedroom and I gaze at the wild creature that stares back at me. Smallish face with huge black hair matted and tangled with myriad pale yellow streaks in all the wrong places. I stand and laugh until I sink to the floor and my laughter turns to tears.

'You're still alive,' she says as she hugs me and it's true, but I haven't got Jenn. I haven't got Jenn. I haven't got Jenn.

'No hairdresser could ever match that,' Layla says and gets her phone out to take a photo. And I weep again. I didn't take a photo. I had Jenn in my arms and I didn't take a photo.

'Will you cut it for me?' I ask. 'I can't go to work like this.'

'How short?' she asks.

'All off,' I reply. So before I eat or drink or talk about what has happened, I sit down and Layla cuts my hair short-short. Almost shaves my head so I'm left with blonde frizz. My brown skin looks darker contrasted with the light bright hair. I like it. I look like Saul, except blonde instead of black. In my mind, I see his head from the back and then from the side, clear and sharp as a photo. Head not broken. Handsome like he used to be.

Layla cooks for me and brings me drinks. Listens while I talk. I give her back the money she lent me. I watch as she walks to and fro in the kitchen. Her hair is almost completely grey now but she moves as gracefully as ever. She's a little fatter than she used to be. Looks thicker, more 'comfortable' but still beautiful. It's her face. I should be thinking about Joel. About Jenn. But I can't face those thoughts. Not yet. Instead, I look at Layla and think about beauty.

'Is it skin-deep?' I asked in life lessons long long ago.

'Oh, no,' said Layla, always ready with an answer even if these turned out later to be wrong. 'Beauty comes from within.'

I used to think that it wasn't true, but now I'm not sure. I think of Carolyn who has a beautiful spirit which shines out of her eyes but her body isn't beautiful or her face. And then there's Kandin. His body is beautiful and he knows it and uses it, but I'm not at all sure about his soul. Beauty is external, I think. It is three dimensional with hills and hollows. It flows with movement and the beauty doesn't break. Like a vase when you turn it might change but will preserve its essence. Ah, the essence. Now isn't that an inside thing?

'What are you thinking about?' Layla asks me.

'I'm thinking I've got to get ready for work,' I reply. I've already texted to say that I'm back and coming in.

In less than ten minutes, I'm out of the house.

***

Kandin doesn't cook so he takes me out to eat. Not for long expensive dinners because I can only go with him at lunchtimes. Every evening I have to work.

'Can't you have a night off?' he asks me every few days.

'No,' I say.

'Why not?'

'Because I would lose my job.'

Kandin sighs in frustration. 'I can pay you not to work,' he says, but I shake my head. I already owe him for the house. I don't know how I'm going to pay him back, but I'll find a way. I won't stay indebted to him forever. But I'll be always indebted to Layla, I think. And Joel. I don't want to think about Joel at the moment. And there's Saul. I don't want to think about him either. My head is full of doors that have to be kept locked.

'Tell me more about your work,' I say. 'What kind of research does your father do?'

Kandin looks irritated. Unlike last time, he seems unwilling to talk either about his work or about his father. 'What work does your father do?' I repeat.

'He's a neuroscientist,' Kandin replies reluctantly, 'I told you last time.'.

'That's interesting,' I say. 'What area?'

'It's none of your business,' Kandin snaps. 'And how I earn my money is private, Aulani. It's no concern of yours.'

'Yes, it is if it involves drugs,' I snap at him.

'Most of what I do is illegal,' Kandin replies 'and you've benefited from it more than once. You got passports and you got a house.'

'Yes,' I say. He's right to remind me about this.

'If you want me to get Jenn here for you, I can arrange it,' he says. 'But there will be a price to pay.'

'What price is that?' I ask.

Kandin smiles at me. 'What do you think?' he asks.

If we didn't already sleep together, I'd think that he meant sex.

'No idea,' I reply.

'Oh yes, you do,' he says and then I look at his face and I do know what he means. Know who he means. The prize he wants is Joel.

'You mean Joel,' I say and his smile gets a little wider. 'I could never agree to that,' I tell him and he shrugs.

I've killed one man to secure my freedom. I can't kill another to free my daughter. But my thinking is twisted, Joel's death would not be to secure Jenn's freedom. It would be to satisfy my needs. My need to have my daughter by my side. Jenn's needs are already fulfilled. She is cared for and happy. She doesn't need me.

'You could get Jenn without killing Joel.'

'I could,' Kandin replies, 'but then you would not be involved. I need your total commitment to me. I'm getting less sure of you, Auli. You've started criticising, but you still want the spoils. Joel is the price you will have to pay. If you want your daughter, you'll have to give me Joel.'

'And why would you want him?' I ask. 'Are you jealous?'

Kandin laughs at this and doesn't reply. It was a silly question.

'Joel's bothering me,' is all he will say. 'He's irritating. We can do without him, Auli.'

We? How have we suddenly become 'we'? I look at him with new eyes. His face is as beautiful as ever and he has the same soft sexy drawl. He's still the golden boy. In looks.

I watch the way he gets up and goes to refresh his drink. And mine. Like a cat, slow and easy but always ready. Ready to pounce. Ready for the kill. To get money. Power. Or just for fun. This man is dangerous so why have I not seen it until now?

'What kind of a man are you?' I ask but without heat. It's a genuine question expecting an answer, but Kandin merely smiles. I need to be more careful. I change the subject, hopefully without him noticing. I change it to something that Layla told me never failed with men (or women either, I expect) but which has already failed sometimes with Kandin.

'Tell me about yourself,' I say. 'What were you like as a baby? As a little boy?'

This time he relaxes and I press my advantage. 'Have you got any photos?'

I settle myself back into the large leather couch he bought recently. It doesn't look that big in this spacious room. He can afford to buy leather because he's got a good aircon system. Otherwise, the leather would be awful in the summer heat or at least that's what he says. I know nothing about such things. As it is, it feels luxurious. My aim is to pass the time with him for half an hour and make him think that everything is good between us. Then I'm going away to think about what to do.

He brings three large green photo albums and plonks them down on the glass table in front of the sofa.

'Only three?' (I'm being sarcastic.)

'It will do for a start.'

I pick up the first one and start leafing through page after page of angelic-looking baby Kandins. First steps. In the park. On the swings. At the beach. Sometimes with Chrissie, but mainly just pictures of him alone.

'Where's Chrissie?' I ask.

'Mostly, she's taking the pictures,' he replies, but there's a hesitation. I read between the lines and realise that Chrissie wasn't there much when he was small. Kandin defends her but he didn't like it. He felt neglected. Suddenly, I stop. There's a picture of Saul sitting on the beach in Melbourne. Impossible.

'Who's this?' I ask trying to keep my voice under control.

'It's my father,' he says, 'it's Lucas.' And he turns the page.

**

'Where exactly did Saul come from?' I ask Layla when I get back. She's got a pile of ironing in front of her.

'Buka,' she replies. 'I told you.'

'And how did you meet him?' I ask. Layla looks up from the blouse with the iron raised in her hand.

'What's up, Auli? Why all these questions about Saul?'

'I saw a picture of someone who looked exactly like him in Kandin's photo album, but he told me it was somebody else.'

'Who did he say it was?'

'His father. Lucas.'

'That's not so strange,' Layla tells me. 'Lucas might be one of Saul's cousins. If you see people from a certain angle then they sometimes look like someone else.'

I'm listening and she might be right but the shock is still bouncing around in my head.

'I don't think I could be mistaken, Layla.' I see her look at me as though she's making a decision about whether to say something or not. She decides to speak.

'When someone you love goes away,' Layla starts, 'you long for them so much that they start to appear every-where. You see them in other people.'

'What do you mean?'

'It's in the turn of the head, the lift of an eyebrow, the swing of a leg. But it's someone else. I mean that you can see someone in the distance with the same walk and before you can think, you run to catch up with them. They turn and it's someone else. You hear the loved one's voice and your heart leaps. You look up but it's another voice, not even a voice, just a sound that your brain has magicked into existence because it yearns. But the person you want is not there.'

'Does that happen to you?

Layla sighs and doesn't answer. 'Another thing,' she says, 'is that your memory of the person becomes blurred with the strain of looking for them. They start to look dif-ferent.'

'How do you know this?'

'It's happened before, Auli. Saul is not the first man I've lost.'

I see Layla looking into the distance. Seeing and not seeing. She's not here. Hope she doesn't burn the blouse. She's got that faraway look she sometimes has. The look that Saul never liked. I used to think she was just remem-bering her past, but perhaps she was thinking of a lost someone. Eventually, she speaks again.

'When it happens like that and you keep seeing the one you think about, it is not always because they are dead. It might be the result of an argument. A falling out. They leave. Or you go. Or you are taken away. It means that the relationship is broken before its time. You were not ready for it, so you try to get it back. You don't mean to, it just happens. It means that you are not ready to lose that person.'

'Oh yes, I am,' I say under my breath. 'Totally ready.'

'And it's a long time since you saw Saul.' She pauses. 'In any case...'

'What?'

I see that Layla is filling up with anger, but trying to control it, trying not to say what is on her mind. She manages it and gives her attention once more to the next blouse she is methodically ironing. Mother Layla is back. She gives me a quick look and almost smiles.

'You might not remember him clearly,' she finishes matter-of-factly.

We haven't talked much about Saul. About what he did and about how I killed him, but I know that Layla thinks about him as much as I do. When I allow myself to think about it, I can't believe that she has forgiven me.

'Have you forgiven me, Layla?'

'Not yet,' she replies, and she puts the iron down but stays standing where she is.

I don't know what to say. I stay silent.

'But I'm trying, Auli. I keep on trying.'

We don't talk about him anymore. I knew that I shouldn't have raised the subject. I knew that, but the picture was such a shock. I look at Layla's face as she gets back to the ironing and I change the subject.

'What do you think of Kandin these days?' I ask and she shrugs.

'He's not bad.'

'I've changed my mind about him,' I tell her. 'I don't like him anymore. I think he might be dangerous.'

Layla looks surprised and asks me why, so I try to explain. I don't mention what he is planning for Joel or the fact that Kandin has been dealing drugs but I tell her about the hacking. About how he said he was making his money.

'It does sound bad,' she says.

'How bad?' I ask.

'Could be very bad,' Layla replies. 'Haven't you read about how elections are being rigged in various countries? About how various political groups are paying firms to manipulate people's voting preferences?'

'No,' I say. 'I haven't.' To be honest, I haven't bothered with the news for ages. My mind has been full of worries about Jenn and Joel.

'You should,' Layla says. 'The world is changing, The powerful are getting more tools to manipulate people and make them do what they want. It's already happening through targeted ads on social media. They are usually aimed at the poorest people, the vulnerable and they're targeted for all sorts of things.'

'What kind of things?'

'One thing was slimming tablets.'

'Slimming tablets?'

'Yes, persuading people to buy slimming tablets that didn't work and all sorts of things like that.' I feel doubtful about this.

'Google claims that targeted ads are helpful,' I say and I see Layla smile.

'You're always defending Google,' she says. 'You're wrong, Auli. It's dangerous for any single person or corporation to have so much power.'

'Targeted ads are supposed to help connect people with local businesses and stuff like that,' I persist. It's true that I defend Google. I think they've done an amazing job with Google maps, Google street-view and all sorts of other stuff. All free. 'And, in any case, you can just ignore them,' I say. 'I get loads of targeted ads, but I just ignore them.'

'Me, too,' Layla says, 'But lots of people don't. Or can't. The data that Google gathers (and Amazon and Facebook and all the others) helps to pinpoint the vulnerable. They know what kind of toothpaste you use and whether someone you love has just died. They know that information is power. And they use it.'

I nod. I'm sure she's right but at the moment, I can't concentrate on global problems because all I can think about is Jenn and the danger Joel is in.

'I'm sure that Kandin wouldn't get paid for nothing,' Layla goes on. 'What exactly is the research that he's passing on?'

'I don't know exactly,' I admit but I know where he's getting it.' At this, Layla looks up amazed and starts to laugh.

'It can't be very secret then,' she says waving the iron in the air. 'If he told you where he was doing the hacking.'

'I think it is,' I say. 'He didn't mean to tell me. I caught him off guard and he wanted to boast.'

'What was he boasting about?'

'That he was getting the information from Lucas,' I say. 'From his father, who told Kandin that he'd never amount to anything.'

And at last, Layla packs up the ironing, puts away the board and comes to sit with me.

'What are you going to do about it?' she asks me.

I shrug my shoulders. 'What do you suggest?'

'We could go to Oxford,' Layla says. 'We should go and find Lucas and tell him what's happening. We ought to stop Kandin passing on information like that.'

31

Going to Oxford is a stupid idea. Layla is losing her sense of reality. The person I have to worry about is Jenn. She's much more important than people's voting patterns being manipulated. I suppose she shouldn't be, but she is. In any case, I point out, we've got no visa for the UK. And we can't get one because our tourist visas for Australia are about to run out, so once again we need Kandin's help. Even if we had valid passports, any mission to stop his evil activities and help save the world is aborted before we can get off the ground. Literally. It costs a fortune for a return ticket to Oxford. We discuss once more what we're going to do about Kandin's hacking activities, but there's not much we can do. Not if we want to survive. I go out to take the rubbish and Saulie Bird hops out.

'Hello,' I say to him but it's a weary greeting. Saulie Bird cocks his head and hops towards me. Looks quite sprightly despite his bad leg. 'How are you this morning?' Already he's seen enough of me and hops back. Doesn't even croak. But I like him. I've grown fond of him and wonder how he's managed to survive with his injury. His eye is always bright and he seems like an omen of hope in a depressing world. My friend the crow.

Since I last talked to Kandin, I've seen him again and nothing has changed. Even if we could have afforded it and had no problems with passports, the problem of Joel and Jenn is what is becoming ever more urgent, not pie-in-the-sky projects like going to Oxford. There is a feud developing between Kandin and Joel and it doesn't look set to end well. It was Joel who first introduced me to Kandin and I realise now that the police must have been turning a blind eye to his activities, but I'm not sure why. I never asked. I was more concerned with getting a passport and getting to safety. Everything worked fine except for having to leave Jenn behind. And that was Joel's fault and perhaps a little bit mine, too, for not being careful to keep my activities with Kandin a secret.

I can think of plenty of reasons why Joel doesn't want Jenn to come here, but his recent change of attitude can only be because of what Kandin has been doing or saying. Either it's the drugs or it's because Joel now knows that Kandin and I are seeing each other. Surely Joel must have known that already or guessed. But now Joel has cut me off from my daughter and it's driving me crazy. What has Kandin said to him? I wish I knew. I don't trust Kandin these days. Don't know what he's doing or what exactly his plans are.

Maybe Joel wants Jenn to grow up in PNG and that's understandable. I do, too, but I can't live there and I miss her and Joel must understand that. He always said that he did and that he would bring her to me. I haven't spoken to him since he let me escape from Scarface. I've tried ringing him but he won't pick up. I texted to thank him but once again there was no reply. I can't say much in case Kandin reads it and I don't want him to know that I'm trying to talk to Joel. I think I'll try emailing to see if I can arrange to speak to him. I need to talk to Joel privately, but I need to be careful how I organise it. Mustn't forget that Kandin is a hacker. And that he's got his eye on both me and on Joel.

The first problem is how to keep my emails private. I can't use Layla's account because Kandin will be monitoring hers for sure. I could set up an alternative email address but Kandin is an excellent hacker and is probably monitoring all my online activities. I could ask Faisal, my work colleague if I could use his email. At this thought, my brain lights up. Yes, yes, yes. This is a possible solution. I'm sure I haven't mentioned Faisal to Kandin. Not even to Layla. He's one of the kitchen hands at work and he fancies me. Has asked twice if I would go for a drink with him before work.

'Thought you weren't supposed to drink,' I said when he asked.

'I meant coffee,' he replied. 'You're right. I don't drink alcohol.'

Twice I've said no. Two illegals together. Disaster. He comes from Bangladesh. Don't know how he got here because we never have the opportunity to talk not even in breaks. There's always someone around and it's understood that we keep quiet about our pasts. We all pretend to have lives that are perfectly fine and none of us says much. There's no-one else I could ask, but Faisal might say yes. Most of the other illegals are from Syria. Occasionally Iran and one guy from Eritrea. That's counting all the ones I know in both Layla's restaurant and mine and not only the ones who are here now but the ones who have already 'passed through'. We're the only females. And Layla is the only old one. Some of them call her aunty but she doesn't mind. They mean it nicely.

Yes, Faisal might do it. I'm going to ask him but when I get to work, he's not there. Patience, I tell myself as I rinse food off plates and stick them into the dishwasher, clean the floor, check the pans, empty the dishwasher, hang the pans on the wall - in the correct places - stack the hot plates in cupboards, on and on. It's noisy in the kitchen. There are always food mixers whirring, steam gushing, fat frying. Worst of all is the noise from the coffee grinder. It's sporadic, deafening and it shakes fit to explode.

After the place closes, I go into the public area and start cleaning in there. Another normal night. Occasionally, I've been given a uniform and asked to wait tables, but that's only when Glenn (the manager) is desperate. Normally, he keeps the 'extra' staff well out of sight. Layla says it's more or less the same where she works. I've only been into her place once. It looks posher than the one where I work.

I've grown to like my new look with super short hair dyed blonde. I think I look more like an African and less like a PNG woman with my hair cut like this (although I feel a bit guilty about that - I'm proud of being PNG). Glenn was pleased when he saw the new hair cut but that was because of hygiene. He's always going on about keeping hair tied back and the danger of people dying because of a hair dropping on to a plate or into food. What he's bothered about are customers complaining or an inspector dropping in and finding, horror of horrors, a hair. As I've said, my hair was quite big before. Glenn was always moaning about it. I was given a strange white hat to wear but my hair would still manage to bounce out here and there. Always full of bounce.

I notice that men look at me more since Layla cut it like this. My head is more or less shaved. It just goes to show that the soft feminine look I had before doesn't seem to do it for them as much as the hard, clear profile. I suppose it's a hard look altogether. Elegant I hope, but definitely hard. What I like best is the contrast between the colour of my skin and the bright blonde hair. It makes my skin look darker and I like it.

I've changed my earrings, too. I used to wear (fake) pearl clusters or fish (especially green fish) in my ears but now I've swapped to large gold hoops. Sometimes small gold hoops depending on my mood, but almost always hoops. One of the people who likes my new look is Kandin. He hasn't said much but I can tell. And I bet one of the people who wouldn't like it would be Joel. He would think that I didn't look feminine enough. If I can get Faisal to let me use his email, I'll send Joel a selfie. I bet I'm right. We'll see.

Funny, how the little things like hair-cuts and earrings get mixed up with the big things like getting Jenn back and working out how to get in touch with Joel and warn him about Kandin. That's what I'm thinking about while I am unloading the dishwasher about halfway through the shift when Faisal walks in. Hallelujah (see how Saul persists). I thought I'd have to wait until tomorrow night but here is Faisal now. I straighten up and give him a quick smile before turning back to my plate stacking duties. Before the night is over, I manage to arrange to meet him for a coffee tomorrow before work. Sevenish. He looks pleased.

Every morning if she's not doing housework or going out to meet Carol, Layla studies and at first, I used to read, too. Books are expensive here if you get them from bookshops and I don't like reading online (my laptop's too big and my phone is too small), but the thrift shops have got a treasure trove. There's a Vincent de Paul near here and they've got loads of good stuff, clothes too. Recently, however, I've gone back to old habits. I've started drawing again. I drew a lot in Keroko and now I'm doing it again. For me, it's like meditation. Better. I'd like to get a decent drawing of Saulie Bird, but he never hangs around long enough. I've got half a sketchbook full of Saulie bird attempts. I'll get him sooner or later.

'Why don't you take a photo and draw from that?' Layla asks me and I suppose I might have to do that eventually, but the image in the head is better somehow if you can keep it long enough to throw the lines on to the paper. I'm getting obsessed with the bird, but I don't tell Layla what my crow is called. Another thing I haven't told her is what Kandin is threatening to do to Joel.

I can trust Layla absolutely (which is weird when you think that it's Layla who always tells me not to trust anyone) but I think I'll be burdening her if I confide my fears over Joel. No, that's bullshit. The reason I don't tell her is because I don't want her to think badly of Kandin. Or at least I don't want her to think any worse of him than she does already because I fear she might refuse to let him help us. We're going to need help with our passports soon and there's no-one else we can ask. I had an argument recently with Kandin when I accused him of having no principles.

'You are completely immoral,' I yelled at him, 'you're just a pragmatist.'

'So are you!' he replied calmly.

I'm beginning to think that he's right about me, but I wish he wasn't.

***

Layla is surprised that I'm leaving early for work and I tell her I've got a date at which information she looks even more surprised. She knows me. If I were interested in somebody, I would have said so. Well, maybe not in so many words but she would have known. I see her notice that I haven't even bothered to do my nails. I've got some black varnish. Well, it's dark red really, almost black. Sweet as. But I'm saving it. It's expensive.

Faisal is already there when I arrive and I do like him. I mean I like what I know of him which isn't much. But Layla is right. I don't fancy him. We sit with the coffees and he offers to buy me a cake but I refuse. I know how hard it is to earn money and I'm sure he needs his as much as I need mine. Almost certainly he needs his more because I've got a house. Yes, I am a pragmatist. Kandin is right. I don't like him anymore, but I haven't offered to give back the house and I'm still planning to get his help for the passports. It was easy in the first place because I liked him a lot. It's taken a long time to realise how dangerous he is. And unpleasant. I've been a fool.

'Are you married?' Faisal asks me, and I almost laugh. At least he's direct and he's wasting no time in getting things established.

'No,' I reply. 'Are you?'

'I was,' he says and in answer to the look on my face. 'She died.'

I don't ask him about her, but I understand why he's told me. He's trying to give our relationship an honest foundation and he is honouring his wife. I find myself hoping that we'll become friends. Proper friends, not lovers but there's not much time so I need to ask him for what I want.

'I need your help,' I tell him and see his face close down. There's an immediate withdrawal of the beginnings of our friendship.

'What kind of help?' he asks.

'I need to get in touch with someone in my country,' I tell him, 'and I'm being watched. Can I use your email to send him a message.'

'Who's watching you?' he asks. 'Is it the police?'

'No,' I assure him. 'I promise you, Faisal. It's not the police.'

'What will the message be?' he asks.

'I want this person to ring me,' I say and hesitate. 'He's a friend and I urgently need to speak to him. But I can't ask him to ring my phone. That's being watched, too. At least I think it is.'

'Go on,' he says.

'Do you have Whatsapp or Skype?'

'Whatsapp,' he says. 'Skype is not worth having. No end-to-end encryption.'

'Skype's changing,' I tell him because I've looked it up, 'or it's changed already. It does have end-to-end encryption now.' Faisal shrugs and I smile at him. Whatsapp is fine. He might be right. It might be better. Why do I always have to argue about everything? 'Could I arrange the call for a prework time like now and ask my friend to ring me on your Whatsapp account?'

'I'll think about it,' Faisal says. He looks anxious and disappointed. He knows I don't fancy him. He's sensitive. He knows why I wanted to meet him and that it was only for this.

'I do like you,' I tell him. 'And you're right. I don't want sex or a romantic relationship. But I do hope we can be friends.'

I see him relax a little. He doesn't smile but he regards me with a gentler gaze.

'Thank you for that,' he says. 'I'll let you know about the other thing.'

Faisal says nothing that first night nor the next one but on the third night, he tells me that he'll help me and we arrange to meet again as before.

32

It's time I went to see Kandin. I haven't seen him for nearly two weeks. I start feeling edgy when I don't hear from him because I don't know what he's doing and I don't trust him.

My plan to get in touch with Joel has worked and I've spoken to him twice. Faisal was there both times and has heard everything, but I've managed to warn Joel that Kandin is planning to kill him. It is true that both Kandin and I are pragmatists, but we are not the same. I can't quite believe that Kandin is contemplating murder as though it were no more important than winning a game of cards. To begin with, it seemed almost like a joke but slowly the truth of how Kandin is and the way he will behave sinks in and shocks me. On the other hand, it is clear that Joel is not shocked. He takes the information calmly and seriously.

When we manage to talk, I tell Joel that I still want Jenn back.

'She's safer here,' he says.

'How can that be?' I ask. 'If you're in such danger.'

'I'm fine,' he says. 'I'm in the police, remember.' As he says this, I see Faisal almost rip the phone out of my hands, but he doesn't. 'Jenn's safe in the village,' Joel goes on. 'She's happy, Auli.'

'She must miss me,' I almost wail.

'No,' Joel says. 'We don't talk about you. She's fine.'

It's time to go. I tell Joel I'll let him know if I get any more details and warn him that I'm going to have to come back to PNG. I have to try and get Jenn in order to keep

Kandin calm. If I don't agree to that, Kandin will know that I've been in touch. Joel says he understands and tells me not to worry.

After the phone call, I try to smile and behave normally but I can't manage it.

'Tell me about it,' Faisal says. 'I'm your friend remember.' So I tell him. I sit there and tell him much more than I had planned to let out and he listens with kindness. Doesn't offer any suggestions. There aren't any, but he listens and I appreciate that.

***

And now it's Wednesday. I've got a day off. The first in a fortnight and I'm going to see Kandin. He's picking me up to take me out for a meal and then we're going back to his place. I haven't told Layla what's been going on but she has observed my 'dates' and my face. She knows that Kandin is coming to take me out tonight.

'What,' she says, half teasing me, 'no nail varnish for Kandin either. He is falling out of favour.'

'Of course not,' I say although the truth is that I very much want to do my nails for Kandin. He always notices how I look. I can feel his eyes on me appreciating me and I like it. So I almost desperately want my nails to be dark red and glinty for Kandin but manage to stop myself because I knew Layla would notice. What does it matter, I ask myself and can't answer that question. Apart from my naked hands, I'm looking quite glam. He buzzes and I grin at Layla as I go out.

'Where are we going?' I ask as we take off. He's got a new car. It's black with silver wheels and a roll-down top that's rolled up. A two-seater sports car, but we can't go fast. This is Melbourne. 60 kph at the moment and soon we'll be down to 40 when we hit the inner city. When he stops the car and I see where we've arrived, my heart sinks.

'Come on, Auli,' he says. 'Or is it Lani?' (Lani is what the people at work call me.) Kandin takes me to the diner where I've been meeting Faisal. 'Thought we'd try somewhere different,' he says.

We go in and he leads me to the table where I usually sit with Faisal.

'I know what you want,' he says with one of his special Kandin smiles and goes off to order a coffee for me but nothing else and a plate of pommes frites, an avocado salad and a beer for himself. 'How are you?' he asks. 'Haven't seen you for a while.'

'You've been spying on me.'

Kandin nods.

'You've no right.'

Kandin smiles.

'Haven't you got anything better to do?' I ask him. Aha, I've got him this time. A look of annoyance flashes across his face but is gone as fast as it appeared.

'Of course not,' he replies with the familiar drawl. 'You're my whole life, Auli. I fill it up with you.'

What I'm trying to work out now is how much Kandin knows and how he's going to use the information. Does he think I'm dating someone he doesn't know about? Or does he know that I've been contacting Joel? I'll have to try and find out.

'What's he like then? Faisal?'

'Very nice,' I reply.

'OK in bed?' he asks.

'Sweet as,' I reply. I still don't know what kind of game Kandin is playing. I'm going to have to wait. I can see that he's waiting for me to react. To tell him more. To get angry but I pick up my coffee and slowly sip. I'm getting to be as good at this as he is.

For the rest of the evening, we talk about Chrissie. Apparently, she's visiting and wanted to stay but Kandin refused.

'I thought she could do no wrong,' I say. 'Why don't you want her at your place?'

'Because she would be in the way,' he replies. 'At times like tonight when I'm taking you home.'

'But you're not,' I say. 'I've got a headache, Kandin. I'd like to go home now. You can phone Chrissie and invite her back.'

Kandin doesn't miss a beat.

'OK,' he replies. 'That's not a bad idea. Come on then, Lani. I'll take you now.'

I kick myself when I get home. First of all, I'm hungry. He didn't offer me any food in the cafe. Secondly, I could have tried to find out what he's been doing and what his plans were if I'd gone home with him. If I'm here and he's there, I'm not going to find out anything. What a waste of an opportunity. What a waste of a night off. I bang about so loudly in the kitchen looking for something to eat that Layla comes to see what's wrong.

'Nothing,' I tell her. 'Nothing at all.'

I feel like texting Kandin to tell him I've changed my mind, but I can't do that. I sit with a bowl of tomato soup out of a tin and work out how I can manage to see Kandin again soon without losing face. As it happens, I'm saved the trouble although the new arrangement is not quite to my taste. I'm about half-way through the soup and sitting with a soggy piece of toast in my hand when the phone rings.

'How's your headache?' he asks.

'It's getting better,' I reply.

'Oh good,' he says, smooth as usual. 'I'm ringing to say that Chrissie would like to see you. Are you free on Saturday morning?'

'I'll have a look,' I say and make walking about noises before picking up again to say, 'Yes, I am.'

'OK,' he says. 'Pick you up about 10.30.' Before I've had time to ask him anything and in particular why Chrissie wants to see me, he rings off. At least I'll see him again soon, I think, although I might not get a chance to talk to him at all if Chrissie's there. I look for another tin of soup but there isn't one. I'm starving so I make four pieces of toast and eat them with Extra Special Blackcurrant Jam (that's what it's called). And after that, three apples. They don't grow in PNG but I've discovered that I like them a lot.

***

Early on Saturday morning, I go outside to take some rubbish to the bin. It's windy out. Actually, I'm going out to say hello to Saulie Bird, but he's not there. I don't confess this to anyone but on the days when the bird isn't there, it feels as though my life is falling apart. Sometimes I think that it's actually Saul himself out there, his spirit inside the bird, but I tell myself not to be stupid. Layla brought me up to use my brain, to ask questions and to think about things. Not to be superstitious or to believe in 'gut feelings' although I have to admit that I often do. There are more things in this world than meet the eye. Things that are still not explained, but they do exist.

'Saulie Bird,' I call. 'Saulie,' but there's no sign of him. It's cold this morning like winter again. We've been in Melbourne for over a year! I'm about to go back inside when he hops onto our path from the pavement. Just as though he's coming back from somewhere. Coming home. 'Hello, Saulie,' I say, suddenly cheerful, so pleased to see him. 'Have you been for a walk?' Instead of stopping with his head cocked to one side and then hopping off behind the bins as he usually does, he hops towards me. Almost to where I'm standing. Then he stands and looks at me. Head on one side as usual. Always the same side I think. I hold my breath hoping that he's going to come even closer, but he turns and hops away.

'You're up early,' Layla says to me when I go back inside. 'Are you ready for Kandin?'

She knows that he's coming to pick me up and she's asked me why Chrissie wants to see me.

'No idea,' I tell her. 'I texted Kandin and asked him but all he said was that Chrissie likes me.'

'And does she?'

'I haven't seen any evidence of it,' I say. 'And I've never liked her.'

Layla knows why I'm going this morning so she, too, is hoping that Chrissie doesn't stay long so that I get the chance to talk to Kandin. I want to find out what's happening with his plans for Joel.

'Let's hope she just drops in briefly.' Part of me fears that she might want to take me on as a project. Poor little PNG girl sort of thing which makes the anger rise up in me at the very thought. I've heard about Australians doing that. Can't stand the thought of do-gooders from any-where. But I have to admit that it doesn't fit with Chrissie. She doesn't seem to care about people at all so far as I can gather, 'poor' or otherwise. Not even about Kandin.

Layla sympathises and makes a pot of tea. There's plenty of time before Kandin comes because it's true, I am up very early.

'If I could only get Jenn back and Joel safe, I'd be happy,' I say.

'And what about reporting Kandin to Lucas?' Layla asks.

'I'd almost forgotten about that,' I say. 'It would be good if we could, but have you any idea how we could get enough money to fly to Oxford?'

It wasn't a question but Layla replies.

'Lotto?' she suggests.

'I've already won it once and got a house, remember.' She laughs.

'Well, a second time wouldn't go amiss. Maybe I'll win it this time.'

'You'd better buy a ticket then,' I say. 'Buy us one each.'

***

Chrissie is waiting in the house for us, Kandin tells me when he comes to pick me up.

'Is she staying with you?' I ask.

'No,' he says. 'I told you before.'

'Why does she want to see me?' I ask again.

'I told you,' he says. 'She likes you.'

I'm getting nowhere so I shut up and soon we arrive. We go in and I see a second breakfast waiting for me. Orange juice, coffee, bagels, chocolate croissants, chopped melon. I wonder who has prepared it but don't ask. I'm sure it won't have been either Chrissie or Kandin. They are both allergic to housework and food preparation of any kind. The most they can manage is drinks. Like mother like son.

'Hello, Aulani,' Chrissie says and for a change gives me a warmish welcoming smile.

'Gdday,' I say taking off my coat and going to sit down.

'Nice haircut,' she tells me. Yes, I think to myself, I'm dyed just like you now except that you're dyed black and I'm dyed blonde. But mine looks better. Chrissie's hairstyle has hardly changed since I first saw her in the hotel at Three Mile. Still jet black and still solid-looking, set in a shape that looks as though you'd have to get a hammer to break it. Wouldn't think that a comb would make any impression. Maybe she's a mind reader because she starts to talk about seeing me in the hotel. I thought she didn't remember. She's never mentioned it before.

'Do you remember when we met in the hotel?' Chrissie asks me.

I nod and notice that Kandin looks surprised. He doesn't know that I met his mother before. It seems so long ago. Jenn not even conceived and she's getting big now.

'Did you ever find your mother?' she asks. I shake my head and a sudden hope rises up. Perhaps she's discovered something and that's why she wanted to see me.

'Have you found out anything?' I ask directly, but she shakes her head. Sorry, no. It is all as she said before. That building was a hotel, not a hospital and you couldn't throw anything out of the windows. All the windows have louvres with flywire on the outside. It's funny, I'd almost forgotten about tracking down my birth mother. Life has been so all-consuming, there has been no time for my own affairs. I make a renewed pledge to myself to try again once I've solved the problem of Jenn and Joel. And reporting Kandin to Lucas. Not much in the way then....

We make polite chat. I ask Chrissie if her business is going well and she says yes. She asks me how my work is going and I say fine. And that's about it. There's nothing more to say and I do my best to hide my pleasure and relief when she says that she must be going.

'You don't like her, do you?' Kandin comments after she's gone.

'Not much,' I reply. 'Do you?' I'm being cheeky, I know, but I don't care. I don't think that Kandin is ever honest about his feelings for Chrissie.

'I love her, Lani. She's my mother.'

'Don't call me, Lani,' I say. 'I don't like it.'

'It's what Faisal calls you,' he says.

'That's because everyone at work calls me Lani.'

'I like it,' he says. 'That's what I'm going to call you from now on.'

He doesn't ask me any more questions about Faisal. Instead, he goes to get me a G&T.

'We've only just had breakfast,' I tell him. 'I don't want one.'

'Yes, you do,' he says. 'I've made it for you specially. Look it's got a slice of orange in it, just the way you like it. Not lemon like everyone else has.'

'OK,' I say. I suppose I do feel tense after talking to Chrissie. At least it's relaxing drinking gin and there's plenty of time to sober up before I have to go to work this evening and I say that.

'You're not going to work this evening,' he says and I put down my drink and go to get my coat.

'Oh yes I am,' I say. 'I need that job, Kandin. You're not going to stop me from going to work.'

'You like cleaning and washing up, do you?' he asks and catches my arm to stop me putting my coat on. 'I'm not getting rid of your job,' he says. 'But you're throwing a sickie tonight. I've already organised it. I rang to say I was your brother and you'd got a stomach upset. Said you'd be back tomorrow.'

I'm furious. 'You've rung to say I was sick with a stomach upset? You must be out of your mind. I'll lose my job.'

'Of course, you won't,' he says. 'In any case, Lani, you're going to have a stomach upset any time now,' and as he speaks I feel myself heave as I rush to the bathroom. I've only had a few sips. How could he do that to me? Why? But there's no time to think about anything as I heave and retch until I can barely crawl out of the bathroom and all thoughts of going to work begin to look impossible.

33

Almost the whole of my Saturday afternoon is spent in Kandin's bathroom as I alternately retch and curse. I try to work out what's behind it. Is it that he wants me here today for some special purpose I have yet to discover? Does he want me to lose my job? Or is it just punishment for my seeing Faisal (which I somehow doubt but it might be)?

'I hate you,' I tell him for the first time ever, although of late, I've begun increasingly to dislike him. Have to admit that I've been too aware of our need for his services to want to antagonise him altogether, but he's pushed me over the edge.

'No, you don't,' he replies. 'You love me really, Lani and you always will. You're mine and you know it.'

I would like to kill him. He is annoying beyond belief.

'Stop calling me, Lani,' I snap. 'I won't talk to you if you call me Lani.' I don't know why it irritates me so much. I like being called Lani at work. Kandin just smiles. At least he doesn't head over in my direction or try to put his arm around me.

'Don't you want to know what I'm going to do to Joel?' he asks changing the subject to something he knows will get my attention and force me to talk to him no matter what he does to me. 'And don't you want to know what's going to happen to Jenn?'

He waits for the answer he doesn't need to hear.

'Tell me,' I say but he's making me wait.

'Would you like another drink?' he asks and watches as I get up and go to the tap to get myself some water.

'There's some ice water in the fridge,' he says but I ignore him as he knows I will. The tap water is quite cool without being put in the fridge. Cold actually. I need something to eat, something to settle my stomach so I go to the fruit bowl and contemplate a banana.

'You can inject bananas through the skin,' he tells me as I pick it up and take a chance. It tastes fine and I eat it slowly.

'What about Joel and Jenn?' I ask him. 'What are you planning?'

'You want to save them, don't you, Lani? Both of them.'

Kandin knows that I will always want to save them. I'd been hoping to convince him that I would sacrifice Joel for Jenn, but Kandin's assessment of my intentions is spot on. There probably isn't any point in my denying it. I don't reply.

'I'm going to have both of them killed,' he says. 'Unless...'

'Unless what?'

'Unless you do exactly what I tell you to do,' he says.

So he needs me. For some reason he needs me. It's the only hope I've got and I need to find out more.

'First of all, tell me why you want Jenn killed, Kandin? I can't believe you mean it. I thought you were working to keep her safe for me. That you gave me the house so that Jenn could come and live here. And I can't believe that you're the kind of person who could kill an innocent child. Either you're lying or you're a monster.'

'Monster,' he says.

I wait for him to say more.

'Jenn is the only way I can get you to do what I want,' Kandin says. 'I don't have a choice.' Then he adds, 'Sometimes people have to be sacrificed, Lani. It happens. It can't be helped.'

Is this the person I used to love who is saying these things?

'Go on,' I tell him. I'm going to eat another banana.

'Have a good look at it,' he says as I pick my second one from the bowl. 'Can you see any needle marks, Lani? Can you be sure it's all right?'

'Tell me about Jenn and Joel,' I say again, ignoring him and biting into the banana. Within minutes, I'm rushing to the bathroom again.

'You're a slow learner,' he calls through the door. 'I warned you about the bananas. It's all about playing with people's beliefs,' he shouts over the noise of the water flushing. 'I thought you knew about that.'

I spend another hour in the bathroom and after that, Kandin offers me a bed for the night. I tell him that I'm going home and he drives me.

'I'll pick you up on Monday evening,' he says as I get out of the car.

'I'll be at work,' I say.

'I don't think so,' he replies.

***

Kandin is right. I will be available to see him on Monday. I turn up for work on Sunday to find that I've been fired. No point in arguing. I go to empty my locker and find a note from Faisal asking me to meet him tomorrow at the usual place, but I won't be able to go because Kandin is picking me up and I wonder how on earth Faisal has managed to get the note into my (locked) locker. There's no opportunity to speak to him or to reply before I leave. I'll have to try and work out how he's done it and whether he's done it by himself or not. My fear is that Kandin is behind the note that Faisal has sent, but how can he be?

It's Monday morning and I decide to confide in Layla. I've been outside to say hello to Saulie Bird, but he's not around. Perhaps he's gone walkabout again. I need to talk things through with someone and she's the only one I can trust. I haven't seen her since Saturday morning because she has had two nights off. Two nights! Heaven. It felt like heaven, she said (unlike my two nights off which have felt more like the opposite). She's been to stay with Carol for the weekend.

'Have you got time to listen?' I ask and she closes the book she's reading and gives me her full attention.

'Let me make some coffee first,' she says.

I don't wait for her to finish making the drinks. I launch straight in and tell her what Kandin did to me. Layla looks shocked.

'Cut him off, Auli,' she says to me. 'We can find ourselves somewhere to rent. We don't need Kandin.' She comes over to where I'm sitting and puts the coffee down then gives me a hug. 'I mean it,' she says. 'We can manage without him. You mustn't go back there again.'

'There's more,' I tell her and explain that Kandin knew that I'd been meeting Faisal and took me to the cafe where we met. 'And the last part,' I say, 'is also worrying.'

'What's the last part?'

'After they told me I was fired, I went to my locker to collect my things and there was a note there from Faisal.'

'What about it?'

'How did he get a note into my locker? I keep wondering if Faisal is secretly in league with Kandin. What do you think?'.

'I think you're being paranoid,' Layla says. 'Kandin's clever but he's not god. Not all-seeing nor all-powerful. I don't know how Faisal did it, but it doesn't seem likely that it's anything to do with Kandin.' She stops to sip her coffee. 'If Faisal were in league with Kandin, it would make more sense for him to make sure that you kept your job. And he wouldn't have let you know that he knew about your meetings. Not if Faisal was informing him about what you were doing.'

I suppose she's right. I get up and make another cup of coffee. We're drinking instant. Can't afford anything else.

'Do you want some more?' I ask and she shakes her head.

'Will you go and meet him for me, Layla?'

'You mean Faisal?'

'Yes. You could explain why I can't be there and ask if he could meet me tomorrow in a different place. What about *The Cockatoo*? It's only five minutes further.' Layla looks dubious and I carry on. 'You could ask him how he managed to get the note into my locker.' I stop and look at her. 'Most of all you could ask him if he's had any messages from Joel. I need to know about Jenn and what's happening in PNG.'

Layla says she'll think about it. I'm surprised by her reply. I would have thought that she would agree immediately, but I have to accept her answer. Not sure why she's hesitating, but I need to go out to get some groceries so I leave her to get back to her books and think it through.

We're nearly out of rice and there's an urgent need for one or two other items. Washing powder is one of them so I make a list and go and do the shopping. When I get back, she's gone.

I text her in veiled terms to see if she has decided to go and meet Faisal but there's no reply so I mooch around wondering what's going to happen with Kandin this evening. I would go and see him even if it were not about Jenn and Joel. I don't like him but I do need him. We need his forging services and his link to all sorts of other services. Kandin has been useful more than once. I admire Layla for her principled stand but I can't match it. That is I don't want to match it. I want to survive. At any cost, I ask myself? The answer might be yes.

I don't know what to do with myself. I've already eaten and I've painted my nails. I open the fridge to see if there's anything I can nibble on but all I can find is a punnet of mushrooms. I help myself to one and eat that. I read an article recently about how mushrooms are good for the brain and my brain needs all the help it can get.

Kandin is late but eventually, the buzzer goes and I go down to meet him.

'Would you like a drink or something to eat?' he asks with a grin as I step into his house, but I don't bother to reply. He looks me up and down in that way he has of somehow making me feel admired. Other men do it and I feel like a piece of meat but when Kandin does it, I feel a sense of satisfaction and for a minute, I bask in the sensation before reminding myself about how unpleasant he is. And how dangerous.

'I've got something for you,' he says and hands me a bundle of what look like travel documents. I look through them and see a return ticket to Port Moresby. My passport is there, too.

'How did you get that?' I ask holding it up and Kandin shrugs without bothering to reply.

'I'll have to go back for some things,' I tell him but he shakes his head. 'And I'll have to tell Layla.' Again he shakes his head.

'No, Auli. You're not going anywhere until I take you to the airport tomorrow. We're travelling together.'

I try ringing Layla but once again there's no reply.

'Where is she?' I ask as realisation slowly hits.

'Quite safe,' Kandin replies. 'I wanted to make sure she was properly occupied for 24 hours.'

'Why?' I ask.

'To make sure she doesn't get in the way.'

'What have you got planned?' I ask him.

'You'll see,' he says. 'It will work better if you don't know in advance.'

I feel desperate. Somehow I've got to get in touch with Layla so that she can meet Faisal and send a message to Joel. Even if I don't know exactly what will happen, I can warn him that we're coming. I have an idea. If Kandin has somehow stolen Layla's phone (which would account for her not answering) then there is one last way that I can get in touch with her. I'll text Carolyn and get a message to Layla that way. The problem is how I can do that without Kandin finding out. If we went out, it would be easier.

'How about an evening out?' I suggest trying to sound casual. 'It's ages since you took me dancing.'

'We can do it here,' he says and attaches his phone to the speaker. The Gotan Project starts to play something rhythmic and Kandin starts to move. 'Come on then, Lani,' he says. 'It takes two to tango. Come and strut your stuff.' 'Strut your stuff'? Where has he been lately? That's not Kandin's language. Except of course everything is Kandin's language. He borrows with impunity and not only language. He reaches for me and pulls me closer, then stops.

'Why so stiff, Lani?' he says. 'I don't think tonight's a good night to take you dancing.'

I'm not doing very well. I'll have to think of something else. In the end, I'm forced to try and text from the bathroom. It's the only place where I can go and lock the door and at least I can turn the tap on so he doesn't hear any noises from my phone. I go and try.

'Tell Layla to send warning to Joel,' I text. I haven't mentioned Faisal so if Kandin does intercept the text, at least Faisal will be safe. Two seconds later there's a reply.

'Layla here. Phone gone. Will do.' I send back two kisses and wipe the messages. The tap is still running and I pray that Kandin is not monitoring my phone. Even if he is, it's not much of a warning that I've sent. Kandin has told me no details at all of what he plans to do in Port Moresby. Only that there will be a death.

'Whose death?' I ask but he won't tell me.

34

Kandin has thought of everything. Or nearly everything.

'You couldn't have packed better yourself,' he says proudly after I've loaded in the underwear, jeans, shoes, shirts and jumpers he's chosen for me for the trip. He's even remembered toiletries and moisturiser. He's got the shampoo right, too.

'All except one thing,' I tell him.

'What's that?' I can hear that he doesn't believe me.

'Nail varnish,' I say. 'And remover. I need my nail varnish.' Kandin is annoyed. He aims for perfection.

'I'll deal with it,' he says. 'What is it called?'

'Witch's Blood,' I reply and he can't stop a smile.

The plane leaves at eleven so we have time for breakfast before we have to check in. I refuse to either eat or drink except from the tap at his house so he gives in and we set off early to have breakfast at the airport.

We are sitting with coffee, orange juice and almond croissants (that I like even more than chocolate ones) when someone comes up to Kandin and puts a large package on the table. I hope it's not a drug deal but don't believe that Kandin would allow anything suspicious to be openly visible.

'Here you are,' he says and hands me the package.

It's the Witch's Blood and a huge container of nail varnish remover. Don't know where I'm going to put it so I hand the varnish remover over to Kandin. He can carry it. For once, he doesn't argue. He leaves me eating while he goes to check in but comes back quite quickly saying I'll have to go with him.

'Let me finish this,' I say reluctant to hurry such a rare thing as an almond croissant but he's impatient. Kandin has supplied me with trolley luggage that is bright sky blue with large white polka dots. He obviously doesn't care about attracting attention to ourselves. His luggage is navy, much more subdued. I'm surprised he didn't me get some shocking pink luggage and say as much.

'I nearly did,' he says. 'It was a toss-up between the pink one and this but I decided the blue was better. Don't you like it?' he asks.

'Very discreet,' I reply.

When we get to the check-in, I understand why he was trying to do it for me. I discover that we're not going to Port Moresby at all. We're flying to London.

It's a reprieve. I feel a huge relief that I don't have to face the showdown with Joel yet. Perhaps not at all? Hope sprouts like a weed.

'What are we going to do in London?' I ask, half expecting the answer I receive, but still not sure why it would be happening at Kandin's instigation.

'We're going to Oxford,' he says and my guess is confirmed. I try again to get some information out of him.

'Why are we going to Oxford?'

'Chrissie wants to see you,' he replies. 'And so does my father. Lucas.'

'Any chance of telling me why?'

'I think Lucas has got a project that he thinks might interest both of us,' Kandin says carefully.

'Does he know you've been hacking his research?'

'Of course not.'

'And what about Chrissie. Why does she want to see me?'

'No idea,' Kandin says, 'but she keeps saying she likes you. Don't see why she can't like you in Melbourne, but no, she insisted she wanted to see you in Oxford. It's Chrissie who paid for our tickets.'

'Does Lucas know that Chrissie is going to see us there or what she wants?'

'I don't think so,' Kandin replies and by this time I know as much as he does.

The flight passes in a long boring haze. Kandin has remembered to buy me a book for the trip but he's got the wrong one. Something I would never choose to read. It's sci-fi - the sort of thing that he would read. And I thought he knew me well. He notices that I'm not reading it and asks me why.

'It's fantasy,' I say. 'Not my thing at all.'

'Well, you read Murakami,' he comments.

'Yes,' I agree. 'Murakami is different.' Kandin gets his own book out and ignores me. His whole body is sending the message that he did his best but that I'm not satisfied with anything. He thinks I'm awkward. Well, I didn't want to come and he didn't consult me. He can't expect a prisoner to be good-tempered, however well looked after. But he does and is not at all pleased that I'm not grateful. Tough.

I watch films, sleep a bit, attempt to read the in-flight magazine which manages to be more boring than you might think possible. They're all like that, Kandin tells me and points again at the book that he bought for me, but it's become a matter of pride for me to ignore it so I go back to the magazine. We stop in Singapore and have to get off and then on again. After that, it's straight through to London and we arrive on a grey day at 5.30 in the morning.

'Have you been to London before?' I ask and Kandin nods. I haven't, of course, and can't help being excited to be landing in a place that I've heard so much about. I've read novels set in London and I've seen the old Inspector Morse series set in Oxford. Some of the movies I've watched were set in London and now here I am. If I think about movies, it seems that they're all set either in the USA or the UK. Occasionally in Australia. Hardly ever anywhere else. I've never seen a movie set in PNG and I remember Saul complaining about the lack of our people on tv. When I think of him, I seem to remember the old kindhearted Saul. The torturer has largely disappeared. Buried, I suppose. Kandin would be surprised to know that I'd killed a man. He thinks he knows me.

It's cold and grey when we step outside but it's supposed to be summer. A light rain is falling but we're soon marching through miles of corridors and walkways that stretch between the plane and the customs area. If you include the long shuffle through the passport queue, it's nearly an hour after the plane lands before we're through customs and out into the airport proper. I'm tired so I'm grateful for Kandin taking charge and leading the way down tunnels and into lifts until we finally emerge into the air again at a coach station. There are coaches to Oxford every twenty minutes at this time of day so we don't have to wait long. In a short time, there I am sitting next to Kandin on what's called the Oxford Tube (except it's a bus) in a daze of unreality. In about an hour and a half, we arrive

in Oxford city, but it passes in a blur. We get off at Glouces-
ter Green and Kandin gets a taxi to take us to Lucas's
house.

When I get out of the taxi, I finally start to feel nervous.
Kandin checks the door number against info he has on his
phone, but the taxi has got it right. The place where we are
standing is Princes St and it's the correct address. Kandin
leads the way up the short path and bangs on the door
knocker. I stand behind him so am able to hide my shock
when Saul opens the door. It isn't Saul of course. It can't
be, but this man looks more like Saul even than the man I
saw in the photograph.

35

'Welcome,' Lucas says to both of us. 'Come in.'

He sounds like Saul as well as looks like him and I can't get used to hearing his voice. A voice that I had never thought I would hear again. Lucas and Kandin talk to each other in the kitchen while I collapse on the sofa and try to take in my surroundings. Lucas pops his head around the corner and asks me if I'm all right? Would I like to go and lie down? His smile is the same as Saul's. He really does seem to be the same man, not somebody similar. Perhaps I've landed in an alternative world.

The house is lovely. Small but with interesting shapes. It's old. I expected a tiny flat like Carolyn's but Lucas is sharing a house with other students, so it's the whole house and we've got it to ourselves at the moment because his house mates are away. It's just off the Cowley Road apparently. Lucas says we got off the coach at the wrong stop. Should have got off at St Clements just around the corner. He puts on a pot of coffee for us. Good coffee. Not instant.

There are pictures all over the walls and underneath my feet, there are polished floorboards and a rug. Quite different from the floorboards in Kandin's house. These are old boards. I'm too tired to look properly and don't know if it's a good idea or not to be drinking coffee but it smells excellent and I gratefully accept. We are offered food, too, but neither Kandin nor I are hungry. It feels as though we've been eating non-stop since we left Melbourne and all I want to do is to drink and rest.

I'm not sure if I'll be able to sleep but I urgently need to be alone to cope with the shock of seeing Lucas who looks like Saul, so I accept the offer of somewhere to lie down. Lucas shows me upstairs to a tiny bedroom that is next to the bathroom. It's painted dark pink and there's a fig tree in the corner of the room in a pot. The small green leaves look lovely against the dark pink wall. I look out of the window and see a large tree dominating the back gardens and when I look closer, I see that it's full of cherries. There are sheds right at the back and a ginger cat sitting on top of a wooden box. Nobody around. I can hear birds singing. Not the same as Keroko. Or Melbourne. These are Oxford birds.

I think I won't sleep, but I do and when I wake up, it's the middle of the night. I must have slept the whole day and halfway through the night. All I remember is getting up a couple of times and going to the bathroom. I peer at my watch and see that I'm right. It's nearly 4 am. I'm thirsty so I decide to go down to the kitchen and get something to drink. I try to walk quietly but every stair creaks. It looks as though someone has left the light on downstairs but when I get down there, it's Kandin. He's sitting at the table doing something on his laptop. I wish I'd got mine here, but mine's in Melbourne. At least I've got my phone and I remembered to put it on charge before I went to sleep.

'Hello, Auli,' he says and I note the Auli. It feels as though he likes me more when he calls me Auli rather than Lani. 'Are you making a cup of tea?'

'No,' I say, 'I just want a glass of water or orange juice or something.'

'The fridge is through there,' he says pointing towards the kitchen which leads off the living room at the back of the house.

'Did Lucas talk to you about his project?' I ask.

'No, he wanted to wait to talk to us both together and he said I should let you sleep.'

'I can't believe I slept the whole day and most of the night,' I say. 'Have you slept much?' Kandin shrugs as though to imply that he's superior and doesn't need to sleep.

'I don't get jet lag,' he says, but I don't believe him. I raise my eyebrows and leave it at that.

'I can't imagine how I could possibly contribute to any of Lucas's projects,' I say.

'Neither can I,' Kandin says brutally. 'You haven't even graduated from high school.'

'That doesn't make me stupid,' I shoot back.

'No, but you're probably quite ignorant,' Kandin says, 'and you don't have any computer skills.'

'It's true that I don't have any special computer skills,' I say, 'although I'm sure I could learn how to do anything that you can do.' At this point, Kandin pulls a face at me. It's clear that he considers his hacking skills second to none and is sure that his father is going to ask him to use them for the project. He's probably right, but I don't like his judgement that I'm stupid and ignorant because I haven't finished high school.

'I've read a lot,' I tell him. 'I bet I've read more than you have. All you do is play on your computer all the time.'

Kandin smiles his usual arrogant smile. I'd give a lot to remove it and one day I will. I take my juice and go back upstairs. Go to the toilet and almost die when the flush sounds loud enough to wake the whole street never mind just the house. Then I remember that there's only Lucas here apart from us so I calm down a bit. Later on, after breakfast, Lucas takes us on a brief tour of the city. He'll show us more later he says. Just wanted us to feel where we were. Feel? Centuries of history he says as we walk through the narrow streets and look at gargoyles and old buildings, mostly yellowish. It's the local limestone Lucas tells us. We go for a walk by the Isis until we get to a pub called *The Head of the River* and while we're sitting outside with a beer and some pommes frites that the English call chips, Lucas starts to tell us about the project that he thinks we might like to be involved in.

Kandin is right that Lucas is interested in his hacking skills but not merely his hacking skills. What he wants is for Kandin to experiment to see if he can do more than extract particular sets of data.

'What else would you want me to do?'

'No details yet, but one thing would be to explore program vulnerabilities and find ways to secure them.' Lucas looks at Kandin who nods.

'That's fairly standard,' Kandin says. 'What are the project aims?'

'They are not yet clearly formulated,' Lucas replies, 'but it will be an investigation into how belief systems are constructed and maintained. What strengthens them and what makes them weaker? How pre-set are people's predispositions to certain types of behaviour in their pre-birth neural circuitry? Could these predispositions be changed?' He stops and looks at us. 'Does that sound interesting?

238

'Yes,' we both say together and once more Kandin looks at me with a kind of irritation. He can't understand why Lucas would want to talk to me about it at all.

Lucas turns towards Kandin. 'You have impressive skills,' he tells his son and I watch Kandin swell (literally) with pride. His chest sort of puffs out and he sits differently. 'I'd much rather have you on my side than hacking my research like you did last time.' I see shock skim over Kandin's face.

'What do you mean?' he asks.

'You know what I mean,' Lucas says. 'I don't want to discuss it at the moment, but I do want you to be aware that I know about it.' He gives Kandin no chance to reply because he turns quickly to me and starts to explain how he thinks I might be able to contribute.

'That's one part of the research,' he tells me. 'The other areas we want to explore are to do with powers of the mind that are as yet not well developed in most people, especially telepathic powers that can be used to access information and powers that can be used to control people's behaviour.'

'Do you mean special powers?' I ask.

'We can call them that for the time being,' Lucas says. 'Do you have any special powers, Aulani?'

'I'm not sure,' I reply. 'I think so.'

'That's an excellent answer,' Lucas says looking pleased. 'Would you be interested to work with us to find out?'

'Yes,' I say. It sounds extremely interesting and I find myself wanting more than anything to be included in the project.

'I'm sure your particular sensitivities would be very helpful,' he tells me. 'I hope you don't mind, but I contacted Layla to ask about you. I'm aware that you've not taken any formal examinations and I needed to know about your interests and abilities. She assured me that you were an excellent student and that you have the kind of questioning mind that would be well suited to assisting with research.' Lucas turns once again to both of us. 'If you agree to take part, you would both be employed as research assistants.' He takes a sip of his beer. Lucas is a slow drinker. Kandin has already finished his. I can see Kandin nodding enthusiastically, quite unlike his usual laid-back demeanour.

'I'd love to,' I burst out and feel myself glowing. I'm grateful for Layla's report of my abilities and flattered to be asked, but more than that, I'm interested in the research he is outlining.

Lucas looks pleased. 'That's excellent,' he says. 'We can talk some more about it in a few days time. There are a couple of other people I need to talk to first.'

As we walk back along by the river, my head is full of questions and excitement. I almost forget that we still have to go to PNG. That Kandin still wants to kill Joel. That I still haven't got Jenn back and that all these things hang in the balance. That I am using a fake passport and that I am not safe in my own country. For a few minutes, I put all that to one side and let the excitement of the research project give me hope and happiness.

36

'How long are we staying here?' I ask Kandin that evening. Lucas has gone out to see someone and we are alone in the house together.

'Not long,' he says. 'I've booked for us to fly out on Saturday.'

'Lucas will be disappointed,' I say, thinking that it is me who will be disappointed. I want to find out more about the project and I've read about Oxford. I want to explore, go for walks along the river, visit the Ashmolean, try out the pubs along the Cowley Road where I've already heard live music pounding out.

'We'll be back,' Kandin assures me. 'But we've got business in Port Moresby. Have you forgotten?'

No, not forgotten, Kandin but I was hoping that you had.

'Chrissie's arriving this morning,' Kandin tells me.

'Does Lucas know?'

'Yes, she's been in touch with him because she wants to take us all out for a meal this evening.'

'Is she staying here?'

Kandin laughs. 'No, of course not.'

It's difficult to believe that Kandin is planning to kill someone. He looks so angelic and uses his charm at every opportunity. His attitude towards me is variable. He tells me I have to help him bring down Joel because Joel is threatening his 'activities'. And why do I have to help him I ask? It's payback time, he tells me. I got the house. Now

I have to pay back. Do I remember that I asked how I could thank him? And that he told me that he'd think of something. He laughs. Can he really be so cold and calculating?

'This is a man's life you're talking about,' I say. 'A man who has saved my own life on three occasions.'

'Doesn't matter,' Kandin says. 'Every dog has its day.'

***

I miss Layla. I've tried texting her, but it's clear that she still hasn't got her phone back. There's no point in texting Carol again. I already messaged to say that we were in Oxford. I'll let her know when things change - if I can. As I get ready to go out for the meal with Chrissie, I stop to marvel at where I am and what's happening to me. I'm in Oxford. I'm going out for a meal with Lucas, who is doing a doctorate in Oxford (Oxford!), and he has asked me to contribute to his research. That's the best part. That somebody thinks I'm capable of contributing something. The fact that Kandin, too, is going to be part of the research team is a burden I'll have to put up with. I have a shower and carefully apply the Witch's Blood. Then I dress and am pleased when I regard myself in the mirror.

We go to a restaurant in town. Walk there. It's not far and when we arrive, Chrissie is already sitting at a table she has reserved for us. She looks different tonight. Nervous. I've never seen Chrissie looking nervous before. I wonder what she's got to be nervous about and whether I'm imagining things. We order and while we're waiting for the food to arrive, we hardly manage to get a conversation going. Like us, Lucas is baffled as to why Chrissie wants us all together for a meal. We asked him and he doesn't know.

I'm beginning to think of him as Lucas now, not Saul. I'm going to ask him about Saul when I get the chance. Did they know each other? Stuff like that. Maybe they are related. I think that's very probable.

It's not until the main course is served and the waiters are well out of the way that Chrissie starts to tell us why she wanted to see us here.

'There's something I've got to tell you,' she begins croakily as though her voice needs a bit of practice. We look at her and wait. 'It affects all of you,' she says, 'and me too, of course.' None of us says anything. 'Of course, it won't change anything,' Chrissie says, 'but I can't bear it any longer. The not being able to say it. I need to tell you. All of you.'

Her nerves are affecting us. Even cool Kandin looks on edge.

'What is it?' Lucas asks. 'You're making us all nervous. Who have you killed and where is the body hidden?' It is an attempt at a joke, but Chrissie takes him seriously.

'No, Lucas,' she says. 'I haven't killed anyone.' She pauses. 'But I might have done.'

'It is about Grace?' Lucas asks. 'Are you going to tell us what happened to Grace?'

'Grace died,' Chrissie says. 'What I told you in the first place, Lucas, was correct. Grace was still-born. She died before she arrived in the world.' I see Lucas clench his fists in an attempt to keep his temper.

'Then why, Chrissie, why did you send me on a wild-goose chase. Raise my hopes that I had a daughter somewhere?'

'I wanted to hurt you,' she says. 'You were leaving us and I wanted to hurt you so I made it up and knew that

243

you'd go looking for her. And knew that you'd hate me for sending her away. Which I didn't do. But you should have been hating me for something else.'

'What's that?' Lucas asks.

'You do have a daughter,' Chrissie says.

Now we're all baffled. If Grace died at birth, where does another daughter fit in? We wait for her to continue. Even Lucas says nothing, but I see his hands clench again.

'She's here,' Chrissie says. 'It's Aulani.'

I feel as though I've been punched in the stomach. What does she mean? And how dare she say things like this in a public place. Chrissie turns towards me.

'I'm your mother, Aulani,' she says and my spirits do more than sink. If it's true, it's a terrible thing to find out. I've never liked Chrissie. I can't bear it.

'Have you gone mad, mother?' Kandin speaks. 'How can Aulani be your daughter. Her birthday is almost the same as mine.'

'Yes,' Chrissie says. 'It's more than that, Kandin. Aulani's birthday is exactly the same as yours, You're twins.' She looks at us all. 'And yes, all of you are right. I didn't want to have children. I didn't want Grace. I was glad that she was still-born, and I was depressed when I got pregnant again. I didn't want a child. I didn't want one and I certainly didn't want two, so I chose the first one. You, Kandin,' she says, 'you were the first one, and then a girl was born.' She doesn't look at me as she carries on speaking. 'There was a window with no louvres - I think they were being repaired. I pulled the flywire back and threw Aulani out of the window.' She looks at our shocked faces. 'That's why nobody noticed there was a baby missing,' she says. 'Nobody knew I was having twins and they saw Kandin. Nobody looked for another baby.' At last, she turns to me. 'I just hoped that nobody would find you outside and bring you back in. But it didn't happen. You disappeared and I breathed a sigh of relief.' A slight pause. 'I'm sorry, Aulani.'

I've had enough. I can't take any more of this. I get up, grab my bag and rush out of the restaurant.

***

I've no idea where I am. I've been walking for hours. It's late. Dark although there's a moon. I'm by the river but not where we walked yesterday. I think I'm near Iffley. I saw a sign somewhere. I'm not going back. I can't bear to see them. Any of them. At least Chrissie won't be in the house but Kandin and Lucas will be there. I can't face them. As I've walked, I've had one thing after another hit my mind. The colour of Jenn for instance. I expected her to be dark. Saul was very dark, but she was light-skinned. Light brown. Like Layla. Like me. Like Joel. No sign of Saul's skin and it must have been because I'm half white. I'm shocked. I can't bear it. I don't want any white skin. Can't imagine anything worse than Australian blood. I feel like killing myself. Pouring my bad blood into the ground where it belongs. I don't want any of Chrissie's blood mixed with mine.

My phone rings again and again, I ignore it, but I look to see who it is. It's Lucas. I get up and walk further. It's quiet here. There's no-one about. I think of killing myself but I don't want to do that. I can't bear it, but I do want to live. There are people I love. There's Jenn. She's happy without me but she might need me later. And I definitely need her. What about Layla? She's been my real mother all my life. How would she cope if I died? I can't do it. Layla has given up so much for me. She's loved me for so long. And there are things I want to do with my life.

There's a text and I read what it says.

'Where are you, Aulani? Please let me come and find you. Lucas.'

How strange that it's Lucas. The person I know least is the one who wants to look for me. Not Chrissie (who is 'sorry' for throwing me out of the window). Not Kandin (who has spent so much time with me). I text a reply.

'I'm by the river. Near Iffley, I think.'

'Stay where you are. I'm on my way.'

So Kandin is my brother. And I don't like him. And I've had sex with him. Incest. And Chrissie is my mother. And I don't like her. I always dreamed of finding my family. My birth family. But I never dreamed it could be so awful. That you could find people you didn't like. A family that you hated to be part of. I thought I would feel a connection. That it would be like coming home. But it isn't. It's unbearable. Worst of all is the Australian blood. Kandin doesn't mind being mixed race but I do. I hate it. But there's nothing I can do about it.

And strangest of all, there's Lucas. He looks like Saul. Two fathers who both look the same. One of them dead. Killed. The other one looking like the first. Sounding like the first. My biological father. But the thing that I've hardly admitted to myself is that when I look at Lucas I see the Saul who tortured me. In my dreams, I've seen a smiling Saul. Almost always smiling. The kind one. But when I look at Lucas I see the one who cut me and ripped me apart. And now he's coming to find me.

For a long time, I sit and wait, watching the water, seeing bubbles here and there and a few ripples. I think I see a rat. Maybe it's a water rat. What does a water rat look like? It disappears over the side of the bank and into the water. I'm cold. I've got a jacket but I'm still cold. At least it's not raining. In the distance, I see a figure approaching and as he gets closer, I see that it's Lucas. Tonight he doesn't look like Saul as I was afraid he would and I'm relieved. He looks pleased to see me and sits down on the bench beside me.

'Can you talk?' he asks. 'Do you want to?' I shake my head and Lucas lights a cigarette and starts to smoke.

'I don't smoke often,' he says. 'Just occasionally. Do you want one?' I shake my head again.

'I've never smoked,' I say, and then, 'Did you know Saul?'

'Saul?'

'Saul who married Layla. Layla is my guardian and my mama, the one you contacted to check on my school work.'

'Of course, I know him,' Lucas replies. 'He's my cousin. Lived with her up in Keroko for years and then disappeared. So I heard.' Slowly I see that Lucas realises that Saul, too, was my guardian. Not just Layla. 'Was he a good father?' he asks me.

'Sometimes,' I reply.

'He was religious,' Lucas tells me. 'Still is, I expect. I don't think he will ever change. It was the missionaries. They got him young,' and Lucas smiles at me. 'We were surprised that he stayed with Layla after she was accused of sorcery. Saul was always talking about driving out evil

247

spirits. That's what he believed was happening to people who were accused of sorcery. He thought they were possessed.'

It makes sense, I think. That's what Saul was doing when he tortured me. Driving them out. Driving them out. Driving them out. Lucas notices that I'm beginning to shiver.

'Shall we go home, Aulani?' he asks me gently and I nod. We don't talk about what Chrissie has said. It's too big. I like Lucas. He's gentle and in some ways, he's like Layla. I feel I might be able to trust him. Not Chrissie. Not Kandin, but possibly Lucas. If only I can stop seeing Saul when I look at him.

37

The noise is deafening, droning on and on. It seeps through the earplugs so I take them out. They're uncomfortable anyway. I'm sitting next to Kandin on a Boeing 747 on our way to Darwin. London to Darwin and then we change and catch Air Niugini up to Moresby. I'm going home but there's no joy in it. I'm terrified. We don't talk about what will happen but every so often we've been talking about what Chrissie said.

'It doesn't make any difference,' Kandin says. 'We're still the same. I'm me and you're you.'

'Of course, it makes a difference,' I say. 'You're my brother. I'm your sister.' I pause to let the weight of that sink in. 'We used to think we were not related.'

I look at him and Kandin shrugs.

'Jenn is your niece,' I go on, hoping that will help to keep her safe. It should do.

'I don't care,' he says. 'It doesn't matter. I don't know her. She's the same as before. Your kid.'

'And what about us?' I say looking at him meaningfully.

'Well, what about us?' he asks picking up my hand and brushing the back of it with his lips. 'What's changed?'

'You're impossible,' I say and I mean this seriously.

'No,' he replies. 'I'm honest and unsentimental. It's a good way to be.'

I put my earplugs back in and try to forget about him. Try to forget about everything. I've tried again to contact Layla. Wanted to tell her that I was on my way to Moresby but I can't get in touch. I tried Carolyn but got no reply from her either, so there's nothing I can do about that. I did my best to send warnings. It was all I could do.

When we get to Darwin, we're both so tired that we hardly say a word and when we finally arrive in Moresby, I hardly have time to feel the pull of my motherland and how good it feels to be back when I'm whisked off in a taxi (a hot and uncomfortable taxi with no aircon - what did you expect Kandin says) to the Frangipani Hotel. Kandin has booked us in together so I'm having to share a double room with him although I see with relief that there are two single beds.

'We can push them together,' he says wickedly, deliberately provoking me, 'although we need a good rest before tomorrow.'

'Why? What's happening tomorrow?'

'You'll see,' he says.

***

The PMV is hot, dirty and dusty but cheerful. With every swing and lurch it feels as though it might fall apart, but it doesn't. I've had my instructions. I have to abduct Jenn like last time and take her on the bus to Gordon's market where Joel will come to get her and then Kandin will kill him. And here we are. I'm sitting with Jenn on my knee and feeling so happy just to be with her again. It's as though it's completely normal, but it isn't. I'm taking part in Kandin's plan to kill Joel. I don't understand how he can do this and I don't understand how I can have agreed to it. I suppose I believe that he will hurt Jenn if I don't. This morning I sat with him over coffee and tried to talk to him.

'Why me?' I ask Kandin. 'Why do you need me and Jenn to be involved in your battle with Joel?'

'It's the only way to get him to come to a place of my choosing.'

'And if I refuse?'

'Then I'll kill Jenn,' Kandin replies calmly. 'That's easy to do and Joel will see that I mean business. I'm being nice, Auli. Can't you see that I'm being nice? Doing it this way means that Jenn doesn't have to die to punish her daddy.'

Shock doesn't begin to describe how I feel about this. Unreality and disbelief is a better description. In the past, I have often thought that I was shocked by Kandin's behaviour but part of me always saw his side of things. So the part of me that went along with it all could be excused. But not this time. He talks about my daughter's life as though she were no more important than a fish or a bird who could be struck down at will. He seems to feel no guilt or shame and no regret at involving me in the evil act he intends to commit. But I believe he is serious so I don't have a choice. All I can do is to pray that Layla has managed to warn Joel. It should have worked. Joel won't know the day, but he'll be alert waiting for Kandin to put his plan into action.

Getting Jenn to come with me was easy. I don't know how she managed to remember me, but she did.

'Mama,' she shouted when she saw me and raced into my arms. There was so much noise going on all around that nobody noticed. Kids screeching. A radio playing loud pop music and women working in the garden, absorbed in what they were doing so I was lucky.

'We're going on the bus,' I told her.

'Same before,' Jenn said. She remembered it all. No wonder Joel adores her. Who would not?

'Yes,' I said. 'Same before. Going to Aunty Shantelle's.' But Jenn didn't like that part.

'Going Papa. Same before,' she said so I went along with her.

'Yes,' I said. 'Going Papa.'

I sit on the bus and my mind fills with horror at the thought of Jenn watching her father get shot. Worse, there is the knowledge that I will be responsible for his death. The man who has saved my life three times. I suddenly realise what I can do. I can get off the bus early. I can get off with Jenn at the next stop and hope that Joel doesn't rush up to the PMV. It might be worth a try.

'Are you ready?' I ask my daughter. 'We're getting off next.'

'Off next,' she repeats happily. 'Off next.' Then, 'Going Papa,' again and again. Jenn talks non-stop.

Eventually, the bus reaches the outskirts of the city and I look around. Perhaps one more stop, I think to myself. We'll have to get to Aunty Shantelle's and it's quite far. No point in going to the hotel because I haven't got Jenn's passport with me. It's in Melbourne. Kandin wouldn't let me go back to fetch anything. And I've got no money to pay for another ticket. While I'm considering all this, the bus shudders to a stop and people start to get on. I think I'm seeing things when I see Layla. She smiles at me and waves and I can't believe it. I've no idea how she got here and on to this particular bus but it does seem like a miracle. She comes to sit down beside me.

'Jenn,' I tell my daughter. 'This is Aunty Layla.'

'Aunty Layla,' Jenn tries to repeat. 'Aunty Layla.' Then 'Going Papa' she informs Layla before she turns back to look out of the window because the bus sets off again.

'Layla!' I say in amazement. 'How did you get here? How wonderful to see you.'

'No, Auli,' Layla says quietly. 'It is not good to see me. I've come to make you do as I say.' What does she mean? Layla opens her handbag and points inside. She's got a gun. Layla with a gun? I start to laugh and reach for it myself. It must be fake. But she holds my arm. Vice-like. Her grip is like iron. She's old. She can't be as strong as she feels.

'Yes, I am,' she says answering the question I haven't asked. 'I am strong, Auli. Much stronger than you are. And I do have a gun. It's loaded and I am going to use it.'

'Going Papa,' Jenn starts chanting over and over, but Layla tells her to be quiet and the child shuts up.

'Saul's daughter,' Layla says and nods at Jenn. Again this is not a question. She's not asking me. She knows.

'How did you find out?' I ask and she half laughs half sobs but quickly controls herself.

'Joel sent a picture of Jenn to Faisal. It was for you but I saw it. I saw immediately that she was Saul's child. You've lied to me, Auli. All these years, you've lied to me.'

'I thought it would upset you,' I whisper.

'Upset me,' Layla echoes and the sound rings in my ears despite the noisy bus. 'Yes, Auli, you could say that.'

'So why are you here?' I ask her.

'I agreed to kill Joel for Kandin,' she says surprising me. 'And he thought you might get off the bus early so we arranged for me to get on here to make sure that didn't happen. I'm going to kill Joel when we get to the market.'

'But why?' I ask. 'You always said you liked Joel. That he was a good man.'

'That was before I knew,' she says.

'Knew what?' I ask. Nothing is making sense.

'He is the grandson of the man who accused me,' Layla says.

'What difference does that make?'

Layla looks at me almost with contempt.

'I don't think you're a PNG girl. If you were, you would understand. You would never ask such a question. It's payback, Auli. Didn't I teach you about payback in life lessons? You didn't learn, but now you will learn the hard way. The hardest way because it's you who I am going to kill first.'

Jenn cuddles into me. She's gone quiet and tense. She knows that things are going wrong. I hold her tight but how can I protect her? What can I do? Layla has stopped talking and we travel in silence as the bus lurches and bumps. Layla has taken the gun out of her bag and is sticking the end of it into my side, right next to Jenn's leg. I wonder if she's taken the safety catch off or if it even has a safety catch. That's what I've seen in the movies. If the gun is ready to fire then it's a miracle that it hasn't gone off already as we're thrown about by the PMV. This driver obviously loves swinging around corners. He'd go on two wheels if he could.

My mind is in turmoil. I struggle to think straight. I can't accept that Layla and Kandin have been working against me although Kandin wouldn't see it like that. Kandin, in fact, is quite straightforward. He puts himself and his interests first and anybody else's concerns hardly register. He must have been delighted to find that he could get Layla to shoot Joel for him and me to get Joel to the appointed place. Kandin doesn't have to do anything. He can just stand and watch.

But Layla! How can she think like this? How can she think it is right to shoot a man who has never done her any harm? Who has done the opposite. Who has helped to save her.

'Have you been in touch with Joel?' I ask and I see Layla smile.

'Of course,' she says. 'You put me in touch with him via Faisal.' She stops and moves slightly so that the end of the gun changes position. I can feel it pressing against me. 'I tried to teach you,' she says, 'but you didn't learn the most important lesson.'

'What was that?' I ask but I know what's coming.

'Don't trust anyone. Not ever. And especially if the person is close to you.'

There is nothing I can say to this so I ask something else.

'Does Joel know?' I ask. 'About Jenn?'

'Oh yes,' Layla tells me. 'I emailed him immediately. I made sure that he knew.'

The PMV stops again. The next stop will be ours. Not long now. I've read that your whole life is supposed to flash before you as death approaches, but it doesn't. At least not for me. I feel Jenn heavy and uncomfortable on my knee and I'm aware of the end of the gun pushing hard into my side. My mind is a blank. One last try. I decide to speak to Layla one last time.

'Don't you love me, Layla?'

'No, Auli,' she whispers. 'I hate you. For killing Saul. For having his child. For lying to me and taking the best part of my life.'

The PMV comes to a shuddering standstill with a final rock from side to side before it is finally still. Jenn is still quiet and the three of us get up to leave the bus. Layla has stepped back so that I can go first. I am carrying Jenn. My child is anxious and tense. We step off the bus on to the dry caked ground and are surrounded by people. I put Jenn on the ground as fast as I can and shout, 'Go, Jenn. Run. Go find Papa.' She runs and the gun digs into my back.

'It's the end,' Layla says. 'Say your prayers, Auli, if you've got any prayers to say,' and I hear a click and then a bang. I fall on the ground and for an instant everything is black. When I open my eyes and stare at my body, I am covered in blood. But it's not mine. Slowly I see that it's Layla's blood. Joel has shot her.

He is leaning over me trying to help me up.

'Mama, mama,' Jenn is shouting, but her voice sounds distant and someone is holding her back.

'Are you all right?' Joel asks me but I can hardly hear him. I shake my head and try to speak.

'I can't hear you,' I say as I look around at the mass of people who are moving backwards and forwards and pointing and staring at us.

'It's the sound of the shot,' Joel says. 'You'll hear again in a minute.' I see that some men are covering Layla and taking her away. Layla. My Layla. My mama. I lie on the ground and cry. Great heaving sobs for Layla. For my mama and for all that she's ever meant to me.

38

'Come on, Auli,' Joel says. 'We need to leave this place,' and he helps me up and leads me to a police car parked on the grass. 'Get in,' he says, and I do.

He takes me and Jenn to Bomana to the Police College where he has a house. I am surprised when we arrive that we have to stop at a gate with a sentry box where the guards on duty salute Joel and raise the bar to let us through.

'Papa's house,' Jenn shouts as we stop outside. 'Papa's house.' She seems to be fully recovered as I watch her run around. The shooting doesn't seem to have affected her. She knows this place, and she's happy here.

'This is where we live,' Joel explains once we get inside. 'Jenn goes to visit in the village, but this is our home.' I hear someone coming up the steps and taking off their shoes on the veranda. A young girl appears in the doorway.

'Mama Nanna, Mama Nanna,' Jenn shouts and rushes into the girl's arms.

'This is Prinanna,' Joel tells me. 'She's my wife, Auli.'

'Hello,' I manage to say. 'Pleased to meet you,' and Prinanna smiles at me. She takes me into the back of the house and shows me where the shower is. She gives me clean clothes and takes my bloodstained laplap and blouse and asks if she should burn them. I nod.

I'm beginning to hear again and that helps, but I can't seem to stop trembling. Joel says it's shock and Prinanna finds a blanket to wrap around me so after the shower, I sit in a chair wrapped up and slowly begin to feel warmer. Joel gets a beer for himself and one for me and Prinanna says she's going to take Jenn for a walk.

'Back soon, Mama,' Jenn shouts to me as she leaves with Prinanna, 'Back soon.'

Everything feels unreal. Joel. The house. The girl. I try to get a hold on my feelings, but the sight of Layla's blood on my clothes and the memory of her body lying on the ground is more than I can bear. Layla is gone. Layla can't be gone.

'She was going to kill you,' Joel says. 'I saw the gun. It was the only way, Auli.'

'But she wouldn't have killed me, Joel. Not really. I can't believe it. Layla loved me. Layla has always loved me.' Joel doesn't look convinced but doesn't argue with me. He drinks his beer and watches me drink mine. 'Where is Kandin?' I ask, remembering that I hadn't seen him at all.

'He's in jail,' Joel tells me with satisfaction. 'Awaiting trial, but he'll be convicted.'

And then I remember something else.

'What did Layla tell you about Jenn?' I ask. I have to admit that Joel doesn't seem at all upset about anything. In fact, quite the opposite. I've not seen him this relaxed in all the time I've known him.

'She told me that Jenn was Saul's daughter,' Joel says and laughs. 'As though anyone would believe that. Layla was obsessed with Saul you know. I don't think you ever realised, Auli.' Joel takes out his phone and shows me the picture of Jenn on the home screen.

'Look,' he says. 'We've got exactly the same skin colour and she's got my mouth. Everybody comments on it.' Then he becomes serious.

'I want to ask you something, Auli. Actually,' he says, 'I want to beg you.' I look at his eyes and see how much this means to him and I know what he's going to ask. 'Please leave Jenn with us. You can see her whenever you want. You can take her for visits, but please let her live here with us. Prinanna loves her and Jenn is happy. There's another one coming and Jenn will have a brother. I know you love her, but she's settled here and happy.'

What he doesn't say is that he can't bear the thought of life without her and I can understand that.

'I'll need to think about it,' I say. 'I can't think straight at the moment. Can't think at all. I don't know what I'm going to do without Layla.'

'All right,' Joel says and sips his beer. He's drinking slowly. 'There's one last thing I need to tell you,' he looks pleased and I wait to hear what it is. 'You can be issued with a legal passport now. It was Layla who was convicted of sorcery. You were only suspected of it and all charges against you have been dropped. Now that she is gone, you will be left alone.'

It's all too much to take in and I'm exhausted and still shaky. Can't think and can't even get up out of the chair.

'Can I stay here tonight?' I ask. 'I don't want to go back to the hotel. And could somebody fetch my things?'

'Of course,' he says and he brings me another beer.

I need as many as possible.

39

The circle is swept and I'm cooking kaukau under the house. Keroko is as wet and as green as ever and the jasmine thrives. There are new banana suckers growing by the side of the house and the little frangipani tree that Saul planted when I first arrived has nearly reached full height. It's a sturdy tree bearing the waxy flowers that Saul loved best.

For Layla and myself, it was always the hibiscus even though they are one of the commonest flowers in the country. Layla and I never thought that things had to be rare to be beautiful. Layla and I. Layla and I. Layla. Layla. Oh, Layla. Her name drifts into the trees. Frangipani and hibiscus grow better on the coast but they manage up here. And we liked the devil's lilies, huge white bells that hang their heads. We liked. Past tense. The 'we' is all past tense. I am alone. I am alone and I am never alone.

I came here after Kandin was put in jail. I attended the trial and saw his face, full of disbelief. He hadn't thought that it would happen. Chrissie didn't come, but Lucas did. Flew from Oxford to be here to support his son. I don't know if Kandin is worth supporting or if he even notices. I suppose everyone is, but Kandin doesn't seem to need people like the rest of us do. I suppose I might be wrong about this. I came here to put my mind in order before I go to Oxford to help Lucas with his project but putting my mind in order is as hard as ever.

I have explored myself to see what I can do and I find there is quite a lot. I can leave my body like I did before and come back safely. Limited space travel. I can go backwards to previous times and places, but willy nilly. No control. I can't go forwards. Limited time travel. I can do silly things like cut a pack of cards and know which card will be face up. I can examine my opinions and consider their opposites. I can regard facts and walk around them to see what they look like from the other side. I am practising these things.

I've drawn and painted a lot. It's my form of meditation. I've covered every surface in the house with my drawings. They're on the walls, the doors, and the ceilings. Joel comes to visit regularly and likes to look at them. He brings Jenn so I'm getting to know her and when she's here, we draw together.

Jenn lives with Joel and Prinanna and this arrangement works well. Jenn is a happy child. Already beginning to read which is unusual at her age. Her little brother was born two weeks ago and they say he looks just like Jenn except perhaps for the nose.

Secrets that cannot be shared are heavy to carry. I am the only one who knows who Jenn's father is. Jenn doesn't know. Joel doesn't know because he wouldn't believe it when Layla told him. Lucas and Kandin don't know. Does it matter?

Now that Layla's gone, I'm the only one who knows that I killed Saul, but is she right? Would Lucas come to kill me if he knew? Would there be payback? Would a father kill a daughter to avenge a cousin brother? Would a girl be worth less than a man? If Lucas knew why I did it, would he understand? I think he might, but I'm not going to risk it.

Let the dead sleep in their graves as someone once said. Except of course that they don't. That is the last place you will find them. I see Saul everywhere and find his spirit in birds and in the leaves of trees, in the way they rustle and create shapes and faces if you stare at them long enough. But I don't see Layla's face. Layla seems to be gone.

The biggest problem is my blood. I haven't meditated long enough, haven't painted long enough, haven't sat and stared for long enough to be able to accept who has made me or what it means. I do not yet know who I am.

The food is ready and I'm hungry when I hear a shout.

'Aulani, are you there?'

I'm surprised, but I know who it is.

'Let me in,' he says as he stands at the entrance to the path. I pick up the broom and go to greet him. I'm surprised that he waits. Why does he wait for me to let him in?

'Hello, Kandin,' I say. 'What are you doing here?'

'Chrissie got me out,' he says. 'She paid a large sum of money. Apparently, I am worth a lot.'

'I'm sure you are,' I say, 'Come and put your things inside. The food's ready so you're just in time. Come and eat and then we can talk.'

I'm not surprised to see him, but neither am I pleased. Kandin is my enemy. My brother and my enemy. I knew he would come, but I'm surprised that he's out of jail so quickly. I calculate. He has been in prison for only six months. We eat and then we talk a little. He goes to bed early because he's tired. It's a long climb up the mountain.

The next day I get ready to set off with him. I had been hoping to go alone and would have preferred that, but Kandin has got the tickets for us to go to Oxford. He is trying to take charge as he did in the past. He doesn't understand that things have changed. He tells me we are due to leave in three days time.

We are both ready now, so I close the door and I open the circle to let him out.

'Give us a kiss, Auli.'

He hasn't changed so he doesn't know that I am not his friend.

'No,' I reply.

Kandin shrugs then walks towards me. He doesn't believe my answer. Doesn't care.

'Give us a kiss, sis,' he says.

I put down my bilum and look at him, then I point.

'Look at the bird over there.'

He looks at the ground under the tree and sees the bird that I am pointing to. The bird is hopping about on the ground. The bird stops. Cocks his head. Looks at us.

Kandin seems uncertain but he looks at the bird before turning back to me.

'No, keep looking.'

He turns back to look at the bird and we watch while the bird hops, stops then flies away.

'Look at the bird, the other bird.'

'The bird has flown. What should I see?'

I smile and pick up my bilum while he pulls a face.

'You've got older, Auli.'

'We can go now,' I say and he shrugs, smiles and sets off down the track.

I have a choice. I follow.

I choose to go.

Life is not clear, but it's a lovely day and a little tune rises up inside me.

THE END

Acknowledgements

Huge thanks to all my beta readers especially to Michael Kerrigan, Jill Tennison, Pat Eva Berger and Chandra Masoliver.

I am grateful to my friends and my sister Caroline Timus in Papua New Guinea.

For inspiration from Melbourne, I thank my family in Australia.

For inspiration from Oxford I thank Itsuki and Makiko Matayoshi and Zoltan Patai-Szabo.

For unfailing encouragement, technical help and inspired editorial suggestions, I am grateful to Francis Booth.

For never ending patience, good humour and helpful comments I thank Paul Way-Rider.

Want to read more?
Novels by Eliza Quancy

Good Girls are Quiet *(family drama)*
Daniela watches her parents fight and finds that only the dog is reliable, but her father doesn't like the animal and Dani's crying drives him mad. He tells her to be quiet. Good girls should always be quiet. Her mother, Esme tries to argue with him and dreams of escape, but Dani's father is determined to control the family. The child becomes increasingly distressed until things blow out of control in ways her parents did not foresee.

SECRETS series

The Saulie Bird (Secrets: Book 1)
Thank you for reading this book.

On the Slow Train (Secrets: Book 2)
In an attempt to bury the past, Lani moves to the UK to work on a research project in Oxford, but her demons won't leave her in peace. She cannot trust anyone and memories rise up to the point where she is sometimes no longer sure of what is real. Despite the need to be careful and keep herself hidden, Lani starts spending time with housemate Maria, who offers girls' nights out and a chance for a laugh. From time to time, they argue bitterly, but Lani's loneliness begins to recede and a possible way forward opens up.

www.ingramcontent.com/pod-product-compliance
Lightning Source LLC
Chambersburg PA
CBHW022033240626
47154CB00007B/2386